ONCE UPO

IN SOUTH ARMAGH

To Ciaran
with Love

OLIVER MURPHY

and Thanks

GULLION PRESS

BY THE SAME AUTHOR

Books and Stories

Belleek – A Celebration

A Fight For Freedom

Josie

The Final Kick

Stage Plays

The Candidate

The Will

Wedded Bliss

Radio Plays

On Active Service

DEDICATION

This novel is dedicated to the people of South Armagh.
Their unique culture, and rich heritage
has to be experienced to be appreciated.
An open door and a warm 'Céad Míle Fáilte' awaits everyone to
this idyllic countryside, once known as the Barony of the Fews.

Jesus of Nazareth king of the Jews
Save us from Johnston king of the Fews

John Johnston 1684 – 1749 Chief Constable of the Fews [South Armagh]

First published in 2023 by Gullion Press

ISBN-13: 9798859805389

Cover Design by James Smith
smith.james.design@gmail.com

GULLION PRESS

gullionpress@gmail.com
@gullionpress
www.facebook.com/gullion.press

1

Overhead a helicopter buzzed, menacing like a gigantic bee. An oncoming car flashed its headlights, the second one in a row. Julia got the message, but there was no turning back now. Soldiers lay along the roadside, faces painted green. What would it feel like to be shot? She slowed down and stubbed out a lipstick-tipped cigarette in the car ashtray. Please God it would just be another checkpoint. She edged forward and kept a steady, non-threatening pace until she reached a soldier who had his hand raised in a stop gesture. He wore a maroon beret and sergeant stripes on his arm. A youth with his hands raised stood by a car pulled in on the roadside. Another soldier, also wearing a maroon beret, was pointing a rifle at his head. This was the elite British paratrooper regiment.

She glanced at the youth. It was Donal Cahill. As far as she knew he wasn't involved, but that might change soon. She often heard Rooster call the soldiers who gave the local population a hard time, 'recruiting sergeants.

She rolled down the window.

'Driving licence,' said the sergeant. She handed it over but he didn't need to read it. 'Turn off the engine and step out of the car,' he ordered.

In spite of her situation, Julia couldn't help but savour the English upper-class accent. It spoke to her of glamorous ladies and handsome men waltzing to Strauss at exciting soirées in big houses, surrounded by green lawns and rose gardens. A world beyond her dreams.

With both hands, she pulled her skirt down over her knees as best she could before complying with his demand. He instructed her to open the boot and stood back as she did so. They would never open the boot themselves in case it was booby-trapped. Having satisfied himself, the sergeant intimated with his rifle for Julia to stand on the bank while he rummaged through the boot, which only contained bags of groceries. It was always wise not to have tools or equipment that might be viewed suspiciously. After the boot had been searched, he checked the inside of the car before finally turning his attention to Julia.

'Are you a fucking quartermaster?' he said in the same accent.

'Why are you asking me that?' said Julia innocently.

She knew he was referring to the groceries, using them as an excuse to harass her. But she wouldn't be cheeky. She wanted to get home. Responding in kind to the Brits was a sure-fire way of being detained, and at the very least being made to stand on the road for who knows how long, like they were doing with the Cahill lad. Julia felt a moment's pity for him. Then she thought this would make him hate these guys all the more.

'There's only you and that lazy man you keep, so why do you need so much food? No brats around to eat it,' said the sergeant. 'If you need assistance to get some, maybe our lads can help out. Private Hensky, come here . . . on the double.'

Another soldier ran up. 'Yes, Sergeant.'

'If this woman wanted a brat to eat all this food, would you help her get one seeing her husband can't do it?'

Hensky looked at Julia and spoke. 'Be glad to help out, Sergeant.'

Julia said nothing. They were trying to get a reaction from her and then they would all have a good laugh.

'Tell your bloke when you get home that if he asks nicely one of our boys will do the necessary.' Both the sergeant and soldier sniggered. Julia kept an impassive look on her face.

'Okay, you can go,' said the sergeant, handing Julia her licence.

She got into the car. Another helicopter suddenly appeared over the brow of a hill and swooped down before hovering a couple of feet off the ground in a cloud of dust and noise. Above the bedlam of the whirling blades, Julia heard the NCO bark an order to the troops. Almost before she had started the car engine, the soldiers were cramming themselves into the helicopter. She saw that they were taking young Cahill with them, and watched them fling him roughly into the chopper. She would have to get word to Rooster. The local guys would know if he knew anything, and how much damage he could do by having information squeezed out of him.

The helicopter rose in the air and sped away at a forty-five-degree angle. The stretch of road, which hardly more than a minute ago resembled a military outpost, was now bare and desolate. In spite of herself, Julia had to admire the speed with which they could disband and disappear. It was all about helicopters, their main asset in the fight with the IRA. Until the Provos could get weapons capable of taking them down they would never be able to compete. In earlier uprisings, volunteers could hide out in mountains and launch attacks at will. Guerrilla warfare wasn't so easy now. Choppers had changed everything.

Sonny Mone, secondary school teacher, and at this moment Saturday morning home decorator, rubbed little bits of paint from his hands before filling the kettle and plugging it in. The table in the middle of the kitchen had chairs and a desk lamp placed on top. The floor was covered in old newspapers, and the sink had worn bedsheets draped over it. In spite of the chaos Sonny decided the room was starting to look brighter already. Julia had picked *Sunshine Yellow*. He cleared a spot on the table, which was also littered with painting materials, and picked up a book. Finding the page where he had left off, he sat down to read while waiting for the kettle to boil.

Sonny loved to read. His mother had told him that if he learned to like reading, he would never be alone. She said, 'There are times in your life when you will be alone, have no doubt about that. You might be in hospital, God forbid. You might be in jail like your father.' Then she tousled his hair. 'And maybe when you're married your wife won't talk to you.'

His mother in her time had been a famous local beauty, with sallow skin, brown eyes, and black hair. Sonny not alone looked like her, but he also had her gentle, easy-going personality. His Mediterranean looks were the cause of nicknames at school, but none of them stuck. In any event, Sonny wasn't his real name. He had been christened Patrick James Joseph, which was as many names of the Easter Rising leaders that his father thought he could get away with. But somewhere along the line, Patrick James Joseph became known as Sonny to everyone except his father, who until the day he died aged fifty-nine always addressed him by his full Christian names.

'Patrick James Joseph,' his father had said as he lay on his death bed dying from cancer, and holding Sonny's hand. 'Stand up for your principles and be a man.'

However, his father's beliefs didn't match his. His father was a dedicated physical force republican, but in Sonny's view killing someone didn't change that person's mind about anything. All it did was make that person's loved ones want to kill you. And on the cycle would go, hurting everyone and fixing nothing. That viewpoint in South Armagh was bound to cause Sonny problems.

At this moment he had another cause for conflict that was just as pressing: Julia. Was that her car on the driveway? Sonny checked the paint can. Still three-quarters full. And no good excuses either. Where did the time go? He hadn't read that much.

One hand on the steering wheel, her nails coloured a soft shade of red, and one hand holding a cigarette, Julia wondered how much of the painting would be complete. It wasn't as if she didn't know about Sonny's mindset before she married him. From the moment she saw the handsome guy with the Italian looks at the carnival dance she had to have him. She knew about his pacifist views, but she thought that after they got married, she would convince him he was wrong and change his thinking. But that didn't work out.

Sonny left his book down and went to open the front door. 'Hello, darling, you're back,' he yelled.

'Help me in with the groceries,' she said, opening the boot and taking out a couple of bags. Sonny followed her into the house with the rest. She looked at the clutter on the floor, and the general untidiness of the room, and the book Sonny had been reading sitting open on the table top.

'My God, Sonny, is this all you have done?'

'If you are doing a job you have to do it right,' said Sonny, cheerfully. 'The paint you picked is a lovely colour.'

'The colour didn't hold you up, it was this damn book,' said Julia, picking it off the table. 'Jesus. *Plato's* . . . what is that word? *Sym* something?'

'Symposium. It was written more than two thousand years ago.'

Julia shook her head resignedly. She began emptying the bags. 'I was stopped by the Paras at Connelly's Corner.'

'They are there regularly. Here let me give you a hug.'

'Go away, you're all yucky.'

'What did they say to you?'

'Just the usual bullshit.'

Julia didn't want to tell him what they really said. It would only start another argument. Sonny had his heart set on at least four children, but he wasn't the one who'd have to carry them and curtail his whole life for years on end. They had talked about having children before they got married, but didn't all engaged couples do that? It was only when the reality of it set in that maybe you realise your whole way of life could be inhibited by squalling babies. Anyway, who would bring babies into the world the way it was just now?

'I would kill them myself if they laid a finger on you.'

Julia tutted. 'You don't do much to annoy them, never mind kill them.'

'Don't let's go over all that again, Julia.'

'When I'm stopped and harassed like that, I wish I were a man and I know what I'd do.'

'I know you don't understand, but it might be more difficult being a man and not plotting to kill and maim, which is what you're talking about. Sometimes I feel like a black swan in the clutch because my thinking is out of sync with most other people.'

Julia had heard it all before. She picked up the book. 'What is this about that's two thousand years old?'

'The nature of love. People get mixed up between love and lust.'

'My God, Sonny. You really are getting worse every day. Sitting on your arse reading a two-thousand-year-old love story.'

'You're upset after that run in with the Paras. I'll make you a cup of tea.'

'For Christ's sake, I don't want tea. I just want you to get this damn room finished.'

'I'll have it finished by this evening and get the place cleaned up. I know it's a mess. Try and have a little patience.'

'Patience, my God,' said Julia, wearily.

'Here, have this cuppa.'

'They took the young Cahill lad away with them on the helicopter. I better ring his mother and let them know what happened.' She got up and went into the hall where the telephone was located.

Sonny picked up the book, marked the page he had been reading and put it on the windowsill. He could hear Julia on the phone saying that Donal would be fine. 'They'll hold him for a few hours and then release him,' she said. 'It was just harassment rather than anything serious.' What Julia was doing was like comforting a sick person waiting on the results of a test. Both knew as much or as little as the other.

Julia hung up and came back into the kitchen.

'Drink the tea,' said Sonny. 'Do you want a biscuit or anything?'

'I want this kitchen finished so that I can see where I'm going.'

'Another couple of hours and I will have it like a new pin,' said Sonny, swishing his arms around like he was swaying with the crowd at a rock concert.

Sometimes Sonny's light-hearted attitude drove Julia crazy. She knew that he knew it as well, which made it all the more annoying.

'What else did the army guys say to you?' asked Sonny.

'The usual guff.'

'It's always best not to respond. You never know what you're dealing with. Maybe a psycho with a gun, or just as likely a teenager who would pull the trigger out of fear if a crow cawed.'

'I think I'll have a lie-down.'

'Will I come with you?'

'You have to finish the kitchen.'

'Maybe we could get lucky and start a new Sonny or Julia.'

'I need a holiday, that's what I need.'

Sonny tutted. 'Lying on a beach somewhere getting your skin prepared for cancer cells to seed and grow, is that what you want?'

'You're such a stick in the mud.'

'I just hate holidays. Airports, tickets, foreign languages, not knowing what anyone is saying to you, and if you meet someone speaking English then you're happy, and you speaking English to people at home every day.'

'The point is to get away, see somewhere different, and learn something new.'

'And all the time be looking for news from back home, wondering what's going on.'

'You're a hopeless case.'

'Let's see if things settle a bit, then we can go somewhere, okay?'

Julia rubbed her forehead. 'I have a headache after those soldiers. Have you a meeting tonight?'

'No, nothing tonight.'

'How is the new wave of peace and contentment progressing?' asked Julia.

'You're just being sarcastic now. We're only throwing ideas around at this stage.'

'I don't think there's any support for a peace movement the way the Brits are behaving.'

'Maybe peace movement isn't the right word. The idea is something that will stop the hassle for everyone, just like for you today, and the Cahill lad.'

'Well, I wish you luck with it because you will need it, that's for sure. Can we go out to Mulligan's for an hour or so later? Not that there will be much excitement there. I can almost tell where everyone will be sitting, and your one on the stage squealing like a chicken getting its neck wrung.'

'A chicken getting its neck wrung would be in no position to squeal,' said Sonny.

'You can imagine it,' said Julia. 'Rooster the fanatic sitting in one corner drinking black tea because Mulligan daren't refuse to make it. If it was anyone else who asked for tea, oul' Mulligan would soon tell him he's running a pub not a restaurant.'

'You're funny, Julia.'

'Then in another corner, nosey Mick Ryan who sides with everyone in order to hear more. If God and the devil were having an argument, he would be agreeing with both of them.'

'The heroic Plank Murphy in another corner,' said Sonny.

Julia took a sip of tea. Why did Sonny mention Plank's name? Did he do it on purpose? Probably not. Sonny wasn't sneaky and sly like that.

'Anyway, if there's music on at least your friend Alice will be working,' said Sonny. 'She always covers the lounge when it's busy.'

'Some friend.'

'What do you mean?'

'Nothing. I'm off for a nap. And I'm taking this book with me to have a browse through it. Also, in case you start reading again and forget about the painting.'

2

Mulligans was the only pub in the village. There had been two others at one time but not anymore. Both had run out of time due to the age of their owners, so in reality, it was their owners who had run out of time. Nobody else kept the other pubs open. The troubles had curtailed people travelling at night, not to mention the danger of being raided by the army. Those not involved were just as likely to suffer as those active in the resistance.

Julia and Sonny entered the premises via a narrow block wall passage that protected the front door from drive-by shootings or bomb grenades from Protestant militants. A lookout, or what Mulligan called a security guard, welcomed them in. It was a boring job standing there all night, and while he would get free drink from the bar, the pay was mediocre. Better than a farm or building labourer though.

There was a smattering of patrons sitting at the bar. Willie McArdle was talking to John Quinn. Quinn had to sit back a little from the counter because of his huge belly, which he would pat with both hands and proudly call his 'conference'. Willie was a wholesale vegetable dealer. Like many others, he minded his own business when it came to politics and the troubles. Even though the 'civil unrest' (as Bobby Patton, a Protestant, and another regular in Mulligan's delicately termed it) impacted everyone, people tried to live their lives as normally as possible. Mulligan himself, a tall thin man going bald and wearing a white apron around his waist, was behind the bar.

The panelled walls were covered in pictures of local football teams and artefacts made in prison by IRA inmates. A huge harp, carved from bog oak and decorated with ancient motifs, sat on a little ledge specially constructed to hold it. The maker had been in Sonny's class at school. He was now buried in the republican plot.

Bat-wing doors led into the snug. The snug's original intention was to cater for ladies who wanted to have a tipple away from the glare of male customers in the main bar. On the opposite wall to the snug, folding doors opened out into a ballroom of sorts. This was a recent addition. In the centre was a small dance floor, and against the back wall a tiny stage for the band. Mulligan called the extension the West Wing, even when someone pointed out it was actually to the east of the original building. He responded by putting a sign on it saying, 'The West Wing Auditorium'. Along with a degree of stubbornness, Mulligan fancied himself a publicist. During its construction he pondered having the whole room oval shaped, like the oval office in the real West Wing, but financial considerations came into play. With Mulligan everything revolved around economics. It was rumoured that when the local coffin maker died and there was a clearance sale, Mulligan bought his own coffin at a knockdown price.

Sonny and Julia sat at a table against the wall. Sonny went up to the bar and ordered Julia's usual, vodka and orange, and a bottle of Black Label for himself. Mulligan told him he would be opening up the West Wing shortly, and that there would be a group coming on stage to entertain. Back at the table, Julia grumbled that at least they might have something to listen to.

Sonny said, 'Do you not like listening to me?'

'Don't be daft. I'm listening to you morning, noon, and night.'

'Aren't you so lucky?'

'Lucky isn't the word I would use. There's Alice coming in now.'

'She covers the West Wing when there's anything on,' said Sonny.

Alice and Julia had been friends since their school days, and Alice had been one of Julia's bridesmaids four years ago. Alice hadn't married and wasn't known to have any romantic involvement, not that she hadn't had plenty of offers. Julia once said to Sonny, 'Mulligan didn't employ her only for her bartending skills.' Sonny had thought the remark a bit bitchy but didn't say anything.

On seeing Sonny and Julia, Alice came over and greeted them warmly. Julia said, 'I love the way you have your hair. It's cute.' After a pause she added, 'And young.'

Alice had her hair over her shoulders. 'You're the expert,' she said, acknowledging Julia's experience as a hairdresser. 'It's not too young, I hope. Is this skirt too short do you think?'

She was wearing a black knee-length skirt, white blouse, and a gold chain with a cross around her neck. Her shoes were two-inch high heels, which Julia thought would be unsuitable considering she would be on her feet all night, but she kept her thoughts to herself. For some people, looking good was more important than being comfortable.

'I think the skirt is okay,' said Julia. 'Is that skirt too short, Sonny?'

'How would I know? It's fine.'

'Aren't you a man? You're supposed to notice these things,' said Julia.

'I only notice the things you're wearing,' said Sonny, putting his arm around Julia and giving her a peck on the cheek.

Julia knew he was messing, but nonetheless she enjoyed it in front of Alice. 'No, the length is okay,' she said to Alice. 'You look lovely.'

'Thanks,' said Alice. 'And so do you.'

'What about me? How do I look?' said Sonny.

Julia pushed him away playfully. 'Alice always thinks you look good. Don't you, Alice?'

'Mulligan is glaring at me,' said Alice. 'I better get my skates on or I'll be sacked.'

'No fear of that, Alice. Don't think Mulligan hasn't noticed the short skirt and the cute ponytail.'

'What do you mean? Do you think he'd have notions about me?'

'I'd say he'd be more interested in the customers having notions about you.'

'You have to try and look good behind the bar,' said Alice.

'You look just lovely,' said Julia sweetly.

Sonny picked up his beer. 'If you have it, flaunt it, that's what I always say. Look at Dolly Parton. She didn't hide her assets behind a whin bush.'

'I'm no Dolly Parton,' said Alice.

'You're far nicer,' said Sonny.

'Oh, I love you too,' said Alice. 'I'm away. The group is getting their gear ready. I'll see you two later. The "special attraction" will be singing tonight. You know who that is?'

'Yeah, we know,' said Julia. 'We can't wait.'

Alice laughed. 'Will I see you at the meeting?' she said to Sonny.

'All being well.'

'Am I invited?' said Julia.

'You know we'd love you to be there,' said Alice.

'I'm sure. Anyway, what ye are at is not to my way of thinking.'

'Yeah, we know that. I better go. See you, Sonny.'

As Alice moved away, Julia said, 'Do you really think she is nicer looking than Dolly Parton?'

'That's like asking is a Ford nicer than a Volkswagen.'

'So, if you had your choice which one would you choose?'

'A Ford or a Volkswagen?'

'You know well what I mean. Which would you choose to have? Alice or Dolly Parton?'

'I have my Maserati here beside me. What would I want with a Ford?'

'Yeah, yeah, yeah,' said Julia.

After what seemed like interminable checking of the microphones by repeating, 'One, two, three,' and, 'Testing, testing, testing,' the two lads on stage began by playing some country quicksteps. Sonny sat back and relaxed and watched Mulligan behind the bar wearing his melancholy, resigned expression. Mick Ryan, a kind of local sage (mostly because he agreed with anyone's opinion, and therefore they thought he was smart) once said that Mulligan's look was common to all good bar workers. It implied, 'I understand how you feel.' Mick argued that once an apprentice barman had acquired that expression, he had his time served. Some never got it, and thus would never make a successful living.

Sonny's observations were interrupted by Julia saying, 'My God, she's at it early tonight.'

'Who?' asked Sonny.

'Look at the stage . . . you're one.'

The woman on stage talking to the group wore a blue miniskirt, black stockings and high heels. The red open-necked blouse showed off her curves to best advantage, while around her neck a white bandana gave her a gipsy look, emphasised by jet-black hair over her shoulders. Lipstick, red as a summer sunset, and the magic of cosmetics made her face seem like it had the skin of a baby – although babies don't have blue eyelids.

'Jesus. Red, white and blue,' said Julia.

'What do you mean?' said Sonny.

'She's wearing red, white and blue.'

'I don't see it.'

'Blue skirt, red blouse, white scarf.'

'It's a black skirt as far as I can see, unless I'm colour blind.'

'Oh, it's blue all right.'

'She might be a stranger, but she's not daft enough to be wearing red, white and blue in Mulligan's.'

'Don't be fooled. She knows exactly what she's doing. She's acting the innocent and getting the attention she wants.'

'Why would she want to stand out so much?'

'Because she's an English tramp and likes making all the silly men's eyeballs pop out, that's why.'

'You're being too hard on her. For a start, you don't know if she's English.'

'She's English, okay, and she is flaunting it. Wait until she starts singing. A crow would sound better.'

The lounge had started to fill up. Now and then a single guy would come into the bar and be served by Mulligan. Alice looked after the lounge. Her busiest times were at the beginning of the night, when people were coming in and ordering drinks before settling down, and again at the end of the night, when they were stocking up before the shutters came down.

Sonny nudged Julia and told her he saw Plank Murphy going by the stage in the lounge. 'He must have been there before we came in.'

Julia immediately looked through the open door but couldn't see him.

'He'll be down at the back of the lounge,' said Sonny. 'I sat beside him at school. Do you know he is called Plank because the teacher said he was as thick as a plank?'

'My God, how many times do you have to tell me that story?'

'It's just interesting that now he goes around as if he's something special.'

Julia was about to say something when they both noticed Rooster walk into the public bar. He had long hair, once obviously black but now a dirty grey colour, hanging down his back and tied in a ponytail with a piece of red thread. Other than that, he dressed similar to any other sixty-something man in the locality. He wore grey trousers and an open-necked check shirt, a grey pullover and a zip-up jacket. His face was nondescript, except he was blind in his left eye which was permanently closed. He approached the bar in a slow deliberate gait, the seeing eye encompassing everything around him in a manner that reminded Sonny of a cat prowling in a hedgerow. Mulligan, already engaged in pulling a pint of Guinness, nodded to him.

Leaving the pint to settle, the barman reached under the counter and retrieved a mug. He plugged in a kettle normally used for boiling water to make hot whiskeys. Mulligan didn't have to take the man's order. It would be a mug of tea, no sugar, no milk. The man settled himself on a stool and gazed into the mirrors behind the bar, which offered him a view of everything.

'Rooster comes in every night,' said Julia.

Sonny didn't respond because just then the lady on stage began to sing 'Sean South of Garryowen'.

'Where did she learn the words?' said Sonny.

'All she sings are republican songs, if you can call it singing,' said Julia.

Sonny asked Julia if she wanted another vodka and she nodded her head. He went up to the bar. There was no table service at Mulligan's. Overheads were kept to a minimum. 'If I don't give it out, I don't have to take it in,' said Mulligan. 'I'm thinking of the customer as usual.'

3

While Sonny was getting the drinks a man approached Julia. It was Mick Ryan, well known to agree with everyone in the conversation, no matter the debate.

'Hello, Julia,' he said.

'Hello, Mick. I didn't see you come in. Where have you been?'

'I was in the east wing, which according to Mulligan's compass is really the west wing, but better known to all of us as the lounge. What do think of her?' said Mick, referring to the woman on stage. 'Straight from the Milan Operatic Society.'

'My God, but she's woeful,' said Julia.

'The fellas say she's very sexy.'

'Yeah, like a praying mantis is sexy.'

'I'm just sorry I ever got my ears syringed,' said Mick. 'Before that I wouldn't have been able to hear that jackdaw. I had to get out of the lounge because of the screeching.'

'Whatever she does for a living, it's not singing.'

'Scotty thinks she's a meteorologist.'

'Why a meteorologist?'

'He saw her looking up at the sky one day.'

'It's a wonder he didn't say she was an astronomer.'

'Johnny the Post says she has doctor in front of her name, and that she's an anthropologist, so she can't be Irish.'

'Maybe she's a psychologist, being a doctor and all?'

'Scotty argued she can't be a meteorologist if she's a doctor.'

'Why?'

'Because whoever heard of a doctor giving out the weather on the wireless?'

Julia took the last sip from her glass. 'God help us.'

'Alice told me she was looking for a drink called Pimm's, so she must be English,' said Mick.

'Sherlock Holmes wouldn't have a look in with you.'

Sonny came back carrying the drinks and greeted Mick warmly.

'Julia and me were just discussing the nightingale on stage,' said Mick.

'Did ye reach any conclusions?'

'Only that she's English.'

'And she's not a professional singer,' added Julia.

'Ye didn't get very far,' said Sonny.

'They say Plank has a *grá* for her,' said Mick.

'Who said that?' asked Julia, sharply.

Mick said that Sean O'Rourke had brought it to his attention. How Plank was watching her. 'Like a cat watching the milk jug.'

'Sean O'Rourke,' said Julia, contemptuously. 'His own wife left him because he was the cat watching the milk with other women.'

Mick nodded his head in agreement and said, 'O'Rourke has a reputation for being fond of the skirt. As for Plank, his interests are himself, money, women, pints, and his country, in that order. Anyway, besides the fact that she's English, I would have thought she was a bit on the mature side for him.'

Julia stood up and announced she was going to the lounge. She said she wanted to ask Alice something. Sonny nodded okay.

Mick took out a crooked pipe and began to clean it with a little penknife.

'Then there's the other side of it,' he said. 'Why would your one be interested in Plank, and him a Catholic?'

'It might divert his attention and take his mind off the glorious struggle for a united Ireland,' replied Sonny.

Mick leaned toward Sonny almost instinctively, and said in a low voice, 'You're the only one in this place, Sonny, who would be that flippant, and things so bad.'

'I don't think I am being flippant. Plank is okay, but he thinks he's another Michael Collins.'

'He could end up unfree to do anything, with your one like a stone around his neck.'

'What, you mean married to her?'

'No, some people aren't meant for marriage. Plank being one of them.'

Sonny was quiet for a moment. He knew that Mick and his wife had separated years ago, but he'd never found out why.

He asked, 'So what happened in your case?'

Mick finished cleaning his pipe. He closed the penknife and slipped it back into his pocket. 'The sad truth is she was cheating with Billy Preston behind my back.'

'I'm sorry,' said Sonny.

'There's nothing as hurtful as a wife who betrays you.'

'Yeah, it must be bad.'

'Anyway, Preston was a Protestant.'

'What has being a Catholic or Protestant got to do with it?'

'They say Protestants are all descendants of Henry the Eighth, and everyone knows about the length of *his* malooja. So, what would the English woman be doing with a wee wizened Catholic like Plank?'

'That's funny,' said Sonny. 'Anyway, she might be English but she knows more rebel songs than the Wolfe Tones.'

Mick sucked his pipe a couple of times, checking that it was ready for filling. He retrieved a plastic pouch from his pocket. Opening the flap, he dug his thumb and forefinger in to withdraw a portion of brown tobacco and proceeded to roll it in the palm of one hand with the heel of the other. Sonny thought it was calming just to watch him. The routine of preparing the pipe, kneading the tobacco and so on, was like a sacred ritual. And if it was soothing to the onlooker, it must be ten times more relaxing for the smoker. Perhaps this was why pipe smokers were always perceived as calm and full of wisdom. Maybe the addiction lay in the tranquilising preparation ceremonies rather than the nicotine. When Mick didn't light the pipe but instead put it in his breast pocket, Sonny thought he must be on the right track.

'It's always foreigners who are the greatest patriots,' said Mick. 'Where did I put my cap? I don't want to go without it.'

'Are you not going to light your pipe?' asked Sonny.

'I'm trying to cut down. Where did I put that cap?'

'Jesus, I was right,' said Sonny, pleased with himself.

'Right about what?'

'It's not the smoking of the pipe that's important, it's the filling of it.'

Mick laughed. 'You're right. But you have never been a smoker or you wouldn't say the smoking bit isn't necessary. Where did I put that damn cap?'

'Here it is,' said Sonny, retrieving it from under the seat. 'You won't need it tonight. It's dry for a change.'

'Don't laugh when I tell you what its main function is.'

'I won't laugh. Tell me.'

'To take it off when the national anthem is being played.'

'Are you joking?'

'In spite of being hammered down for years, we can still stand proudly for our national anthem. Removing my cap has a special significance for me.'

'Jesus, I will never look at a cap the same again.'

'My oul' uncle Mick used to even take it off when the national anthem was being played on the TV.'

'Is it from him you got the idea?'

'Maybe. What's passed on is very important.'

'I detect something in your tone, Mick.'

'I like you a lot, Sonny, and Julia is such a lovely girl. And I hope you produce lots of boys so that maybe someday our wee club will win the county championship.'

'Okay, Mick, tell me the "But".'

'Sonny, none of us can ignore what's going on. The way they are killing our neighbours. There is collusion between the security forces and the loyalists, and there's information being leaked from somewhere. We all must stand together or go down together.'

'Were you talking to Julia?'

'Why do you ask?'

'She was on to me this morning about the same thing.'

'I'm not surprised with her background. Everything follows on from our heritage as it were.'

'It's not so simple, Mick.'

'You have even a far greater inheritance than Julia. If your father were alive today, he would be leading the struggle.'

'Do I have no say in my so-called inheritance?'

'I don't think you can escape it.'

'I don't want to be a replica of my father.'

'Ah, he was a great man.'

'I'm *not* my father. When will people realise that?'

'I suppose it hasn't been easy for you.'

'Can you understand my position?'

'I can't disagree with it.'

'It's like I have never been my own person.'

'I can understand that. The son is never going to be as good as the oul' fella was.'

'It's as if I was always walking in his shadow.'

'But this is about our neighbours, Sonny.'

'You don't have to tell me. Nowadays, even Johnny Bennett, my closest friend at school, hardly says a word to me.'

'There's a price to be paid for standing out from the crowd. I discovered sometimes it's best to go along with people.'

There was a pause between the two men. Sonny took a drink of his beer and Mick let his eyes wander around the pub. Mulligan was kept going behind the bar, and the dance floor, seen through the open doors, was filled with couples moving to the music. Sonny wondered if someone should tell Mulligan that he was providing therapy for people. He would love to hear that, but it might mean a cover charge to get in. He could just hear Mulligan arguing that attending therapy is always expensive.

Sonny spoke as if there had been no break in the conversation. 'But that's not all of it, because then there's Julia.'

'What about her?'

'Maybe because of her background I think she doesn't have the same respect for me because I don't get involved.'

Mick paused before answering. 'You know there is a history of rebellion in this area that goes back centuries. Along with your father's reputation, that's a powerful legacy for any young man in the times we live in.'

'I didn't ask for it.'

'You got it whether or not you asked for it. It's what you do about it that matters.'

'But why can't I just be myself? Why do I *have* to copy my father? Why am I expected to think the same as other people? Why does my wife not respect the fact I'm not a rabid republican out shooting British soldiers? Can you answer me that?'

'It's hard. I agree with you there.'

'You would agree with me anyway. If I had said something else you might have agreed with that as well, so I can't take any consolation in your understanding of my situation.'

Mick turned to look at him. 'Let me explain something to you, Sonny, to do with your situation. Sons of fathers, especially sons of noted fathers, seem as a general rule to adopt one of two stances. Either they adore their father and try to replicate him, or I think a more common outcome is they rebel and try to be the opposite to him. It's just a way of coping with the journey we all have to take to become our own man. You have obviously taken the rebellious route.'

'Does that mean I'm wrong?'

'No, it just means pain and isolation.'

'As a matter of interest, what way did *you* cope with the journey to be your own man?'

Mick's voice took on a tinge of sadness. 'The truth is, not as well as you, Sonny. Your path leads to loneliness; mine leads to a kind of shame, you could say.'

Sonny remained silent for a few seconds. 'Is it very private or can you tell me about it?'

'After having analysed you, I suppose it's only fair I tell you my story,' said Mick.

'Thanks, and don't think I'm not grateful to be told, because I am.'

Mick took a deep breath. 'Okay then, here goes. You know the way people say I don't have a mind of my own and just agree with what everyone says?'

'I didn't think you were aware of that.'

'Sonny, everybody knows, unless they are totally ignorant, how they are perceived by others, but very few want to face it.'

'It's not easy accepting the way that people might see you.'

Mick gave a wry grunt and said, 'Anyway, this is my excuse. My father and mother fought the bit out. My dad must have been some kind of alcoholic, but for whatever reason, they were always stuck in each other. And me being the only child was forced to take sides in whatever it was they were arguing about. It wasn't easy because I loved my mother, and my father would use me to bolster his side or be very angry if I didn't. Automatically, over time I developed a way of agreeing with both of them. It worked to some extent. But the downside was I developed it into a way of dealing with everyone. Now I find it difficult to disagree with anyone. It's my way of coping with people I suppose.'

Sonny rotated his beer on its mat. 'You mentioned shame?'

Maybe for the first time ever, Sonny saw Mick get agitated. His voice rose even as he spoke. 'You of all people must be able to understand the shame of how it feels not to have an opinion of your own. To be able to shout out, "You're all fucking wrong, and I'm right!"'

Sonny realised he had touched a nerve. Maybe he had no right to be quizzing his friend. 'I know about having to develop a way of thinking that suits someone else,' he said. 'My father drilled into me the idea of a united Ireland, and his notion that there was only one way it could be achieved: out of the barrel of a gun. I don't know why I rebelled. Maybe it was because that besides all his teaching about a united Ireland, he also taught me to make up my own mind about things.'

'Some would call that a contradiction,' said Mick. 'On one hand he was schooling you to take up the fight, and on the other he was schooling you to be your own man in how you lived your life. But to me that showed the depth of his wisdom.'

'I know that, and I love him for it, but it also makes it harder for me when I don't fight for the things he fought for.'

'The bottom line is things are never black and white. There are always contradictions.'

Again, there was a pause between the two men. Sonny was processing in his mind what Mick had said, while Mick was allowing his thoughts to settle. He rarely, if ever, talked about himself and why he always agreed with everyone. Now that he had told Sonny about it, he didn't know if he felt relieved or embarrassed. In truth there were very few people one could share things with. In this part of the country things were left unsaid, even things, maybe especially things, that *should* be talked about. The troubles permeated everything. And behind closed doors, things were not always as they appeared from the outside. Hadn't Danny Bracken's daughter suddenly emigrated? People didn't just go away to England or the States without some talk of them leaving. The Brackens had relatives in America and the talk was she was going to them. But she had just started college so it was strange.

Talk as little about yourself as possible – it was bred into the people of this region. His uncle told him about Mrs McShane and her husband. The husband said very little in case he would reveal something inadvertently, while the wife never stopped talking so as not to reveal anything. His uncle said that there were two ways of keeping stuff to yourself: say nothing, or control the conversation by non-stop talking.

'I think the banshee has left the stage,' said Sonny. 'So, we have to be thankful for small mercies.'

'I can't get over it,' said Mick. 'Imagine if Plank fell for an English woman?'

'Imagine *any* woman falling for the Plank?'

'Don't be jealous. All the ladies fall for Plank.'

'Only those who can't see beyond the swashbuckling persona he loves to portray.'

'Someone said he uses the English woman to make people talk if they are under interrogation.'

Sonny looked astonished. 'In what way?'

'She stands beside them and sings.'

'That's funny. But you see the problem, that the likes of the Plank would have the power to be interrogating anyone.'

Mick shook his head. 'Yon man sitting at the counter talking to Mickey Beatty and Sean Lundy is the one who has the power. The way they are huddled, it looks as if he is divulging the third secret of Fatima.'

Sonny glanced over to where the three men were having a clearly private conversation. Sonny didn't know much about Beatty or Lundy, but he suspected they were in the IRA.

'Where did Rooster get his power?' he asked Mick, already knowing the answer he'd get.

'You ask him because I don't intend to. And he has it for sure Did you hear about him having Mulligan bar young Kavanagh because there are rumours that he likes guys more than girls?'

'That's terrible, I hadn't heard that.'

'Rooster has a thing about sex,' said Mick, leaning close to Sonny and almost whispering. 'You know the way republicans raise money smuggling? Well, I heard it on the grapevine that some bright spark at a meeting discussing finance came up with the idea of smuggling condoms into the South where they are illegal. That there would be a huge market for them. It seems Rooster blew his top, and declared that if he heard anyone mention them filthy things again, he would have them court-martialled. So, you can ask him where he gets the power if you want.'

'Boo, cowardly custard,' said Sonny, teasingly.

Mick lifted his eyes towards the ceiling in mock frustration and said, 'Let me ask you something, Sonny. Do you know why we are afraid of some things, like for instance sitting down beside a lion?'

'I don't know what you're on about, but tell me why.'

Mick said in a triumphant tone, as if he was announcing a big revelation, 'Because the fear of the lion stops us from being eaten.'

'Ah-ha, so you think Rooster might eat you?'

Mick's tone became serious. 'I said no such thing, do you hear? But I better get back or Scotty will have slipped away without buying his round. You know the Scots?'

'You're at it again. Because he's from Scotland he must be tight-fisted.'

'That proves my point,' said Mick. 'Did you ever see him rushing to buy his round? I'm telling you; you can't shake off you're breeding. I'm away before Julia gets back. See you soon.'

4

The group in the lounge were taking a break when Julia came back.

'Anything exciting happening in there?' asked Sonny.

'There would be more excitement at a wake.'

'Well, exciting people then?'

'Yeah, Tom Jones is after arriving, and Elvis isn't dead, he's in Mulligan's lounge bar.'

'Oh, so do you fancy Tom Jones?'

Julia was getting fed up with Sonny's teasing. 'Are you carrying out a personality test on me?'

'I just want to be aware of the opposition.'

'You needn't worry about Tom Jones or Elvis. They won't be appearing in this godforsaken acre of earth where nothing ever happens.'

'There is a lot of blood being spilt over what you call a godforsaken acre of earth.'

'None of it yours,' said Julia in a swift response. She clamped her mouth closed. God, why had she said that? Sonny was as brave, if not braver than any of them for the stance he'd taken. 'I'm sorry,' she said. 'I didn't mean it like that.'

'It's okay,' said Sonny. 'You're right. Any blood I have I intend keeping instead of having it soak into some roadside shuck. But I'm still an Irishman.'

Even though he accepted her apology, Sonny knew what she was thinking. Like many more in this community, she wanted to hit back at the Brits. They were an occupying force, harassing the people, and he was just standing back and accepting it.

There was silence for a couple of minutes between the couple. Rooster approached them carrying a mug and a pot of tea. He said a warm hello and they both responded in kind. After enquiring how they were doing, he asked Sonny could he have a word with him in private. Sonny said, 'Sure,' and Julia made an excuse to go back into the lounge. Rooster suggested that he and Sonny go into the snug where it would be quieter. When they settled, Rooster remarked that it was a lovely night out. Just a quarter moon – not too bright, and yet enough light to see.

Sonny said, 'Let me guess, a good night for manoeuvres?'

Rooster gave a little gasp, saying, 'Unbelievable. It's like I'm sitting here looking at and listening to your dad. Those were the exact words he said the night I carried him home drunk on the day you were born. A night like this always reminds me of it.'

'I'm sure it was a big night, but I wasn't invited,' said Sonny.

'He declared that one day you would be the leader of a free united Ireland.'

Sonny grimaced. 'A tipsy father's dream for his new son, no doubt.'

Rooster frowned. To Sonny, it made him look unnatural because of having just one eye.

'Come to think of it, you are a bit laid back in that area. How long have you been married now?'

Sonny felt his sex life, or lack of offspring, was none of Rooster's business, but he would keep his cool. 'Julia doesn't be well much of the time.'

'Is everything all right between the two of you? We have to keep the pipeline moving with fit young men eager to take up the cudgels.'

'Like it's my duty, I suppose.'

'Of course, it's your duty. Doesn't it say in the Bible we have to multiply and fill the world?'

It was time to respond. 'We won't be filling the world if they are all killed with cudgels in their hands.'

Rooster leaned forward earnestly, his elbows on the table, his one eye fixed unblinking at Sonny. It made Sonny wonder if the closed eye blinked as well. He would watch out and see.

'Sonny, I know you are an intelligent man. It's a sad fact but nonetheless a true one. We need dead heroes. Listen to Pearse. *While we hold these graves, Ireland unfree will never be at peace.* Those are the people who keep our holy cause alive. One IRA volunteer in jail is more use to us than five on the outside.'

Sonny shook his head. 'That's a ruthless approach to the idealism of young people.'

Rooster's tone became urgent. 'How many did Churchill sacrifice at Gallipoli? How many were used as cannon fodder in the trenches by Haig? How many did that great Irish saint John F. Kennedy send to be slaughtered and maimed in the jungles of Vietnam for a useless adventure, more to do with pleasing the military than for any strategic reason?'

'But if you criticise those, there is no need to ape them.'

'The point I'm making,' said Rooster, 'is that you have to close your mind to any feeling of sentiment or compassion when entrusted with responsibility in such matters. Did Truman have any compassion for the hundreds of thousands he would kill when he decided to drop the bomb on Hiroshima? Did the planners of D-Day think of how the seas would run red with the blood of their countrymen?'

Sonny feigned surprise. 'You're not comparing a dispute about a line on the map of Ireland with world wars, are you?'

Rooster shook his head impatiently. 'It isn't the scale of something that's important, it's the principle behind it. To die in some forlorn Ballymagash ditch from the enemy's bullet is every bit as glorious as to fall on the Western Front. I would argue it's more so because it's about the dispossessed rising up rather than powerful capitalist forces competing against each other. But where were we? Oh yes, Julia and you. If you ever want to talk about it, I have open ears.'

Sonny thought it was time to get to the real purpose of Rooster's talk. 'What did you want to see me about?'

'What were we discussing?' asked Rooster, pretending to have forgotten.

'You were going on about my father.'

'Oh yes. My God, when I think of it, those were the days.'

Sonny was getting more irritated. 'I don't think you took me in here to reminisce.'

'No,' said Rooster, and his face became serious. 'The point is, Sonny, you haven't lived up to your father's expectations.'

Sonny kept calm. First Mick and now Rooster all on the same day.

'People notice the stance you are taking.'

'I'm sure,' said Sonny, drily.

'We could be doing with someone of your intelligence.'

Before he could say any more, Sonny interrupted. 'Well, the truth is I couldn't inflict pain and suffering on anyone . . . even a Brit.'

'What are you saying, boy?'

'I'm saying that I don't feel I could harm another human being, especially for some crazy notion of doing it for your country.'

'My God, crazy notion?' thundered Rooster. He grabbed a floor brush that was lying against the wall. 'On your belly, soldier.'

Sonny started to say, 'What the fuck?' when Rooster roared again.

'I said on your fucking belly, now!'

Anyone else and Sonny would have told them to fuck off. But Rooster was not someone you wanted to fall out with. He got down on his belly. Rooster thrust the brush into his hands.

'Take this rifle and point it at the enemy.'

'What enemy?' said Sonny, genuinely confused.

'The damn enemy facing you, hold your rifle properly, soldier,' Rooster shouted.

Sonny wondered if people outside the snug would hear and peek in. But the band had struck up again, and no one would disturb Rooster if they could help it. Sonny held the brush half-heartedly to his shoulder like a rifle.

'What do you see?' whispered Rooster, as if the enemy might hear him.

'I see a wall, for Christ's sake.'

'What you see is a uniform,' said Rooster with quiet vehemence. 'Not a human being, you see a fucking uniform that represents hundreds of years of pain and suffering inflicted on our people. That's what you see. Listen carefully as you pull the trigger, and you will hear the moaning of countless Irish men, women, and children across the centuries pleading for revenge.'

Sonny lay still on the floor, pointing the rifle and saying nothing.

'Now pull the fucking trigger and do your duty to those voices,' said Rooster in the same hypnotic drone. And then he shouted, 'Bang!'

Sonny startled, and somewhat mesmerised he got to his feet.

'My God, Sonny. I'm talking about our inheritance and how we must embrace it. This has nothing to do with inflicting pain and suffering on anyone. It's about revenge for the pain and suffering inflicted on the Irish people.'

Just at that moment Julia came in to the snug. 'I hope I'm not interrupting anything. I wondered where you had got to, Sonny.' She gave a little start of fear and put her hands over her face. 'Oh God, it's a spider running down the table. I hate them. I can't stand them.'

Sonny stood up. 'Where is it?'

'It's after running under the chair,' said Julia.

Sonny lifted the chair, saw the spider and stomped on it, saying, 'That's one less spider in the world.'

Rooster was watching him. He said, 'What harm was a wee innocent spider doing?'

'I can't stand them,' said Julia.

Rooster shook his head in sorrow. 'You shouldn't have killed it, Sonny.'

'Why not?'

'Because like every other creature, it just wants to live out its life.'

'It's only a spider, for God's sake,' said Julia.

'A spider full of life a minute ago and now it's just a smear of dirt on the floor. Such a waste. But I have to go. Think about what I said, Sonny.'

Sonny stayed quiet. Julia looked between them, and with a hesitant voice said, 'Rooster, now that I have the opportunity, do you mind if I ask you a personal question?'

He gave Julia a sharp look with his one eye. 'Try me.'

'You sure you don't mind?'

'Will you ask the damn question?'

'Is it true that you left a wedding breakfast once because there was a jar of English mustard on the table?'

'Who said that?' said Rooster.

'Oh, somebody. I can't remember,' stammered Julia.

Rooster made to leave. As he was going out the door he turned and said to them, 'We must never forget what the English bastards did to our people.'

As soon as he left, Julia said, 'He didn't deny the mustard.'

'He has a one-track mind,' said Sonny.

'It seems you have to be like that if you want to be successful and reach the top.'

'Who would want to be at the same top as him? I'm going to the toilet. Are you ready to go home?'

Julia nodded and said she would wait for him in the snug. Sonny was only gone a minute when a guy wearing jeans, check shirt and brown cowboy boots came in.

He said, 'I noticed Sonny heading for the jacks. He stopped to chat with Pete Donnelly.'

Julia was both scared and excited. 'God Plank, I'd rather he didn't see us together.'

'I'm only staying a second. When can we meet?'

'Mick said you couldn't take your eyes off that tramp on stage,' said Julia, accusingly.

'No way,' said Plank. 'I only have eyes for you. You know that.'

'I don't know that.'

'All the fellas look at Ruby.'

'Oh, so it's Ruby now. How come you know her name?'

'Don't be so suspicious of everything, Julia.'

'You didn't answer.'

'It's my business to know things. Surely you understand that.'

'That's very convenient.'

'You have no cause to be jealous.'

'I wouldn't be so sure.'

'Well, you can be.'

'Are you sure you're not up to something with Ruby behind my back?'

'Now you're talking daft. When can we meet?'

'I don't know. I feel so guilty, and anyway, maybe you'd rather meet sexy Ruby?'

Plank tried to see himself in the glass of a football team picture hanging on the wall. 'Don't be like that, Julia.'

'If Sonny finds out, what would happen?'

'He won't find out.'

'He adores me.'

'I adore you.'

'More than yourself you mean. Or more than Ruby, and she old enough to be your granny.'

'Nobody would want her. Anyway, she's English.'

'If she was from Mongolia, it wouldn't stop you if you thought you'd get your way with her.'

'You're giving me a hard time, Julia.'

'Sometimes I think it's just sex you want.'

'You know that's not true. Stop giving out to me. When can we meet?'

'Give me a ring tomorrow. Sonny has a meeting tomorrow night. But I'm not promising anything. Go now, quickly before he comes back.'

'Give me a wee kiss to keep me going,' said Plank, leaning down to her.

Julia gave him a quick peck on the lips and said, 'Quick, go.'

When Sonny returned, she was checking her face and hair in her pocket mirror.

5

Donal Cahill was very scared. He was even more frightened than the time he got stuck down the well. Back then he knew that his parents would be looking everywhere for him, and they would hear him shouting. But now they wouldn't know that he had been taken in by the soldiers, and he couldn't shout for help in here. They had made him lie face down on the floor of the helicopter and put their boots on his back. All the time they laughed about what was going to happen to him. They called him a terrorist and murderer. After dragging him off the helicopter they flung him into this room. It had a table and three chairs and nothing else, just four bare whitewashed walls and one big mirror. It crossed Cahill's mind that whoever installed the mirror did a bad job because the edges were rough and unfinished. He wished he had emigrated to join his brother on the building sites in New York. He wasn't as smart as him at school and he never did any exams. His father had wanted him to take up a trade, but farmers and builders always had something on that kept him going. He never played any football or bothered much with anyone. His mother encouraged him to go out to the dances and meet a girl, but he wasn't interested in dances or girls.

That is except for Ann Sheldon, who lived about two miles away from him. He was in love with her and thought about her day and night. She didn't know this but someday he'd tell her when the moment was ripe. In the meantime, he would write letters to her almost every day confessing his love for her. He'd write them and pour out his feelings. How he thought she was more beautiful than an angel and would win the Miss World Contest if she entered. If necessary, he would gladly die for her as long as he died in her arms. In fact, he fantasised about that and could imagine her holding him as he died saving her life and her telling him how much she loved him. He wrote long poems about her. It was hard making them rhyme but that didn't matter. Someday she would read them and know how much he loved her. He never posted them. He kept the letters in the inside pocket of his jacket in case his mother found them in his bedroom. Now the soldiers had found them while he was being searched. They had let him keep his jacket, but the letters were taken. What would they do to them? They would definitely read them.

He could hear English voices laughing and cursing on the other side of the door. He felt cold and shivery but built up his courage to rise from the chair and go over to the mirror. A cut on the side of his forehead that he didn't know about had stopped bleeding. Blood on his hair had matted and some of that had run down the side of his face and dried. It wasn't sore. He was dying to go to the toilet.

The door opened and a huge soldier stormed into the room. He was carrying a sheaf of papers and looked very angry. 'Okay, my pretty fellow, sit down,' he ordered.

Cahill sat down. 'Can I go home?'

The soldier smirked. 'That depends now, doesn't it?'

'I want to go home,' Cahill said, almost begging.

'Okay, then tell us all you know about the IRA.'

'I don't know anything about the IRA.'

The army man thumped the table. 'What do you mean you don't know anything?'

'I'm sorry. I stay on my own and don't go out much.'

'Oh, so you're a fucked-up loner then.'

'I'm sorry,' said Cahill. 'Can I go to the toilet?'

The soldier didn't answer him. 'Do you know the Plank Murphy?'

'Yes, but I don't know anything about him.'

'If you did, would you tell us?'

'Definitely, yes.'

'Would you tell us about other terrorists that you know?'

'If I knew them, yes.'

Cahill felt a flicker of hope. All he wanted was to get out of here. If he was free, he didn't have to do anything.

'Can I go to the toilet, please, please?'

'What have we got here?' said the soldier, spreading the contents of the folder over the table.

Cahill's heart sank when he saw the letters. His interrogator picked up one with a look of curiosity on his face. 'Hmm,' he said, 'let me see now.' And he began reading it. 'My beautiful rose of Armagh, I love you as much as anyone has loved anyone before.' His eyes flicked to Cahill. 'What the fuck is this?' He continued reading. 'I think you are so beautiful, more than anyone else. I promise I will always love you.'

He stopped reading and looked at his captive. 'My God, you're a pervert?'

'No.'

'Who is this girl?'

'She's just a friend.'

'A friend? Does she know about these?' The soldier flipped the letters on his table contemptuously. 'What's her name?'

Cahill spoke into his chest. 'You wouldn't know her.'

The army guy leaned over the table, and with his face almost touching Cahill's, he shouted, 'What's her fucking name, pervert?'

'Ann Sheldon,' said Cahill in a hoarse whisper.

'Does she or her family know about these pieces of filth?'

'I was going to tell her soon.'

'Well, you're not going to tell her soon because it will all come out at the trial.'

'What trial?'

'Your trial for being a pervert.'

'I'm not a pervert.'

'Who do you know in the IRA?'

'I don't know anyone.'

'You're a liar.'

'I'm sorry, I'm not a liar.'

'Do you know Plank Murphy?'

'Yes.'

'Isn't he in the IRA?'

'Some people say he is, but I don't know for sure.'

'You said you didn't know anyone in the IRA.'

'He's the only one I know. I don't know for definite if he is or not.'

'It doesn't matter. You might get to know some more in jail. You'll meet them when you're doing time. I hope they don't abuse you too much.'

'I don't want to go to jail. Please let me go.'

The soldier went over to look at himself in the mirror. He smoothed back his hair with the flat of his hand. 'We will let the judge decide that at your trial.'

Cahill hoped he was dreaming. Maybe he was. Ann and her family knowing about him would be worse than going to jail. Could he say he was guilty and go to jail without them knowing? It would be in all the papers. He was bursting to go to the toilet.

The door opened and another man in plain clothes came into the room. He looked friendly.

'What's going on here?' he asked.

'We have a pervert on our hands,' said the soldier.

Cahill thought this man looked kinder. 'Can I go to the toilet, please?'

'Of course,' said the man. 'Here, I will show you where it is. This way.'

Cahill gratefully followed the man down a long corridor. Sometimes they met soldiers, many of them carrying cans of beer. They all looked at the young civilian with curiosity. Only one of them spoke. 'Enjoy your stay, mate,' he said with a guffaw.

After he relieved himself, Cahill felt a bit better. Before leaving the toilet, his escort warned him about the other soldier who was interviewing him. He said his nickname was Hitler and nobody liked him because they were all afraid of him. 'Try and cooperate as best you can.'

'How can I do that if I don't know anything?'

'Yeah, I guess it's a problem. But if you did, it might help you.'

'I don't know what to do.'

'I have an idea that just might work. Let me see . . . Suppose we tell him you will poke around for information about the IRA when you're let go, and as a reward he doesn't do anything with the letters.'

'How did you know about the letters? He didn't show them to you.'

'I met him as he was coming to interview you. He said that he had dirty letters written by you and he intended to throw the book at you. That's why I looked in to see what was going on. He can be very cruel, believe me. I have had to intervene before for other people. It doesn't always work though.'

'They are not dirty letters.'

The man shrugged his shoulders. 'Maybe not, but the reality is they are what Hitler says they are.'

'That's not fair.'

Then man laughed. 'Hitler doesn't know the meaning of fairness. Leave him to me and let me try and see if I can sort things out for you. By the way, my name is Craig.'

He walked out in front of Cahill, but just as he stepped into the corridor, he saw something that caused him to push Cahill back into the jacks. Cahill didn't know what was going on. This Craig guy was clearly afraid of someone seeing them because they stayed hidden for a full minute. Then he peeked around the door to see if the coast was clear, and he hurried both of them back to the interrogation room.

Hitler was seated at the table, reading through some of the letters. 'Unbelievable, fucking unbelievable,' he said.

'What's unbelievable?' asked Craig, who no longer seemed spooked.

'The stuff in these letters,' said Hitler, pointing to the table.

'I gather you want to prosecute this young fellow. Is that correct?'

'Damn right it's correct.'

'I have a suggestion that might be useful.'

'Oh yeah, what is it? It better be good.'

'Suppose you let this guy go free.'

Hitler interrupted. 'Stop, stop, there is no way this bastard is going free.'

'Please, let me finish,' said Craig. 'You want to get your hands on those terrorists who are killing people. What if, in exchange for you dropping all charges and forgetting about these letters, my friend here found out all he could about the IRA and kept us informed about what's happening in the area? Would you be agreeable?'

Hitler stayed silent as if processing the question. 'I don't know. It would need to be good information.'

'Let me tie you down. If my friend here can bring you some useful information on the IRA, will you promise to give him back his letters and let the entire affair drop?'

'You know I have certain principles,' said Hitler.

'Will you, or won't you?'

Hitler turned to Cahill. 'Do you promise to get me information in order for this thing to end?'

'How do I know you will give me the letters if I do what you want?' said Cahill, feeling braver now that this other guy was here.

Craig butted in. 'I will keep the letters in my possession, and after six months I will return them to you. You know you can trust me, don't you?'

Cahill nodded.

Hitler grimaced and folded his arms. 'Fine, that's it then. Now get the fuck out of my sight and come up with the goods. I'm going fucking soft in my old age.'

'I will show you the door,' said Craig. 'Have you money to get home?'

'I'll hitch it,' said Cahill.

'Good man. You did well in there. Remember, get whatever information you can, and here is my phone number. Ring me every week and ask for Pope Pius and that will get me. Okay?'

'It's a funny name,' said Cahill.

'I'm using that name so that you don't forget. We don't want any mess-ups with the big guy in there.'

They reached the door of the barracks. 'Okay, bye now my friend,' said Craig. 'Be in touch soon.'

Cahill headed up the road. Almost immediately, Hitler appeared at Craig's side, saying, 'The next time you can take my role. I was so sorry for him I almost let him go, the poor bastard.'

'Sorry, my arse. You can't be too hard on these Irish fucks,' said Craig. Hitler was about to walk away when Craig gripped his arm. 'Do you know who I saw in the corridor a while back?'

'Who?'

'Potts. I didn't want to say it in front of Pissing Pete.'

'Jesus, are you sure?'

'I'm fucking sure. He was pointed out to me at a conference one time, his head bobbing up and down like a hen pecking for seeds. It was him all right.'

'I've only heard about him. Wright told me that seeing him around is like seeing vultures in the desert. Something or someone is about to die.'

Craig looked Hitler in the eye. 'Are you sure you're clean? You would tell me if you soiled your bib.'

'Of course, I'm fucking clean. Did you soil your fucking bib?'

'Cool down,' said Craig. 'It's just that Potts isn't here for a holiday. And in his eyes, anyone associated with a little bit of dirt is just as guilty.'

'They say he never deletes anyone himself,' said Hitler. 'That he hates guns and won't even handle one.'

'From the reports I hear, the ones deleted by bullets are lucky,' said Craig. 'Say nothing to anyone, and keep your mouth shut about me telling you.'

6

Sean Lundy had been fascinated by Irish history from the time he was a boy and first able to read. It wasn't just the never-ending wars with England he was interested in. He loved all the old legends and stories to do with Cú Chulainn, and the Brown Bull of Cooley, and Grace O'Malley, the Irish Pirate Queen, and so on. As he grew up and delved into Ireland's past, he developed bitterness towards the English and their role in Ireland over the centuries. He'd dream of being an Irish hero, a patriot prepared to sacrifice his life for Ireland's cause, like all the other famous Irish martyrs. At civil rights marches, he was at the forefront echoing their demand of "one man one vote" even though he wasn't sure what that really meant. When the Provisional IRA came into being in 1969, he was only sixteen. He had to search out IRA leaders and convince them he was nineteen in order to get enrolled as a volunteer. Since then, he had become adept at the talents required to be effective in guerrilla warfare.

Mickey Beatty was always wild. He got into trouble at school for mitching, and when he did attend, he was first in line for disrupting the class. He got into trouble at football matches and regularly got suspended for kicking his opponents rather than the ball. He got into trouble at dances for not conforming to the usual etiquette of not interfering in another guy's romantic activities. He got involved in pub fights, and when the British army were ordered onto the streets and byroads of Northern Ireland, he got into trouble with them as well, and found himself in jails overnight on more than one occasion.

When he applied to join the Provos, there was some reluctance by one or two leaders about accepting such a loose cannon into their ranks. However, this concern was misplaced. Mickey had found his vocation. He loved the danger involved and the thrill of the underdog up against the might of the British Empire. His superiors soon read that Mickey wasn't driven by any sense of patriotic duty, or Ireland's fight for freedom, but rather the excitement of the fray.

Right now, Sean and Mickey were on assignment, planting a bomb in a culvert under the road at a place called Cranky's Brae. Sean, by now familiar with the electrics involved, wired up the device to go off when a remote button was pressed. Everything set, they climbed the adjacent hill and made a hide for themselves in some whin bushes, overlooking the road along which they knew a convoy of British Army trucks would soon pass. A farmer's van had been left in a lane close by. Once they had detonated the explosives they would dash for the van and be across the border and safe in less than thirty minutes.

The two Provos settled in to wait on the convoy. Locals had been logging army movements, though never on paper. When they used such-and-such a road, and so on. They would pass this way tonight, almost for sure.

There was little conversation between the two men. Sean had a bunch of bananas under his jacket, which he shared with Mickey. Being younger, the apprentice as it were, Mickey would press the button setting off the bomb. From reports, there were likely to be anything from three to nine vehicles in the convoy.

The British Army had hundreds of years of experience of ambushes in hostile territories throughout the empire, and more recently in Ireland during the War of Independence. It was better to travel in strength so that if waylaid they were in a position to defend themselves from gunmen. They were not to know that Sean and Mickey had no intention of firing on them. They didn't even carry weapons. The plan was that when the second vehicle passed over the culvert, Mickey would set off the device and they would scarper.

Mickey tried folding the banana skin like a piece of paper. He thought about what would happen when he pressed the button. It would be a massacre – human bodies blown to bits, worse than when dogs went feral and mauled sheep. But he was in an army and that's what soldiers did. Up until now he hadn't felt like he was in an army. The training – how to fire a rife, mock missions in the hills, parading and saluting – it was all great craic. But this was different. He would have to get a grip. Wasn't this what he committed to? To drive the English bastards from Ireland. They never had any compunction about killing the Irish. It was just a matter of pushing the button and getting the hell out of there. Just stop thinking about it. It's like jumping into the icy sea in spring – blank your mind, close your eyes and do it. He could resign later.

Both sides of the conflict knew that convoys had no real purpose other than showing the flag of the occupier. It was about who controlled South Armagh. The officer in charge of the armoured personnel carriers, the Saracens, was Second Lieutenant Roger Saunders. Roger was wealthy, or at least his father was. He was also bright, ambitious, athletic . . . and a coward. His forebears were industrialists, back when men made fortunes on the labour of slaves from Africa. Roger never really questioned where the money had come from. He had his life mapped out. First, he would become an officer in the elite Parachute Regiment. After an honourable discharge, he would run for office in a safe Tory seat. The goal was to be Prime Minister by age forty-five, or at the latest, fifty.

Things went well for Roger. After Oxford, he enlisted in the British Army as prime officer material. When commissioned, he was posted to the Parachute Regiment as a second lieutenant. Six months later his regiment was deployed to Northern Ireland, which he thought was perfect. Close to home. Not too hot. And the posting would help his political career. Seeing action always helped, and you didn't actually have to engage in any close up fighting. The danger was minimal, but it would look great on his CV. Bravery under fire. It didn't mean he had to fire back.

Sometimes the thought came into his head that he was a coward at heart. He tried not to let it settle in his mind, but he couldn't forget the day that a servant had challenged him in his own house. He was home from

Oxford and giving the butler a hard time, really out of misplaced anger because he had lost a small fortune at the club the night before. After the butler brought him cold toast, he slapped the man in a fit of rage. But instead of cowering, the butler calmly invited Roger out onto the lawn to settle these like men. He told Roger that if he refused, he was a yellow-bellied coward. A river of fear coursed through the would-be future Prime Minister and he apologised profusely. The butler knew he was in no danger of being reported to the lord of the manor. After that, Roger could no longer look this supposed subordinate in the eye.

It was just getting dark when the five-vehicle convoy was about to move off. Second Lieutenant Saunders walked over to the last vehicle. He knew the odds. In the unlikely event of the convoy coming under attack, the front vehicle was the most dangerous, the rearmost the safest. Let the plebs in front take their chances. This country needed him alive and well. When he became Prime Minister, he would help these working-class drudges so he felt justified in staying at the back.

He stuck his head in the vehicle. No room at the inn. All seats taken, but he spotted a redheaded private he'd had a word with earlier about the state of his boots. Watson, was it? No, Walton.

'Private Walton, perhaps you'd like a taste of what it's like at the front of the convoy. Take your position in vehicle one.'

Private Reggie Walton scrambled from his seat, and said, 'Sir, yes, Sir.' He ran to the front Saracen and found a place between two other soldiers. A moment later, the order was given to set off, and soon the convoy was trundling along the boreens of South Armagh.

For Walton it was a dream come true to be serving in this elite outfit. He had cursed himself earlier for being called out by Saunders for scuffed boots, but maybe the second lieutenant had already forgiven him. He wasn't a bad sort, really. Bit stuck up, but so were half the officers.

Reggie's station in life had been entirely predictable. His great-grandfather Albert had fought in the Crimean War, and according to family legend was one of the horsemen who rode into the Valley of Death during the Battle of Balaclava. Reggie wasn't so sure of that, but there were ancient looking medals to prove that he had been there at least. Albert's son Ansley fought in the Boer War. He got a medal too. True to tradition, when the time came, Ansley's son Freddie found himself in the trenches on the Western Front during the First World War. He lived to tell the tale and fathered a son named Denis who took part in the D-Day landings.

Incredibly, in this whole lineage of service to king, queen, and country, not one of these Waltons ever got so much as a scratch. There was the odd case of dysentery, a touch of cholera, but none of them got an injury as a result of enemy action. This was a source of pride to Reggie's father. He would declare, 'No enemy bastard ever managed to lay a finger on a Walton.'

Reggie was born and reared in Leeds, and when he turned seventeen, he joined the Prince of Wales's Own Regiment of Yorkshire. He settled well. Soldiering was in his blood after all. But Reggie wanted more excitement than he was getting in the Yorkies. He applied to join the Parachute Regiment, which meant all kinds of tests for suitability. Although he did poorly on the written exams, he excelled in the field. The staff at HQ were convinced that his family history had manifested itself in Reggie's DNA.

Meanwhile, Reggie's father Denis had little time for the Northern Irish troubles. As proud as he was of his son being a Para, when he learned that Reggie was posted to South Armagh, he sneered that it wasn't where soldiers should be sent. Soldiers were trained to fight real wars. Northern Ireland was for poofs. He said, 'Imagine our lads in Normandy, with the Germans spraying their lines and dead comrades everywhere, firing back with rubber bullets and water hoses and gas that would only tickle your eyes? Crimea, South Africa, the Somme, Normandy, those were real wars where soldiers went into battle. Not these Sunday outings going on in Northern Ireland.'

Reggie had listened and said nothing. He knew the family history and had no fear of deployment. If all of his antecedents could come home without a mark from such famous battles, he had little to worry about. He settled in the Saracen and watched the passing countryside as dusk was falling. He narrowed his eyes a little. Did the light just glint off something on that hilltop?

Hidden among the thorny whins, in what was now a little nest warmed by the closeness of their bodies, Sean and Mickey spoke little. Out in the open, a mother sheep looking for its missing lamb bleated plaintively. Water in a nearby drain gurgled incessantly over stones. A badger slinked along a ditch.

Otherwise, all was quiet. Earlier, an old Austin 35, obviously being driven by a drunk coming from the pub, stopped and jerked its way over the culvert, as if the car itself was staggering home. Sean prayed on a rosary for the success of the mission and his own safety. He also prayed for his deceased mother. He asked that she be released from the fires of purgatory. He asked that she look after him. Mickey tried to keep his mind blank and think of nothing, like he heard those mystics in India were able to do.

All at once there was the sound of engines. This was it. Sean tried to say, 'Get ready,' but no words came. On the second try, he shouted breathlessly at Mickey, who had lifted the remote control from the ground.

'I will tell you when to press.'

He could see the front vehicle round the bend towards Cranky's Brae. Three, no four more Saracens followed. They were approaching the culvert. Ten seconds more. Five. Would that bloody sheep ever stop bleating. The first vehicle was crossing over the bridge.

'Now, press the button,' hissed Sean. 'Press the button quick.'

Nothing happened. Sean tore his eyes away from the convoy and glanced at Mickey.

'Press the fucking button,' he shouted.

'I can't, I can't,' wailed Mickey. 'I can't do it.'

'Press the fucking button before they're all away,' Sean shouted again.

'I can't, I can't, I can't.'

'For Christ's sake, give me that.'

Sean grabbed the device from Mickey and flicked the switch, just as the final truck was passing over the culvert. There was a deathly silence that seemed to last forever, and then a boom like thunder. The ground trembled. For a few seconds everything around the whole area, living and dead, seemed paralysed, unable to move.

Sean and Mickey didn't wait to look at the carnage. In a flash they were away over the hill to the laneway where the van was waiting. They started it up and headed pell-mell for the border. In the distance they could hear gunfire. If they'd have looked before leaving, they would have seen the soldiers in a state of utter confusion shooting high powered rifles at random.

Second Lieutenant Roger Saunders was killed instantly when his Saracen passed over the bomb. Although the floor was armour-plated, the blast happened right underneath him, and a piece of shrapnel passed clean through his head. Everyone else in the vehicle survived. Someone had shouted that terrorists were in a field opposite to where Sean and Mickey had lain hidden, and soldiers began firing at phantom targets. This was different from exercises back home. Fear was the driving force here, not a desire to impress superiors. When the soldiers realised there was no one there they ceased fire. As they took stock, Reggie was found dead on the roadside with a bullet wound in his back. He had died of friendly fire. The family tradition survived. It was still the case that no enemy had ever managed to inflict the slightest wound on a Walton.

After the commotion had settled, the farmer who owned the field found two cows shot up so badly that their guts were spread over the grass. Half a mile away a stray bullet went through the window of a farmhouse where a family of eight children were living. No one was injured except the pet donkey in the garden. It had to be put down.

7

Sonny was listening to the early morning news while having breakfast. The broadcaster had just announced the deaths of two soldiers in South Armagh as a result of a terrorist bomb left by the roadside. He read a statement put out by the British Army press office:

'Last evening, under cover of darkness, terrorists thought to have been at least twenty in number mounted a cowardly gun and bomb attack on Her Majesty's forces in South Armagh. Two members of the armed services were fatally injured. Their names are being withheld until the families have been notified. The assailants were driven back, suffering several casualties.'

When Julia came the kitchen Sonny had a depressed look on his face. 'Two more soldiers blown up . . . at Cranky's Brae from what I can work out,' he said.

'May the Lord have mercy on their souls,' said Julia, ladling porridge into a bowl. 'But they wouldn't have died if they'd been at home where they belonged.'

'You know well it isn't that simple,' said Sonny. 'They were just victims, you could say innocent victims, of a far more complex picture. They had lives, mothers, fathers. In all likelihood these two guys were from some rundown high-rise in Manchester or Liverpool or Glasgow, who joined up to escape the misery of their environment.'

Julia sat down to eat her porridge. 'You don't know their stories. You're only surmising.'

His breakfast ruined; Sonny spoke with passion in his voice. 'That doesn't matter now. They are dead, blown to bits just down the road from us. And they aren't the only victims. What about guys who set off the bomb? What's their story? Where does the rage to kill come from? They're normal fellows, part of our community. Maybe we even know them.'

'Remind me to put porridge on the shopping list,' said Julia.

'You're not even listening to me.'

'I am listening to you. Of course, everyone has a story that brings them to whatever place they find themselves in. You just go into things too deep.' As she was clearing the table, she said, 'You didn't finish your porridge.'

'How is wondering about why lads become so hardened that they can kill other human beings be going too deep?' said Sonny, to himself as much as to his wife.

He sat at the table and looked through the window. In the distance, Slieve Gullion had a blue Van Dyke hue to it. An idyllic landscape, yet for hundreds of years that same countryside had soaked up the blood of the conquered, and conquerors, in a seemingly endless struggle for freedom on one hand, and domination on the other. Was the present chapter of the tragedy as simple, or was it feeding on past ideologies? A robin alighted on the front hedge of his garden. He remembered his mother's love for the bird. When she would see one, she'd say it was her husband comforting her. There were families somewhere needing two more robins after last night.

'Anything else you want on the shopping list?' said Julia.

'You haven't heeded one word I'm saying.'

'I have, but remember this is South Armagh. How many centuries has it been since the first English soldiers were killed here? What can we do about it?'

Julia was putting into words almost exactly his own thoughts, except she seemed to feel nothing.

'That's a despairing attitude,' he said.

'It's reality, that's what it is. I'm going to work. What are you doing this evening?'

'I'm going to call with Eric Johnson.'

'You're what? said Julia. 'My God, Eric Johnson of all people. What's that about?'

'Imagine if we could get him to come to one of our meetings.'

'Imagine if we won the Irish Hospital Sweepstakes. It's the same chance.'

Eric Johnson, the son of a scutch mill owner in Blackstown, had a long lineage in the area. He was a Protestant, but having attended a school run by Catholic clergy, he had grown up with Catholic friends, and it being South Armagh, he had been immersed in a culture where respect for law and order was minimal. Some would say non-existent.

His own people had the opposite approach to law and order. The Calvinist and Presbyterian influence called for discipline and self-restraint as the foundations of living a life dedicated to the Lord. So, it was no surprise to Eric's Catholic friends when he decided to join the Royal Ulster Constabulary. It was a good job with good pay, and before the present troubles it wasn't as dangerous. Sonny had phoned Eric to tell him he was going to call over to his house, and Eric gave him a warm welcome when he arrived. 'Come in, come in, my old pal of schooldays past,' he said, giving him a firm handshake before leading him into the sitting-room.

Sonny took in his surroundings. A portrait of the Queen and Duke of Edinburgh hung on one wall. On the mantelpiece, many of the various trophies won by Eric's children had red, white and blue ribbons attached to them. A union flag was furled up in the one corner of the room. Eric was a Protestant and this was a Protestant home so what did he expect?

On another wall there were pictures, some very old, of scutch-mills and people working them. They fascinated Sonny. He knew that for some, this was the story of Northern Ireland. When William III vowed to discourage the woollen trade in Ireland, and to encourage the manufacture of linen instead, he was as good as his word. English and Scottish settlers in Ulster wore linen instead of wool. Belfast had most of its roots in the linen industry. The production of linen was a Protestant industry stemming from the Protestant plantation. Northern Ireland was founded, or at least made viable, because of these mills and the people who owned them. Eric Johnson had his country's history in pictures on the sitting-room wall, just as pictures of Vinegar Hill or Wolfe Tone decorated the walls of Catholic sitting-rooms.

'Sit down, sit down', said Eric. 'It's so good to see you.'

He went to the door and shouted in to to his wife to come in and say hello. A tall thin woman entered the room. She had that typical Protestant sallow skin, and her hair was pinned up, not a strand out of place.

She struck Sonny as being nervous, and when she went to make tea, Eric told him that the present troubles were getting to her. She wouldn't let him answer the door if a knock came out of fear. 'Only we knew it was you this time,' he said.

Sonny agreed that the times were awful.

Eric said, 'I've heard about your plans to hold peace meetings.'

'How? We've barely told anyone.'

'Aren't I a policeman?' laughed Eric. 'We're supposed to know about what's going on.'

'That's really why I'm here. Will you come to one of the meetings and speak at it? Most people will know you, and your appearance would be a powerful statement. Before you answer, I will personally guarantee your safety. Going to the meeting, at the meeting, and coming home from it. They will have to shoot me before they shoot you.'

Mrs Johnson came in with a tray of tea and cake. The tea-set was adorned with pictures of London Tower Beefeaters. Sonny took a slice of cake. Definitely home baked – more Protestant self-sufficiency – and as delicious as only Protestant baking could be.

Eric told his wife what Sonny proposed and the colour left her face.

'Oh God, no' she exclaimed.

'It's okay, love. It won't happen.'

'Are you sure?'

'I'm sure.'

'I hope so,' she said, and she left the room.

Eric turned toward Sonny. 'Let me explain something, Sonny. You said you would protect me, and you might be able to . . . just might, mind you. But you wouldn't be able to protect me from my own, as they are called. I am going tell you something, my friend. There are bad apples in the RUC, and I mean very bad apples. They would be more dangerous to me than the IRA, if I were to do anything like what you are suggesting. You may ask, why stay in the RUC then? Well, it's my career. And there are many good apples as well. Plus, and I hope you understand this, I will not be bullied by the IRA. I'll not quit my job or leave a community where I was born and reared. My breeding is Protestant, and that's thicker than water. I also have a heritage, one that I have a duty to preserve for my children. I am very sorry to have to refuse you. Can you understand my position?'

Sonny nodded. Yes, he understood. It was a long shot anyway, and he valued his friend's honesty.

'If it's any comfort to you, tonight at our family Bible reading, we will pray to the same God you pray to that you are successful in what you are attempting.'

'I appreciate that.'

'Let's talk about old times,' said Eric, pouring more tea into Sonny's cup. 'Do you remember the time we let down the wheels of the master's car at Halloween, and we got a day off school as a result?'

'I do. It was your idea as I recall. I wonder is there any more of that cake left?'

8

The posters and local newspaper ads for the meeting had done their job. Even before the designated start time, the hall was reasonably full. The gathering was almost all male, from their twenties to middle age, and a couple of older guys. Few if any would have been to college. This was a farming community. Not many jobs around here required a degree.

Sonny and Alice, one of the few females present, sat at the top table with three others. In the middle, Frank Brannigan was well- known locally. He was highly educated, very politically aware, articulate, ambitious, and self-interested, just some of the reasons why Alice didn't like him. To her eternal regret, after being pestered relentlessly, she went out with him once. Never had she encountered such a self-centred narcissist. Of course, he was very bright and smart, but that didn't mean he had to be the way he was. He had told her that what all people wanted more than anything was power, and since politics was the easiest route to power, it was in that area that he would reach the top. He said his goal was to do good in the world, and if some people had to be hurt a little in the process, so be it. Alice had listened quietly as he prattled on and then excused herself as soon as she could. There was no second date.

But when Sonny contacted Brannigan and invited him to the first peace meeting, he jumped at the opportunity. Here he could be in the vanguard of a platform that might further his plans. He would act as spokesman, he said. Someone had to do it, and there weren't many volunteers. That's why he was now sitting in the middle.

The other two people at the top table were colleagues of Sonny at the college where he taught. Sean Donnelly had to sit back a little from the table because of the size of his belly. Being that far from a table hadn't yet interfered with his ability to reach the food. When doctors told him to eat less, he always replied that because of simple mathematics relating to distances, the problem would ultimately solve itself. Next to him sat Pete the Pipe who was known for his wisdom, although Pete said that his reputation for wisdom came from the fact that he smoked a pipe. He rarely spoke, preferring to listen instead. He was always afraid of missing something important by speaking himself, and he already knew what he was going to say, so best keep quiet. His pupils loved him.

After tapping on the table with a pencil to call the meeting to order, Brannigan spoke a couple of sentences in Irish and said, 'We all know why we are here. All comments are welcome.' And then he sat down again.

There was silence in the room, broken only by a cough or a match being struck. Someone else was clicking his lighter trying to get it to work. Alice leaned over to Sonny, her face almost touching his shoulder so she could smell his smell. He smelled nice. God, if he only knew what she was thinking. 'You say something, Sonny.'

Just then a voice from the middle of the hall piped up. 'Everyone knows the problem. Derry: so-called security forces massacring innocent civilians. Kingsmill: so-called resistance forces massacring innocent civilians.'

'And what about so-called loyalist forces massacring innocent civilians,' another voice said. 'Don't forget just prior to Kingsmill, local families, little children, being wiped out.'

'Two warring factions. Maybe three,' said Brannigan. 'But what can be done about it?'

Immediately, someone else spoke. 'There aren't two warring factions. There is only one. If the Brits weren't here, there would be no war.'

Shouts of, 'Hear, hear,' from a couple of places in the crowd.

A young voice yelled, 'What do you think if Rodney gave each one of them a slap on the mug? Chase them home to their mammies!'

Another small cheer in the hall, and a few laughs.

Rodney Walsh was sitting at the back keeping a low profile. Sonny had been surprised to see him there. He wasn't big into talking, especially when it came to confrontations. He was more inclined to action, almost always to the detriment of those he disagreed with. Some years ago, this was recognised at football matches where brawls had occurred. One punch from Walsh usually ended proceedings. It was known as the 'Big Clout'. No one knew where the name came from, but anyone who saw it in action knew it was apt. He used it sparingly, but when he was particularly riled up, Rodney would lean back and unleash a haymaker that no one could withstand.

Some friends persuaded him to enter the boxing ring. Sure enough, the first couple of bouts lasted less than a minute. There was great excitement in the area. The local paper had a headline: 'Future World Champion Rodney Walsh?' The story was picked up in the US, and in less than a week two American guys appeared at Rodney's front door. One was skinny with a fat cigar in his mouth. The other, a huge black man, had a nose as flat as a pancake. They offered Rodney all kinds of inducements: fame, women, a million bucks within two years. They would guide his career towards becoming world champion. His nickname was already decided: "The Armagh Ape" with the mantra, "You Don't Argue with the Ape". Rodney wasn't happy about being described as an ape, but they assured him that publicity was the name of the game. Rodney flew out with the two guys the next day.

A month later he landed home with his face still covered in bandages. Some said that he fought at Madison Square Garden on the same bill as Mike Tyson, but was homesick and wanted to come home. Wiser heads suspected he never got beyond some New York neighbourhood gym, where his limitations were quickly exposed.

Wanting to keep the discussions serious, Sonny spoke up. 'The question I put to you all is this: is it worth all the bloodshed? Can there not be a better way forward in the latter half of the twentieth century?'

A babble of voices rose up. Arguments and opinions, some sensible and some silly, took up several minutes.

Finally, Sean Donnelly spoke in a voice that seemed to come from deep in his huge belly, thus adding gravitas. 'Does everyone agree that we should make an effort in some new direction? Hands up.'

Practically everyone in the room raised their hands. No surprise, thought Sonny. Only those with an interest in stopping the mayhem would be here.

Pete the Pipe took the pipe from his mouth and said that he was a school teacher. 'History has taught us that it's only when people themselves rise up and say what they want that things change.'

Brannigan saw an opening. 'A people's movement,' he declared.

A squeaky voice said, 'It's not much of a movement if this is all there is.'

'From little acorns, the mighty oak grows,' said Sonny.

'I wouldn't like to be waiting on this oak to grow,' said Squeaky.

Sonny ignored the jibe. 'I think we should call another meeting in Carrickbawn to build on what we have begun.'

'Yes,' said Brannigan. 'Publicity is key. We need to get it out there that we exist.'

Alice thought that Frank would know all about publicity and letting people know he existed.

Someone suggested that leaflets with details of the next meeting should be attached to the windscreens of cars at Sunday mass. The aims of the group could also be listed. This prompted the question: just what were the aims of the group?

More discussion, sometimes heated. Eventually, it was clear to Brannigan that no coherent set of aims would be agreed upon at this stage. He proposed simply stating in the leaflet that the next meeting would explore ways of improving community life in South Armagh. Everyone endorsed this form of words, and a couple of people volunteered to distribute the leaflets.

When Brannigan saw the success, he was having he thought it was time to strike the iron while hot. 'What if we were to form a little committee here tonight to head up the movement and give it momentum?'

'Will you act as chairman?' asked Joe Patton from the crowd.

Brannigan smiled. 'I don't know,' he said hesitantly. 'I have a lot of stuff going on at the minute. Is there anyone else who would take it on?'

'I propose Frank for chairman,' said Joe. 'Everyone agreed?'

There was a murmur of agreement.

'Okay, I will take it on a temporary basis,' said Brannigan. 'On the condition that Sonny agrees to be my vice-chairman, and Alice act as secretary. Is that okay?' he said to Sonny and Alice.

Both of them nodded. Alice knew Frank wanted Sonny as vice-chairman because of his commitment. After all, wasn't it him that started the whole thing off? But she would become secretary as long as Sonny was involved. There wasn't much work to it, and she'd be able to spend more time with him. Following the meeting, Alice, Sonny, and his two friends from college went for coffee in the local café. Alice would have preferred it if the other two hadn't come.

9

'This place would freeze you,' said Julia. 'I thought you weren't coming.'

She was speaking to Plank who had just breezed into the room in cavalier style. The place was a three-bedroomed terraced house in a town twenty miles from home. It was a typical safe house used by the IRA. With so many similar houses nearby, it didn't attract attention. Neighbours on the street would assume it was unoccupied. Those who used it parked their vehicles in a laneway at the back. Black blinds covered the windows, and noise and lights were kept to a minimum.

'You think I would miss an opportunity to be with you?' said Plank taking Julia in his arms.

'I feel so guilty,' said Julia.

'Don't feel guilty. You don't love Sonny, and everyone deserves a second chance.'

'It's just that he loves me so much, and he is a good man.'

'I love you so much and I'm a good man too. Let's go to bed and I will warm you up.'

'All you're interested in is sex.'

'You know that's not true. I love the very bones of you.'

'What about the English woman? Do you tell her you love her as well?'

'How would I tell her that? I don't see her.'

'You sure you don't bring her here to have sex, like you do me?'

'Don't be daft Julia. She and me have nothing in common. Let's go to bed.'

'In a minute. What have *we* got in common?'

'For a start, we love our country, and we want to do something about the way it's being treated. Sonny is a pacifist, which gets you nowhere.'

'But what lies ahead for us?'

'At some point we can get away and live happily together.'

'Away? Where to?'

Plank continued to hold Julia. He kept rubbing her back. Over her shoulder he stared at the wall as he answered. 'I don't know. Maybe the States, or Australia. We will see. Come on, I want to warm you up.'

Julia let her arms fall by her side. 'This doesn't get any easier for me. Even though it's the third time doing this.'

Plank took her by the hand and led her to the bedroom. 'I just want you to be happy.'

Later, as she nestled in his arms, she whispered to him, 'I don't know how this is all going to end.'

Plank tried to comfort her. 'It will be okay.'

'When will the troubles be over? I don't think ever. And even if they were, what would we do?'

'They will end with a great victory for us. We will have a united Ireland, and we can live our lives free in our own country. That's what's going to happen.'

'What about Sonny?'

Plank watched a beetle clamber over a crack in the ceiling plaster. Why was she always going on about Sonny?

'Sonny will be fine,' he said. He cupped her chin and kissed her again before she could say any more.

The following evening Julia was watching *Coronation Street* while Sonny sat next to her on the sofa reading *Profiles in Courage* by John F. Kennedy. The familiar theme music signalled the end of the soap.

Sonny looked up from his book. 'What was Ena Sharples gossiping about now?'

'Same as usual. If she was living around here with all the squinting windows, she would have plenty to keep her going.'

'Did you ever notice that it's always the people who complain about gossips who have the most to fear?'

'What are you suggesting? That I have something to fear?'

'No, my dear. Just making an observation, that's all.'

'I don't like observations like that.'

'Tell me what your auntie used to say when she was denying things.'

'You heard it a dozen times.'

'Please, just once more.'

'Ok then, if it makes you happy. "Well thanks be to God, and the blessed virgin Mary, Saint Joseph, the holy pilgrimage to Knock, St Gerard's novena, all the saints in heaven, and the suffering souls in purgatory, that I never done that."'

'It's very funny,' said Sonny.

'You're easily amused.'

'Anyway, I don't think there's much gossip in our little village. A lot of the talk is about the troubles, and I wouldn't call that gossip.'

'What about the English woman,' said Julia. 'Isn't there plenty of gossip about her?'

'I don't think you like the English woman. Anyway, I just think its people wondering who she is and what she's doing here.'

'If people really knew about her you could be sure there would be plenty to gossip about.'

Sonny laughed. 'You're just guessing.'

Julia grunted something.

'What do you say we have an early night?' said Sonny. 'We never get an early night anymore.'

'It's the stress of the times we're living in. How can you be relaxed about anything?'

'I'll make you a cup of tea. Then we can hit the *leaba* and I will relax you.'

Julia changed the channel to the news. The headline told of a suspect bomb in a house in Fermanagh and the evacuation of surrounding properties. 'Hassle, hassle, hassle,' she said. 'Nothing only hassle.'

Sonny went to plug in the kettle. 'Some say it's the price of the struggle. If that was the worst price it wouldn't be so bad. But early graves and young people incarcerated are a different kettle of fish.'

'There's a price tag on everything, I suppose,' said Julia.

'A very high one in this case. Do you want a biscuit?'

Sonny made the tea while Julia watched the news. He would prefer not to watch the latest happenings because he found them depressing. What's the point of depressing yourself? Knowing about bombs didn't stop them from happening, and it did nothing for your peace of mind.

'You go on down and I will be in when the news is over,' said Julia.

'Don't be long, honey.'

Later on, the only light in the bedroom came from a full moon between a slight opening in the curtains. Julia stared at the ceiling in darkness. This room needed painting as well. She never liked the colour. It was the builder who chose it three years ago. She had too many other things on her mind at the time – getting the house finished, the wedding, the honeymoon. She'd left the choosing of the colours to the contractor. Maybe a light cream would be nice, or even a light blue. She had seen that on a wall somewhere and it was different. Where had she'd seen it?

She felt Sonny climax and he slid off her and lay on his back. There was silence between them. Sometimes she felt so guilty. 'What are you thinking about?' she asked.

Sonny didn't respond for a few seconds. 'Things.'

'What things?' said Julia, even though she was afraid of what answer he might give.

'I'm thinking of this duvet.'

'What about it?'

'We had such plans before we got married, children and everything.'

'Things weren't so bad then. Now young people are sure to be involved. Think of the pain parents go through with their sons being jailed or shot or who knows. Look at young Cahill, an innocent fella, and his mother so distraught when I told her he was arrested.'

Julia was just making excuses. The truth was she yearned for more excitement in her life, and that didn't include squealing kids. When she was with Plank, she felt exhilarated and had a sense of more adventures to come. She never felt that way with Sonny. It wasn't his fault. Maybe she only wanted him because he was handsome and the other girls were jealous of her. If only she'd known it would be like this – dull and dreary, with nothing to look forward to except being tied down with children. Why couldn't he be like Plank? But would that make a difference?

'Maybe things will settle down soon,' said Sonny.

'You said you were thinking about the duvet.'

'Yeah, maybe I was. It's not important really.'

'It is important. Tell me.'

'It was a wedding present from the Cranny twins.'

'Yeah, I know.'

'When we were first married you said we would never need it. That you would always keep me warm. Now we need it all the time.'

Again, there was silence. Julia felt a wave of guilt overtake her. She remembered saying that, not once but a few times. God, she was so innocent then.

'Everything has changed,' she said. 'Even the old Cranny ladies are dead.'

'You're right, everything changes. But there is one thing that won't change and that is the way I love you.'

Julia squeezed her eyes closed. God, he could make her feel awful. She sat up in the bed, grabbed the duvet and tossed it out to the floor. Then lying back, she turned around to face him, smoothed back his hair with the palm of her hand, and whispered, 'Love me, darling.'

10

This time the meeting was packed, and not just because of the leaflets. The community was still angry about what had happened to Eric Johnson's wife. She had answered a knock on the door one evening and someone shot her, thinking it would be him. Whoever did it, most likely some young guy with little experience. He must have been excited, or even afraid, and pulled the trigger in haste. Luckily, the bullet went through her shoulder and she wasn't mortally wounded, but people were upset. Pete said that was a good thing. In spite of all the mayhem and killings, at least some were still not immune.

Frank Brannigan, Sonny and Alice occupied the top table. Sonny looked around the room. Everyone was more focused. Attentive. There was clearly a wish for something to be done. Frank tapped his biro on the table and a hush descended. He began by welcoming everyone, and he suggested that people refrain from smoking as not everyone liked it. A voice shouted up, 'Is this meeting about stopping smoking? Because if it is I'm out of here. If I want to attend a Quaker meeting, I'll go to Portadown.'

There was a ripple of laughter. Frank responded by saying everyone was free to do what they wanted, that he himself was a smoker, and that it was just a suggestion in deference to anyone with breathing problems, but perhaps those Quakers in the room would tolerate the pleasures of nicotine for the duration of the meeting. The idea of Quakers being present also got a laugh. Pete the Pipe made a show of putting his pipe into his breast pocket.

'Okay,' said Frank. 'Now that we have solved the smoking issue, let's turn to easier problems.'

Sonny was impressed by Frank's handling of the situation, though Alice thought Sonny could do better.

'You all know why we're here,' continued Frank. 'But let me summarise. On my way tonight, not a hundred yards from the house of my birth, I was stopped and questioned and interrogated by a soldier, who for sure didn't have an Armagh accent. It is not an exaggeration to say that every time this happens it feels like an invasion, a rape of my being. Now I know this is nothing compared to what many have suffered, and continue to suffer, which is why we are here. However, it might be interesting if we take that incident from another perspective, that of the soldier. He will say that he is in an army, and soldiers must do as ordered and if we investigate higher up the chain, they will say that soldiers are deployed in a part of the United Kingdom, which is where we happen to live, whether we like it or not. Plus, he will say if the IRA weren't trying to kill his comrades, then they wouldn't be here at all. Each side argues their own justification for what's going on, and in the meantime the populace, that's us, suffer the consequences.'

Frank paused. Sonny could feel the tension in the room. With his use of the phrase "rape of his being" Frank had put into words what many felt but couldn't express. He had fired up the audience with his description of harassment, but at the same time wasn't cheer-leading for the IRA.

'Perhaps,' said Frank, 'we all wish to see the border go and our county united, but this isn't an anti-partition meeting. It's about how we can go about our daily lives and not be caught in the middle of two warring factions. That's how I see it, and it's up to the meeting now to make suggestions.'

Frank sat down and there was silence in the room. A voice said, 'You talk about doing away with the border. There are guys out there happily shouting the same slogans, but if the border disappeared in the morning these same patriots would be totally dismayed.'

Everyone knew he was referring to smugglers. Many of the top IRA guys were big into smuggling. When the border was established, it meant that the price of products would be different on each side. And it wasn't just different prices that made it lucrative for the smuggler. There was always a scarcity of something on one side or the other of the imaginary line. In border areas, smuggling was tolerated by the locals, and few questioned the contradiction of an industry being run by the same people who were literally dying in some cases to demolish its source. As such, the guy who raised the issue at the meeting would get little support, and in fact he was ignored by all.

When no one spoke for a few seconds, Frank said, 'Come on people, let's hear you.' A woman, one of the few present, stood up. She spoke with a cultured accent that wasn't entirely English, more like a mixture of South

Dublin and Scottish. She wouldn't get much of a hearing, Sonny thought. Too upper-class. She'd be perceived as some kind of airy-fairy do-gooder.

She said, 'If there could be a mass movement of people shouting, "Stop the conflict," maybe by holding marches and such, it might make a difference.'

Sean Donnelly stood up. 'We can have all the marches in the world, but at the end of the day, and I don't like to say it, it's only politics that brings about change. I know that many of you will argue that politicians have not solved any of our problems, and that's why the IRA have resorted to the bomb and the bullet. But if you look at any conflict that has ever happened in history, it ended in politics regardless of who won. Ultimately, it will be politics which will end our troubles.'

'What are you saying?' some voice asked. 'That we form a political party and take over the country?'

'What I am saying,' said Donnelly, 'is that when a wind for change arrives it will come via politics.'

'What *is* politics?' someone asked, perhaps trying to be smart.

Brannigan answered, 'Maybe politics is the way humans organise themselves without fighting. You know the way animals fight each other over a mate or over territory. They don't use politics.'

The same smart alec said, 'I know a guy who fought another guy over a woman.'

Another voice: 'The two of them should have gone into politics.'

'I think the IRA and the Brits should sit on the ditch and hash it out.'

'Mightn't be a bad idea.'

'Mightn't be a bad idea if we had four months of summer guaranteed every year as well.'

Frank rapped the table with his pen. This was all going nicely. Plenty of engagement, but was now time to call order. 'There will be local elections next year,' he said. 'What if we put forward a candidate to represent our views?'

Alice glanced at him. She was seething. Brannigan was using them all just to achieve his own ends.

Sean said, 'Mr. Chairman, what are you going to call this new political party?'

'I don't think the name is important,' said Brannigan. 'But it would show everyone what we are trying to do. As Shakespeare said, what's in a name? It won't change the reality of what we want to achieve.'

The lady with the cultured voice stood up. 'I think we have made progress here tonight, and we should be happy about that.'

'I agree,' said Frank. 'So, if everyone is happy, we can conclude the meeting now. Our little committee will arrange when to call the next one. Any objections?'

No one said anything.

'Okay, I declare the meeting closed.'

11

Donal Cahill couldn't sleep at night. He couldn't eat either. He couldn't read or write or concentrate on anything. His mind was all fuzzy. Every time he rang the army number, Pope Pius, or Craig, warned him what the Hitler guy would do if he didn't come up with the goods. But he couldn't discover anything. He went to Mulligan's on several occasions to see if he could get information but nobody talked to him much. Maybe they knew what he was up to. If they did, they would torture and shoot him in the back of the head and leave him in a ditch somewhere. He told Craig about the English woman singing rebel songs. He wanted to know who else was singing rebel songs and Donal gave him some names. But that's all he could find out. He thought of making stuff up, but he knew he would be discovered. He couldn't run away because he had no money and nowhere to go. Hitler would soon turn on him, he could feel it. Or maybe the IRA would get him first. There was only one solution.

Father Brady, the local curate, was a very conflicted man. At seventy-one he would never make parish priest, but he didn't really care. His favourite Bible quote was, 'It is easier for a camel to pass through the eye of a needle than for a rich man to enter the Kingdom of God.'

He applied that dictum to all the perks and rewards of modern life. The conflict in him arose because of his love of country, and the love of his church. The ideal Irishman in Fr Brady's mind (an Irishwoman's role was really in the home) would receive the Lord in the morning and that night inflict chaos and mayhem on the English forces of occupation, giving his life if necessary.

However, when he looked at what the free part of Ireland was becoming, he despaired. People were reneging on their duty towards Sunday mass and the confessional. Rock-and-roll and sex were everywhere. Colleens had no shame or modesty. The Free State government was clearly communist. Things weren't as bad in the North, so if his dream of a united Ireland was achieved would the North become like the atheistic South? He didn't like to admit it, but attendance at Sunday mass was greater in the North because Catholics had an enemy, something they had to protect themselves against. The southerners had no such problem. Protestantism was largely wiped out there, so what was there to oppose?

His primary duty was to save as many souls as possible, so he loved hearing confession. Most other clergy hated this aspect of their work – sitting in a stuffy dark box for hours on end, listening to penitents confess mostly human failings rather than any huge crime against God or man. But Brady believed that however simple these sins were, they merited the sacrament of penance, a gift he had the power to confer. He took great joy in bestowing it on those willing to receive it. He seldom paid much heed to the sins of his penitents. He had heard them a million times before. Women confessing about gossiping or maybe not paying for something in the supermarket. Men talking about having bad thoughts or getting drunk and spending the household money.

Gradually over the years the age-group of those coming to confess got older and older. Rarely did he have a young person sitting in the cubicle waiting for him to slide back the latch. So, when it transpired that he had a teenager waiting on him, his attention became focused.

Instead of the usual, 'Bless me father, for I have sinned,' the young lad immediately said, 'If you commit suicide do you go to hell?'

Fr Brady collected his thoughts. Suicide was the latest curse to afflict his flock. Too often he found himself crying beside distraught parents with no words of comfort to offer.

'Start at the beginning, my child. God loves you. You will never go to hell.'

'It's too bad, Father,' said Donal.

'What is too bad, my son?'

'I wrote love letters to someone but I never sent them. Now the army has them and they are going to send me to jail.'

'You are not going to jail. I won't let them. Tell me the whole story.'

Donal blurted out his entire ordeal of being lifted by the army and being made to act as a spy.

'I would rather die than have go to jail, Father,' he wailed. 'Can you forgive me of all my sins, and for killing myself? Please, please, Father. I don't want to go to hell forever.'

Fr Brady listened, appalled. The English hadn't changed in six hundred years. Every uprising was eventually doomed because of informers, and if you couldn't pay them off you blackmailed them. But he had a problem. He was bound by the secret of the confessional, and could tell no one of this guy's dilemma. Something had to be done. He had to get him to repeat his story to someone else, but to whom?

First things first. He told the penitent that he would give him absolution, but he was to come with him at once and tell his story to someone he knew.

'I can't, I can't. Hitler or the IRA will get me.'

'Then suffer the fires of hell. Because if you don't get absolution and do your penance that's what will happen.' He hated having to make such threats but it was the only way.

Cahill had no choice. He agreed to tell his story to the friend of the priest, and he felt some relief after receiving absolution. Fr Brady exited the confessional with his penitent. He couldn't take the chance of leaving him alone.

When Sonny answered the front door, he was surprised to see Fr Brady and Donal Cahill, but he invited them both in. He apologised for the untidiness of the living-room, and offered them either tea or something stronger. Donal, his face the colour of snow, shook his head. Fr Brady, his cheeks an unhealthy purple hue, accepted a glass of Bushmills. Donal asked to use the toilet. While he was out of the room, Fr Brady told Sonny not to enquire how he had come to know what Donal was about to tell him. Sonny understood at once. The sacramental seal. He was just glad Julia was out visiting her sister. This must be serious stuff.

When Cahill came back, Sonny said casually, 'Did the handle for the toilet stick on you Donal? You just have to keep pushing it. Really, I should get it fixed.'

'I don't know,' said Cahill, not interested in a toilet flush.

'Sit down,' said Sonny, 'and before you tell me your story, I want to reassure you that it won't leave these four walls. We will get it sorted, okay?'

The teenager sat hunched forward with his hands clasped together and jammed between his knees. He was attempting to speak but no words came out.

'Take it easy,' said Sonny.

'Will Hitler or the IRA get me?'

'Nobody is going to get you.'

Donal's eyes swept around the room like a caged animal. 'Can I go to the toilet again?'

'Sure, you can, and keep pushing the handle.'

Sonny replenished the priest's glass. When Cahill came back, he sat down, his head hanging in shame. After encouragement from the priest and Sonny, he repeated the story of the letters. So as not to disrupt him, Sonny kept staring at the flower pattern on the carpet and listened intently. He understood exactly Donal's feelings of love for this young girl. He remembered how he felt about Julia when they first met, the way he thought about her all the time, the silly letters he wrote. Cahill's story was no different. Those army bastards. How dare they put anyone through such torture? It would drive you to tears.

'What can I do? What can I do?' sobbed Donal.

Sonny went over and put his arm around him, saying, 'Don't worry. I can fix it. I can fix it, no problem. But we have to work out a strategy.'

He kept his arm around Donal's shoulder. If the young fellow had been spying for the Brits, whether being blackmailed or not, it would not be so easy to fix. He would have to tread gently.

'I hope you don't mind us coming to you, Sonny,' said the priest. 'There is a lot of talk about the initiative you are taking.'

'No, that's fine. Let me think.' This was serious stuff. He had to keep Cahill occupied. 'You're an odd job man,' he said to him. 'I have a job for you here preparing my garden for sowing out. I have never been able to get around to it. There is a week's work in it. What do you think?'

'What about Hitler and the letters?'

'I will see about that right away. But you have to trust me, okay?'

'If you can keep them from putting me in jail.'

'You start the garden at seven in the morning, all right?'

Donal nodded, and Sonny looked at the young lad sitting glumly. This Hitler guy and the letters weren't Donal's biggest problem. If the IRA got wind of him informing – and they always seemed to know everything, as if the walls had ears – then he was a dead man walking.

12

Sonny tried to stay relaxed and not rehearse what he wanted to say. He looked at the pictures hanging on the wall of the snug. One of the football team photos had his dad in it. His dad was big into the GAA. He had encouraged his only son to be a footballer, but it was all in vain. On one occasion, the underage football coach took Sonny aside and asked him why he was just standing watching the action rather than getting involved. Sonny said he was wondering what it must be like to walk on the moon. He had been watching a programme the night before about the moon landing. The coach just shook his head and muttered something like, 'Another spacer.'

Rooster entered the snug carrying his big mug and teapot in a deliberate way, as if every movement was thought out, like an army general in battle. Sonny studied him. Hopefully, he didn't see this encounter as a battle because if he did there would only be one winner. How to greet him? Everyone addressed him as Rooster and not his real name, which was Richie Ward. Better keep it informal. 'Hello, Rooster.'

'Hello, Sonny, how have you been?'

'Very well, thanks. And you?'

Rooster bent his knee a couple of times before sitting down. 'The oul' arthritis isn't improving, but that's one of the perks of age, I guess.'

'It's a perk I can do without.'

'You have a long way to go yet. Anyway, I don't think your father had arthritis, if I remember right, so it may not be in your genes.'

Rooster lost no opportunity to bring his father into the conversation. Try and keep it light.

'I'm sure there are other better things one can inherit, like a farm of land.'

Rooster poured out black tea. 'For all his love of country, your father personally owned very little of it. But inheritance is a big concept. Anyway, what's on your mind?'

There was no way to make it sound good so Sonny told Donal's story to Rooster straight. The only time a flicker of emotion passed over the IRA man's good eye was when he heard the word 'informant'. Sonny asked him not to let harm come to the young fellow, that he felt he had no choice but now realised his mistake.

Rooster sipped his tea, and when the cup was empty, he filled it up again. After Sonny finished speaking Rooster stared at him.

'Are you not angry at the bastards?'

'Of course, I'm angry, but what can I do?'

'You can sign up like any red-blooded Irishman and make them pay.'

Sonny shook his head. 'I can't.'

'Are you afraid of what might happen to you?'

'I don't think so. I have no stomach for violence.'

Rooster changed tack. 'What does Julia say?'

'You know Julia is a hard-line republican.'

'Your relationship with her isn't always one hundred per cent?'

'I don't know how you know that, but I suppose it's true.'

'What do you think is the problem?'

'I don't know. Maybe she doesn't have enough respect for me.'

'And why do you think that is?'

'Because I don't get involved in the movement.'

'If you got involved, would it improve the relationship? Women are attracted to men of action.'

'I'm certainly not that type.'

'Here is a glorious opportunity to prove otherwise.'

Sonny knew Rooster was trying to manipulate him. He just listened quietly. He didn't want to antagonise him.

'If it's not fear that's holding you back, then what?'

'I know how much you hate the English, and I don't like them either, but I couldn't kill anyone, not even an English soldier.'

There was a pause. Rooster said, 'Because you are your father's son, I will tell you something that very few people know, Sonny.'

'What's that?'

'My stepfather was English.'

'What? I don't believe you.'

'My mother was from around here but worked in England after my father died. I was seven at the time. Even though there were just the two of us, I was happy. That Christmas she was going to buy me a pony because I loved horses. But it never happened. She met my stepfather. He was a drunkard and would beat up on her. But in the end, he did make a man out of me. Do you want to know how?'

'How?'

'I was a weak nervous child afraid of everything, so in the winter he'd make me lie out in the snow naked to harden me up.'

Rooster stood up, walked over to the wall and stood looking at one of the pictures. It was a very old photo of a parish schoolboys' team. 'That's me third from the left kneeling down,' he said. After a few seconds of staring at the picture with his hands behind his back, he continued. 'I will tell you a story. Once we had a litter of pigs, ten of them. I had names for them all. When they were ready for slaughtering, they were taken out one at a time. My stepfather knew I couldn't stand the sight of blood, and while the butcher looked on, he made me cut the pig's throat with a knife. I can still remember the gush of warm sticky red liquid over my hands and arms as the pig bled to death. Did you know that fresh blood has a smell, almost a strange sweet kind of smell? I remember Squealer was the first to die. I made them keep Wee Lucky to the end. She was the last to be born and her mother had no teat for her, so I reared her myself with a bottle. She would come running to me when I entered the sty. On the day she was to die, she stayed sulking in the corner. Maybe she could smell the blood and death. She knew her time had come. Everyone in that situation does.'

Rooster turned back to the table. 'But by then I had come to realise there are things that must be done. I was no longer a frightened little boy. I had power if I wanted to use it. It was up to me. My stepfather died young. Too much alcohol. That's why I never drink. Then as I grew up and read my Irish history, I found out how the English had treated my mother's ancestors, just like he had treated her, and it made me want to do something about it. You remind me of that little boy, Sonny.'

Sonny didn't speak because he didn't know what to say.

'You're very quiet. What have you to say?'

'So now you'd kill any Englishman,' said Sonny, as much to himself as to Rooster.

'I kill those who have invaded my country, who have come here to trample on my people.'

'You didn't want me to kill the spider.'

'Most animals are not doing us harm. It's necessary to kill the pigs so that we can eat. You only kill what has to be killed. Spiders do no harm to anyone and you can't eat them. It would be ridiculous to wonder why it is necessary to kill British soldiers considering the suffering they have caused this nation.'

Rooster drew in a deep breath and said, 'He will have to appear before a tribunal.'

Sonny knew the danger for Donal. You'd never know who would be on the tribunal, or what attitude they might adopt. He said, 'Why? He never gave any information. He didn't know anything.'

'That's the procedure. If he is as clean as you say, then he should be fine. If not . . .' Rooster didn't finish the sentence.

'Can his mother or father be there with him?'

'That wouldn't be advisable.'

'Can I go then?'

'If he is innocent, he doesn't need anyone.'

Sonny couldn't contain himself. 'Jesus, Rooster, you are talking about having a united Ireland. Does this united Ireland not allow representation before the courts? Because if not, it's about the only country in the world that doesn't. Even at Nuremberg the Nazis had representation.'

Rooster grimaced. 'It's not the same thing. Okay, I don't have the last word but I will see if you can be there. I'm pushing the boat out for you. I hope you realise that.'

'I'm very grateful,' said Sonny.

13

The voice on the phone said for him and Donal Cahill to be standing facing the back wall of Mulligan's at eight o'clock that night and they would be picked up. They were not to turn around. At the appointed time the waiting men heard a vehicle pull up. In a flash, they were blindfolded and bundled into the back of a car. Sonny had already decided to try and calculate their journey. He attempted to figure out where they were going by the bumps and turns on the road. At one stage he guessed they had done a complete turnaround three times. It made sense not to travel far in case they ran into a road block. They had been in the car thirty minutes, but it was likely they were only maybe a ten-minute drive from where they were picked up.

On arrival, they were shunted into what turned out to be a bare room in a house. They were told to stand to attention and remove the blindfolds themselves. When they did so, they could just about make out three masked men sitting on chairs behind a table. The glare from some kind of spotlight was shining directly into their eyes, putting their interrogators, all of whom wore white Ku Klux Klan type hoods, in the shadow. Sonny felt a shiver run through him. The windows were covered with dark blinds.

The middle man spoke. 'Donal Cahill, stand to attention and give a full and absolutely detailed account of what happened to you, what was said by you, and by others, from the time you were stopped at the checkpoint.'

There was something odd about his voice, Sonny thought. As if he was trying to disguise his accent.

Cahill tried to speak, but nothing came out. He desperately wanted to pee. It always happened, even during his driving test he had to ask the examiner could he stop at a toilet. In the dentist's waiting room, he always had to go. His throat was dry. He needed a drink of water but that would make his other problem worse. Eventually he began. As best he could he related his encounter from beginning to end. The pressure on his bladder was increasing. He asked could he go to the toilet.

The guy on the left in a Belfast accent said, 'No, that's not allowed.'

Sonny strained his eyes against the spotlight. This guy had no need to hide his accent because he wouldn't be known in this part of the country. He had been drafted onto the tribunal as an outsider.

The middle man asked Donal what names he had given the army men. Donal said he hadn't told them any names. The middle man asked him to describe in detail the room and everything about the location he was held in. He asked him to describe the two army men who interrogated him. The Belfast guy asked him about his time as an informer.

Donal said, 'I'm not an informer,' and the Belfast guy roared back, 'What the fuck are you, then? Didn't you agree to become an informer?'

'Please, please, can I go to the bathroom?' begged Donal.

'Touts always piss themselves. You don't deserve any better,' said the Belfast guy.

The middle man crooked his finger at someone standing to the side and told him to blindfold Donal and take him to the yard. Sonny asked to go as well. It would be a relief to be out of this room, even for a minute.

When they were back again and standing to attention, the Belfast guy resumed his interrogation. He accused Donal of spying for the army and telling them the names of people.

Donal said, 'I don't know the names of people.'

'You're a liar. We know you gave them names.'

'All I did was go to Mulligan's a couple of times. But I didn't get any information.'

'Did you not tell them Plank Murphy was in the IRA?'

Sonny could have sworn the man on the right flinched a bit when Plank's name was mentioned. Was that Plank behind the hood? Donal had forgotten to mention that the army men asked him about Murphy.

He mumbled into slumped shoulders. 'I'm sorry. I forgot about that.'

Belfast thumped the table. He shouted, 'You are a lying bastard. You forgot about it? What else did you forget about?'

'Stand to attention,' said the middle man, 'and tell us what was said.'

Donal straightened himself as best he could. Sonny knew this was all a bluff. Everyone knew Plank was involved, including the Army. Hadn't they lifted him several times but couldn't pin anything on him? Plank didn't mind his notoriety. He was a somebody. Donal wouldn't have been smart enough, but the locals knew that when they were lifted to always tell their questioners about people who were already known to be involved. It made it seem like you were cooperating.

Donal told them that it was the army guy who mentioned Plank, but he wasn't sure if he told them Plank was in the IRA or not.

'You have been well coached by your mentor,' said Belfast, obviously referring to Sonny. 'He has told you what to say and what not to say, isn't that so?'

Sonny's heart-rate increased. He felt a tingle on the back of his neck. The bastard. Who did he think he was?

'I object to your accusation,' he said. 'I've done no such thing. My role here is one of moral support, as anyone is entitled to in this situation.'

'Moral support?' said Belfast, his voice dripping with sarcasm.

It was time to make a stand. 'You understand the meaning of moral support I assume?'

Belfast shouted, 'I understand the meaning of touts like yourselves reporting us to the enemy, and brave men being locked up or worse as a result.'

Standing to attention in front of guys dressed like the Ku Klux Klan was bad enough. To be called a tout was beyond the pale.

'You are sitting there like some kind of Muslim Mullah hiding behind a mask. What are you afraid of? Are you that big a coward you cannot show yourself? I'm not a tout, and I am a better Irishman than you will ever be. I don't want to be judge and jury over people. Are you too ugly to let us see your face?'

Belfast seemed ready to vault the table and run at Sonny, but the middle man held his arm to restrain him. 'Enough, enough,' he said, quietly but firmly.

Donal thought the guy on the right was enjoying all this. Something about the way he relaxed into his chair.

The middle man asked Donal, 'What do you intend to do?'

'I don't understand.'

'What's your plan when you leave here?'

This was the part Sonny feared – what sentence would be imposed. Many sanctions were possible. He wouldn't be shot. That would have happened immediately. He could be made to wear a placard saying "Friend of the Brits" and told to stand in some public location. He could be banished from Ireland for a period. Or they might let him off – totally unlikely, especially with this Belfast guy as a judge. The guy on the right hadn't uttered a word.

'My brother is in the States. I intend to go over to him and look for work. There is nothing here anyway,' said Donal.

Belfast was on the right track when he called Sonny Donal's mentor. Sonny and his supposed protégé had discussed telling the panel about the American brother.

'A wise choice. One that I strongly advise you to act upon immediately,' said the middle man. 'These proceedings are over. You're both dismissed. Take them away.'

Sonny was stunned. He had never expected it to end so abruptly, and in such a positive manner. It must have already been decided. Why was that? Maybe there was nothing in it for the IRA. To punish Donal would reflect badly on them. People knew he was a simple fellow and not a tout. They would eventually find out he was being blackmailed. Also, his family were well thought of. Perhaps they could channel people's anger at the Brits for tormenting this poor lad, but everyone felt that way about the Brits already.

Sonny and Donal had their blindfolds put back on. They were being guided out of the room when a voice said, 'Bollocks to all this. Waste of fucking time.'

A new voice. It had to be the guy on the right. He'd made no attempt to hide his accent either, and Sonny recognised immediately who it was . . . Plank Murphy.

14

Sonny was correcting a pupil's homework on the kitchen table when Julia danced in singing an Abba song.

'*Mamma mia, here I go again, my, my . . .*'

'You're the happy one,' said Sonny.

'Why shouldn't I be?

'You tell me.'

Julia went over and kissed him on top of his head. 'First, I have my health. Second, it's a beautiful day, and most important of all, don't I have a darling husband?'

'Woah there, pull the reins. What's all this about?'

'Why don't we go out and have a meal this evening,' said Julia. 'We never go out, and there's a new Chinese restaurant opened in Castlehill. You love Chinese.'

'Only a Chinaman would be daft enough to open a new restaurant the way things are. But there's more going on here than meets the eye.'

'Don't be so cynical, darling. Just go with the flow for once.'

'Sometimes the flow turns into a waterfall.'

Julia began making tea. 'Well, let it take you over the edge. Enjoy the drop, honey.'

'It's not the drop that does the harm, it's the sudden stop. Tell me what this is all about.'

'Just say we will go for the meal.'

'Okay, but when will the mystery be revealed?'

'Everything in its own time, darling. Remember the Bible: a time to live and a time to die, and so on.'

Sonny loved Chinese food. Maybe it was the sauces. Someone told him it was all sugar and salt – white poison in other words. No matter, they knew how to delight the taste buds. This new restaurant was no different than all the others popping up everywhere. Coloured lanterns with twisting dragons on them. A fish tank in the corner with colourful koi and carp and goldfish drifting around. Deferential little Chinese waitresses – could you call a Chinese girl a lassie? And the familiar Chinese restaurant aroma. He was glad Julia had suggested it. But what was the mystery? She had something in mind. Could he dare hope she was pregnant? That was possible. What else could it be?

The restaurant was reasonably busy. Sweet and sour chicken for Sonny and a curry for Julia, both with fried rice. Sonny always knew what he wanted in a Chinese restaurant, but he would browse the menu anyway as if he'd never seen one before. Julia put that down to his tendency to be always reading something. One of his excuses for never wanting to go abroad was the difficulty of getting an English-language newspaper. She would remind him that they could always go to a place where English was spoken.

After the pretty girl with long black hair and broken English had taken the order, Sonny wanted to know again what the mystery was. Julia took a sip of wine and said, 'All in good time. Let's enjoy the meal.'

Later, when she laid a spoon down in her dessert dish shaped like a boat, she said, 'I'm going on a diet.'

'I've never seen a banana split being part of a weight loss regime,' said Sonny, running a finger along his boat to retrieve any remaining cream and then sucking his finger.

'Don't be doing that in public. You're not at home now.'

Sonny leaned back in the chair. 'I want to lie down and sleep.'

'There'll be no sleeping tonight,' said Julia, causing Sonny's head to race.

What was this all about? There was little said on the way home. The bottle of wine they shared at the meal had brought out Julia's stage ambitions. She sang 'If We Are Not Back in Love by Monday' and other popular songs. Sonny joined in. Singing was just another of her many talents.

As soon as they were in the house, Julia said, 'Into the bedroom, darling. I will be there in a minute.'

Once undressed, Sonny smoothed the wrinkles on the duvet. In a way, it was like a metaphor for their relationship.

Julia entered the room. He blinked a couple of times. Was it the wine? Or was he dreaming? This was definitely what she'd worn on the first night of their honeymoon. It was burned in his memory. An almost transparent dusky pink negligée tied in a bow at the waist barely concealing matching pink bra and panties with white lace edges. She had a cocktail in each hand, Pink Ladies, each one with a cherry on a stick.

This mirage sashayed towards him. Sonny pulled back the duvet and tossed it on the floor. Julia climbed onto the bed. Straddling him, she placed a knee on either side of his face. With arms outstretched, and still holding the cocktails, she gently lowered herself onto him, saying, 'Drink your pink lady, my darling.'

Sonny's mind was fuzzy. Was it the food, the booze, or the last hour of Julia's ministrations? Whatever it was, he didn't want his head to clear. On his back, trying to catch his breath, he murmured to Julia how much he loved her. He felt drowsy. He turned on his side with his back to Julia, and he felt her arms snake around him and her head resting on his shoulder.

'Sonny, darling,' she whispered. 'I have been asked to go to the States. Will you come with me?'

'Hmmm, what did you say, honey? I'd drifted off. You have destroyed me for ever.'

Julia gave a little giggle. 'Hardly likely, my darling. I have been asked to go to the United States and need you to come with me.'

Sonny opened one eye and tried to focus on the crumpled duvet heaped on the floor. An empty cocktail glass was tipped over beside it. What did she say about the States?

'You've been asked to do what?'

'They have asked me to go to America as a representative, and I need you to come with me.'

Sonny got his eyes to focus. 'Who has asked you? And for what?'

'The Provos. They want someone from South Armagh who can describe what's going on with first-hand knowledge.'

'But, why you?'

'You need to have a clean record and nothing they can suspect you of in order to get a visa.'

'It isn't hard to get a visa to go to America.'

'If you are from South Armagh, it is. But you and I are both clean. You especially.'

Sonny was beginning to wake up and understand the implications of what she was saying. He sat up in the bed. 'You are saying the Provos have asked you to go America to promote their campaign, and you want me to come with you. Is that what you are saying?'

'Not to promote the Provos. To let the American people, know what's going on here.'

'Is this what you had to tell me? The big secret?'

Julia pulled Sonny down again. He lay on his back trying to think. Julia snuggled up beside him. 'It's so exciting, darling. We won't have to pay a penny. And it's an English-speaking country. It will be the trip of a lifetime.'

'Is this the surprise you wanted to tell me?'

'Yeah, darling, isn't it wonderful?'

'Yeah,' he said. There was no point in telling her how disappointed he was, or what he was hoping the news might be.

'You don't sound too enthusiastic, honey.' She never expected him to be. But he would come around. She couldn't go on her own as a married woman. It wasn't the done thing.

Sonny didn't reply. He loved her so much and wanted her to be happy. Anyway, that was his duty, to love and care for her in sickness and in health. But the States, with their puffed-up notion of being the most wonderful country in the world, was the last place on earth he wanted to travel to. What would the rest of the peace committee think if he was in America living it up with IRA money? Also, he had to put out of his mind the suspicion that tonight was a honey trap, buttering him up for the big reveal. Even if it was, there had to be more to it. It couldn't just be seduction. Maybe she really did love him as much as he loved her.

'I am going for much the same reason that you are holding your meetings,' said Julia.

'How do you make that out?'

'It's your intention to try and do something about the hassle people are getting. Well, those stories are what they want me to tell the people in the States.'

'We want to get *both* sides off our back.'

'You know that if the Brits leave there will be no more trouble.'

'When are you supposed to be going, and for how long? I would have to take time off work.'

'Honey, I love you so much,' said Julia, putting her arms around him, knowing he had already decided to go.

Was it very wrong of her to say that while having an affair with Plank? But she did love him . . . a little bit, anyway. Did she love Plank? That was different. And did

Plank love her as much as Sonny? Maybe that was different as well. Can you love two people at the same time? Maybe. Yes, if it's a different kind of love.

She pressed herself against him. 'It's just for four days. They have arranged a series of meetings and places for me to go.'

Sonny turned towards the window. A cherry from one of the Pink Ladies was stuck to the bedside locker like chewing gum. He had been naive to think that she might be pregnant. But there was no way he could refuse her. He read once that the only person who has no faults is the one, you're in love with. It's wasn't true. He loved Julia but could see faults in her. But they were only human weaknesses, and didn't everyone have those?

'I don't know if I can get the time off,' he said. 'But I'll do my best.'

Julia was happy. She put her mouth against his back and nipped him. 'I want you again, darling,' she murmured.

15

"Dundalk Democrat - founded 1849" read the sign on the building next to the junction where Sonny sat waiting for the lights to change. 1849 – near the end of the terrible famine. The famine was always used as a stick to beat the Brits, and rightly so. He took in the scene. If a complete stranger was told that there was a war happening less than five miles away, he would find it difficult to believe. It's another country, a local might say. It's not our problem what's going on in the North. Others might rub their hands and say it's terrible what's going on up there, but we don't want it to spread to our side of the border. Was it selfishness, or just the human instinct to protect oneself? Were these lights ever going to change?

One of the dresses in a boutique window had caught Julia's eye. She would love to try it on. It might still be there on their way back. Better not say anything about shopping to Sonny. It was another of his pet hates. She would have to allow him a lot of leeway. Going to America wasn't part of his plans. But Plank was all for it, and he made her promise to bring him home a confederate flag. It was a symbol of rebellion, he said. She had heard Sonny say one time it was a symbol of slavery. Plank wouldn't have had any part in the decision to send her to the U.S. It would be higher up the chain of command. When she was making love to Plank a couple of nights before she left, she felt very uncomfortable, and maybe a little bit guilty. Better to banish guilty thoughts from her mind and concentrate on Sonny during this trip.

'You are very quiet, hubby,' she said.

'Would these lights be stuck do you think?'

He glanced over at her. She looked so lovely in jeans, a white tee shirt and matching denim jacket. With a figure like hers, casual would pass for formal. Maybe it was only him who thought that.

'At last,' he said as the lights turned green.

Thirty minutes later he drove slowly through Castlebellingham, named after some aristocrat whose castle still dominated the little town. Next came Dunleer, a village that had grown around a monastic site. That was where all these settlements came from, he thought. Either the English or the church. Well, maybe along with the Normans. And a few Vikings. God, the Irish were a mongrel race.

Then there was Drogheda. No one could dispute the importance of this area to Irish history, especially with regard to the North. First of all, there was Oliver Cromwell who massacred the people of Drogheda simply because they were Catholic. Then there was the Battle of the Boyne. Different century, different actors, same fight. All to suppress a papist threat to the English monarchy. He remembered Ian Paisley on the news shouting to a crowd, 'Not an inch. Never, never, never.' It was no fluke that the leading unionist politician was a protestant clergyman.

'I know what you're thinking about,' said Julia as they crossed over the Boyne River.

'Tell me.'

'Easy. You're thinking about the Battle of the Boyne.'

Sonny laughed. 'One smart lady.'

'So let that be a warning to you. When we are in the States and all those American cheerleaders are trying to get the Irish hunk's attention, I will know what you're thinking.'

'Yeah, yeah, yeah.'

Julia sometimes wondered why it was she could play around and yet be so jealous if someone else caught *his* eye. Maybe it was a kind of love, this wish that no one else could have him. She hoped so. Better that than selfishness.

16

'God, that's something else.'

Sonny was speaking to himself as much as to Julia. He was looking at the nighttime Manhattan skyline. The black taxi driver said, 'Yeah, man.' Recognising Sonny's Irish accent, he pointed his finger like a gun and said, 'Bang, bang!'

So, they did know about Ireland here, but what did they really know? Sonny pointed his finger back, said, 'Bang, bang!' and then, 'Mafia.'

The driver laughed.

They were staying in a hotel on Sixth Avenue, a few blocks from Times Square. Sonny rose early the next morning and went out onto the street. He strolled along and took it all in. Was it his imagination, or could he really feel an energy in the air? He had never experienced this feeling anywhere else. An atmosphere of excitement, of dynamism, of enthusiasm. It wasn't just him, everyone felt it. It was written on their faces. Great wealth was on display, but it wasn't only for the rich. Everything was possible. His opinions about America were all wrong. He knew now why the USA had been so successful.

A cop told him that the huge railway station was the famous Penn Station. Next was Madison Square Garden, a massive concert auditorium better known in

Ireland for legendary boxing contests. He wondered if Rodney ever actually fought there. In the distance he could see the iconic Macy's Store, and finally, Times Square, where he just stood and marvelled. It wasn't the buildings. It wasn't just the ambience of the place, and the variety of human faces strolling, hurrying, browsing or searching the area that enthralled him. It was something more. He was standing in the essence of America. Not a place, or a piece of earth, or a spot on a map. It was an idea. And Times Square was its soul. He felt like crying out, 'God, this is where I want to be.'

The meeting that afternoon was held in a luxurious hotel conference room. Politicians, dignitaries, and business people, all at least fifty years of age and none of them known to Julia or Sonny were present. Most were men dressed in sharp suits. There were only two women. Both had left middle age behind them some time ago, and both exuded wealth.

One of the women was plump with a low-cut red dress revealing an ample bosom. She was obviously with her husband and never let go of his hand. The other wore a green jacket and skirt. She was tanned a deep Jersey-Cow colour, with wrinkles on her face not unlike a seashell. Over a white blouse, she sported a sparkling necklace that glinted from the lights of the chandeliers. Because of her accent, she reminded Sonny of Barbara Streisand.

Before the main session, food, mostly of the salad type, was available on tables, which were adorned with little tricolour flags and green tablecloths. Sonny and Julia were introduced to so many people that after an hour Sonny stopped trying to remember who they were. Everyone talked and listened earnestly to others. They all wanted to meet Julia, and were either Irish or of Irish decent, and clearly Provo supporters.

When shaking hands, the usual remark was something to the effect of, 'It's very bad over there,' or, 'It's terrible what's going on in the old country.' Some would say, 'We have to win this one.' What struck Sonny wasn't the lack of knowledge that these people had about the 'old country', but the instinctive positivity in their thinking. This was the American way.

After the supper, everyone sat down to listen to Julia speak. There were maybe forty people in the room. Sonny sat in the front row next to the Streisand lady, who seemed to be alone. The other woman clung to her husband in a manner that suggested she was ready to protect him from other wicked females. She kept looking into her husband's eyes, and she listened intently to his every word. Maybe this was also the level of attention an American wife gave to her husband.

Julia stood at a podium to give her talk. She looked stunning in a yellow suit. What she had to say was written down in front of her. She wasn't expected to make a speech. All her presentations were written by the Provos before she left, and they were all much the same. The functions and meetings had been prearranged by Sinn Féin in the States. Their people would be in attendance keeping a low profile. What they wanted were authentic first-hand accounts from the frontline, as it were. Their handler said, 'All you have to do is give an address to a taxi driver, turn up, give the spiel and mingle with the guests. A monkey could do it.'

Julia kept herself from looking at the audience. Better to concentrate on a spot beyond the listeners. She had never felt this type of excitement before. She had to keep calm and remember that they were only people like herself. Just read from the script.

After nervously clearing her throat, she began by thanking everyone for being there and for their interest in what was going on back home. Then she read out a tirade of strident Provo propaganda. She told the listeners of the way the citizens of South Armagh, a Catholic, peace-loving people, had been terrorised by the might of the British Empire. Sonny smiled to himself at the 'peace-loving people' bit. As far back as the 1700s, travellers through the area were advised to make their will first and have a sound horse. Julia recounted how the brave youths of the IRA fought the enemy with inferior weaponry but with moral right on their side, and a readiness to lay down their lives for the cause of Irish unity. So, it went on for an hour. Every so often, when Julia told of some particular torture the Brits had inflicted on the innocent Irish, Barbara Streisand would murmur to herself, 'Oh, my God. Those poor souls.' Whenever the woman spoke, Sonny closed his eyes and tried to imagine the real Streisand. Julia finished her talk with a quote in Irish: *Sáróimid*, or, 'We shall overcome!'

Everyone clapped heartily and then queued up to shake her hand.

Streisand turned to Sonny and said, 'I had no idea. I'm so sorry for what you are suffering.'

Sonny tried to be polite, 'Are you American-born?'

'Yes,' she said. 'My mother was Russian and my father was Scottish, so I'm quarter Irish. Also, my second husband was Irish, which increased my interest in all things Emerald Isle.'

As Sonny tried to figure out the maths that could make her quarter Irish, the woman continued, 'I had arranged to go to Ireland with my second husband who was from Cork, but he got a stroke and died just three months ago. We had him embalmed so he won't decay, and that gives me comfort.'

'That's consoling to know,' said Sonny, who couldn't imagine anything worse than being frozen in time forever.

'And we stuffed Boris also and have him at home in a glass case.'

'Was Boris your first husband?'

'Oh, you're so funny. I like you. No, Boris was my pet poodle.'

'Sorry, I'm not used to the customs here.'

'And I don't know much about Ireland, so we have something in common. Have you got electricity there? But even if you don't, I still want to go.'

Sonny told her she should visit and that she would like it. She wanted to know if the British imposed curfews in Cork because she would want to see the Giant's Causeway. Sonny assured her that there were no curfews in Cork, and she would definitely see the Giant's Causeway.

Streisand leaned over and put her hand on Sonny's knee. It looked dried out like an oak leaf in late autumn. There were five rings on her fingers, one with a huge glinting diamond inserted in it. She squeezed his knee and said, 'You are very handsome. Rugged country men do something to me.'

Sonny felt a shiver go up his spine. Where did she get the rugged from?

Just then Julia appeared and Sonny rose and kissed her cheek. Streisand looked crestfallen. She showed no interest in talking to Julia and moved away.

'God, my heart is pounding,' said Julia. 'This is such a high, better than any drug. The feeling of power, the way they listened to every word I said. I think they loved me.'

'They did,' said Sonny. 'Now, how do we get out of this place?'

'You didn't introduce me to your lady friend. She looks very wealthy. That's an expensive dress.'

'Can we make our escape? I don't want to end up stuffed in a glass box.'

'What are you on about?'

'America,' said Sonny. 'Let's go.'

That same night, Julia had a dinner engagement with a number of businessmen and their partners. There were about twenty people at the table. Again, she was expected to socialise and converse casually with them. On this occasion, she wore a green gown with a white scarf. The Irish Americans had a thing about green, the Sinn Féin guy had said. Sonny sat between Julia on his right and a fat Irish American on his left. The fat man had emigrated from Donegal aged seventeen. He had arrived with nothing only the smell of turf on his clothes. Now he travelled first class, but he wanted to help the old country in her time of need. Sonny wondered if the seventeen-year-old, most likely a shy and innocent Gweedore gossoon, would recognise the boastful loudmouth beside him today.

'Here it's up to yourself,' the guy crowed.

When the meal was finished Julia read her speech. It was almost word for word the same as the one earlier. It went down well, judging by the amount of applause. Sonny managed to extricate himself from his table companion. He had a duty to mingle. It turned out they all belonged to an association of Irish-American New York businessmen. Besides having that in common they were all replicas of the Donegal guy. Boasting about yourself seemed very acceptable. There was no hiding your light behind a whin bush here. But in a way, it was easier to listen to their success stories than to listen to them talk about the 'old sod', and how Catholics were being slaughtered. Clearly, they had no idea of the real situation. While much of their perception was over the top, Sonny's problem in trying to explain what was really going on stemmed from the fact that they were substantially correct. Catholics were being murdered, and it could easily be argued that the Brits were an occupation force. But would they listen to a different perspective - for instance, that the loyalist population had been there for hundreds of years at this stage? Had they not a say in how the country should be governed? These businessmen, all active members of the American

Republican Party, and only a wet day in another country compared to the protestant community in Northern Ireland, assumed the absolute right to have a say in how America was governed.

Sonny found Julia in earnest conversation with three businessmen. He interrupted them saying, 'Can I have my wife back?'

'You are a lucky guy,' said one of the men, in what sounded to Sonny like a real Yankee accent. He stuck out his hand. 'John McDonald, otherwise known as Big Mac. Bog Mayo born and reared, and proud of it.'

He was big all right, and looked to be a fresh sixty-year-old. A navy-blue suit and red tie helped to give him an air of being a somebody. He had a tanned face, high cheekbones and black hair – definitely dyed – like pictures of native Americans seen on the streets. If he didn't know differently, Sonny thought this guy could pass himself off as a Sioux or an Apache. Maybe he modelled himself on them. Sonny couldn't help picturing him dressed in a loincloth leading an attack on General Custer. This guy had charisma and knew how to use it. Still shaking Sonny's hand, he said, 'You have a lovely wife. I hope you take good care of her now, me oul' segocia.'

He was using old sayings from home as part of the charm offensive. Julia seemed enthralled by him.

Sonny extracted his hand. 'I know. She is as rare a creature as the curlew that once adorned the blue skies of Mayo. Are you ready to go, love?'

'Wow, another poet from the old country.'

Sonny said nothing. Why did they all keep calling it the old country? I suppose it could have been worse. He might have said the oul' country. He could see Julia was having too good a time and was not really ready to leave.

'You can go ahead, darling,' she said sweetly. 'I can grab a taxi in a little while. My husband,' she explained to Big Mac, 'needs his rest. He'll be up with the lark in the morning.' And then she added, coyly, 'Do you have larks in New York?'

Julia couldn't understand why Sonny was always wanting to head back to the hotel. Weren't they on holiday? Well, it was a holiday as far as she was concerned. She could sleep all she wanted back home. This was the Big Apple, and she was entitled to enjoy it. Besides, this guy was fun. Maybe he was flirting with her, but all men did that, so what harm?

But Sonny had had enough. He wasn't going to hang around all night listening to a bunch of blowhards. One of the Sinn Féin men organised a taxi for him.

The driver asked if was he Irish, and Sonny said, 'Yeah, how did you guess?'

'That hotel you just came from is owned by an Irish guy. It gets a lot of attention from the cops, if you know what I mean.'

'The mob?'

The driver laughed. 'I've been in this business a long time. I know all the hotels the mob use. I know all the hotels hiding illegal casinos with cops on the take. And I know all the hotels the Irish terrorist's use. Not that I care one way or another. Everyone in this city is a crook. And everyone has a cause.' He caught Sonny's eye in the rear-view mirror. 'Are you an Irish terrorist?'

When he was dropped off, Sonny felt he'd been overcharged but said nothing. Didn't the guy say everyone was a crook in this city?

So, their grand function had taken place in an IRA hangout. The Sinn Féin guys had kept pretty quiet about that. Did Julia know? If so, why hadn't she said anything? There were beers in the bedroom fridge. Sonny drank them all and was in a stupor when Julia came in.

17

Sonny stepped into the Boyne Bar to order a late breakfast and a beer. He surveyed his surroundings. Almost every seat was occupied at ten o'clock in the morning. Other than two girls in nurses' uniforms, and an elderly blonde lady on her own, the rest were young fellas. Definitely Irish by their accents. Maybe they were working the night shifts. At home, Mulligan's wouldn't even open until midday. But this was New York, the city that never sleeps. No troubles here dominating people's lives. Then again, most of the young guys were from counties where there were no troubles either. That was the sad thing. So much of Ireland had no interest in the suffering of ordinary people going on in the North. Sitting here, South Armagh may as well have been on the far side of the moon, even in an Irish bar. A waiter who looked Mexican plonked a plate in front of Sonny. 'Irish breakfast,' he said. The plate was laden with eggs, beans, big thick sausages, black and white puddings, onions, soda bread, thin rashers of bacon and other stuff he couldn't name. He would have to inform Mulligan what a real Irish breakfast looked like.

When he was finished, a woman who he took to be the manager came to take his plate. She had a ready smile. 'The Boyne Bar' was emblazoned on her green blouse, and her name-tag said 'Rita'. She asked Sonny if his breakfast was okay. Sonny said it would do for his dinner and supper, and she laughed.

Sonny said, 'I know your accent.'

'Tyrone,' she said.

'Ah, among the bushes.'

'And you?'

'South Armagh.'

'Ah, among the rushes.'

Sonny laughed. 'Wow. That was quick.'

'Not really. Everyone says "among the bushes" when I mention Tyrone. So, when they tell me where they're from, I say "among the rushes". If you had said Meath, I would have said the same thing, and I'm sure there's not many rushes in Meath.'

'Maybe more heather in South Armagh than rushes, now that you mention it. What if someone says they're from New York? I don't see many rushes on the streets here.'

Rita laughed again, a warm and generous sound. There was something maternal about her. Maybe that's why a lot of these young lads were here. Their own mothers were a long way away. Sonny took a sip from his beer. He asked her if she would like a drink and she said no, but she would rest her feet for a couple of minutes.

Sonny told her he was a teacher here for a week's holiday with his wife, and that he'd always wanted to see New York. 'Have you been here long?'

'Twenty-five years. I've seen it all.'

'Do you stay in touch with home?'

'Not so much these days. But I know how bad things are. Tyrone is no different to South Armagh in that regard.'

Sonny looked around the bar again. One wall had a mural of the Boyne River. He said, 'I've been trying to figure out the real story of America and the Irish. But I'm not getting very far. They all seem so fake. So slippery.'

Rita said there were three types of Irish in New York. 'There are the new Irish like the guys at the bar. That's what I had you pegged as when you first walked in. Then there's the Irish Americans. I'd count myself as one. I'm married to a guy from New Jersey. My children were born and reared here, and I'll probably die here. So, I'm Irish American.' She paused to wave goodbye to the blonde lady who was shuffling towards the door.

Rita turned to Sonny again. 'But then there's the American Irish. Second and third generation. Their first allegiance is to America, which is fair enough. It's where they were born. But it's these old ones who have a romantic view of Ireland. If they're republican minded, as in Irish republican, they raise money for the IRA. And there's a lot of it around. Even the guys sitting at the bar, only here to have a good time, will drop a few bucks in a tin can if they know it's for the struggle. Money is being raised in all sorts of ways and people back home don't know the half of it.'

Sonny looked at the young guys nursing their drinks. It could easily have been Mulligan's on a Friday afternoon. 'What will happen to them as they get older?'

'They all intend to go home when they earn enough. I thought that myself once! Few ever will. They'll get married, divorced, all the usual things people do. Some of them will do well, and some will fall through the cracks. That's America. In time their offspring will become American Irish.'

'Wow, you know your stuff.'

Rita shrugged her shoulders and stood up. 'Yeah, but I better do something to earn my dollars.' She smiled at Sonny. 'Come and see us again before you go!'

When he got back to the hotel room, Julia was standing facing the door in a green trouser suit saying, 'What do you think, darling? Am I like a green leprechaun?'

She did a pirouette in front of a mirror and began going on excitedly about the fashion shops, and how expensive everything was, and how she didn't have to pay for any of it. Mr McDonald, the Mayo guy, had some connection in Macy's, and he told her to charge everything to his account.

Sonny slumped on the bed. 'What? What do you mean you didn't have to pay for it?'

'He has a gold card or something with Macy's. He claims it as a business expense so it doesn't cost him anything. He said I had to look my best if I'm representing Ireland.'

'Jesus Christ, Julia. Can't you see he's courting you?'

'Don't be daft. He has no interest in me. He's big into the struggle. He wants me to impress the donors here and gain their support.'

Sonny sat saying nothing. She had bags of stuff everywhere. What could he do? He couldn't make her take them back. If he started arguing, where would it end? And what would be the point anyway?

Julia stopped admiring herself and put her arms around him, saying, 'Honey, don't be cross if he wants to spend money on dresses. It doesn't mean anything.' She kissed him on the lips. 'I only love you, darling.'

'We have to talk,' said Sonny.

Julia sat down on the side of the bed. This didn't sound good.

'What's the matter?'

'I can't stand any more of these functions. They drive me crazy. For the next couple of days, maybe we can each do our own thing. You do what you came here to do, and I will get in a bit of sightseeing.'

Julia almost sighed in relief. She leaned over and put her arms around Sonny again. 'I understand, darling. But I will miss you beside me.'

'It's only for the next two days. You don't need me moping about anyway.'

'I want you to be happy. And if that's what you want then I will go along with it. I know you will want to see all of New York while you have the chance. I won't spoil that on you. I have a meeting soon, so I will see you back here in the afternoon. You go learn all about New York and then fill me in over drinks later. How does that sound?'

'Yeah,' said Sonny, though he doubted she would have much interest in the history of New York.

Julia stood up and began picking among the bags. 'I wonder which outfit I should wear for the afternoon function?'

18

Sonny was back walking the streets. He was getting a tiny bit tired of all the hustle and bustle. What must it be like to be here all the time on your own? He found himself outside the Boyne Bar again.

'Ah, the rushy South Armagh tourist,' Rita said with a beaming smile when Sonny walked in.

'Have you time for a chat?' he said. 'I will pay you.'

She laughed at that. 'There may be ten million people in this city, but it can be a lonely place if you're over from Ireland and homesick and you don't know anyone. So, it's part of my job description. I listen to your problems and the Boyne Bar has a new regular.'

'I won't be a regular, that's for sure. I'm home in a few days.'

'You never know,' said Rita. 'Okay, what's the problem with our wonderful city?'

'I'm not really a tourist.'

Again, Rita laughed. 'Tell me something I don't know.'

'How do you know that?'

'First of all, you say you're a teacher. A teacher wouldn't be here on holidays during the school year. Secondly, you're from South Armagh. We get very few tourists from South Armagh, or Tyrone for that matter. People on holiday are usually into drinking and seeing the sights, going to the theatre on Broadway. You never mentioned any of that. You were only on about Irish Americans and what they do. So, if you're a teacher you're not a tourist. I don't have to be Columbo to see that.'

'You're right. I am here accompanying my wife who is speaking at functions organised by Sinn Féin. I took a week's leave from work.'

'Ah, fundraising. So that's the game.'

'No, it's about telling people here what's really happening in places like South Armagh. My wife is into Sinn Féin big time. I am neutral. I say let the ordinary people get on with their lives free of hassle from either side.'

'My friend, this trip of yours isn't about some notion of informing Americans. When you think of America, think of the dollar.' Rita rubbed her thumb and two fingers together. 'Money! It's big business. Money is raised by those American Irish, I told you about. Only after they take their commission does the rest find its way to Ireland. And these guys take big commissions. They raise money by targeting the new Irish, who don't know any better, and the old wealthy American Irish.'

'Do you know a guy called Big Mac?'

Rita smiled. 'Yeah, I know Big Mac.' She sat closer to Sonny. 'One of the top guys. He owns the Starry Plough Hotel.'

'One of our functions was held there. A taxi driver told me it was a Provo haunt.'

'Raising money is how Big Mac made his fortune. And he works for anyone. It doesn't have to be the Irish cause. It could be the Palestinians, the Israelis, they are all the same to him, as long as he can take a little off the top. He pretends to be very patriotic towards Ireland, but he's two-faced and dangerous. If I were you, I'd do my best to avoid him.'

She didn't have to convince Sonny of that. But what about Julia?

Rita looked at him critically for a moment, and then a smile crept over her face. She said, 'Sonny, the best help I can give you right now is to tell you you're barred.'

He looked at her in shock. 'What? Why?'

'Look at you. A Paddy with the clabber still stuck to your shoes. This is New York. The Big Apple. Experience what it has to offer and stop pining for a barn of a pub at a forlorn crossroads somewhere in South Armagh. The rain and wind howling outside, and inside oul' men sitting hunched over the bar looking at their screwed-up jaws and watery eyes in the mirror. All the talk is about who's dead and the weather. I know the story.'

She motioned for the guy that Sonny had taken to be Mexican earlier. 'Roberto, let me introduce you to my friend from Ireland. Sonny this is Roberto. Roberto is Cuban and his brother runs a nightclub in Lower Manhattan. He'll give you the address.'

Sonny was about to say that Cuban nightclubs weren't really his thing, but she cut across him. 'No arguments. Get your arse down there and Roberto's brother will look after you.'

The taxi man dropped Sonny off at the Havana Nights Salsa Club. On a huge sign over the entrance, there were red flashing neon figures of scantily dressed girls swaying and dancing to music. It looked both scary and inviting. Sonny took a deep breath and entered.

The first thing to hit him was the throbbing beat of what he assumed was salsa music. The light was dim. Everything was red: red lighting, red seating in the booths surrounding a little dance area, and a stage with drawn red curtains. A few of the booths had young people sitting in them, drinking from straws in hollowed-out pineapples.

The bar was horseshoe shaped. On shelves behind the counter were rows of bottles filled with exotic looking liquors. The barmaid flashed gleaming white teeth at Sonny and asked him what he wanted to drink. What would she say to, 'A pint of Guinness, please'? Best be truthful.

'I don't know.'

'You are Sonny Mone,' the girl said.

'How did you know?'

Again, she flashed that brilliant smile. 'You don't look Cuban to me, and Julio said to expect you. His brother rang and told him you were coming.'

Just then a dark skinned, thin guy of indeterminate age sitting in a wheelchair wheeled himself in from a door behind the bar. His legs were missing below the knee, where his white trousers were neatly tied off. 'Ah, the man from *Irlanda*,' he said. 'I am Julio, and you are Sonny. Any friend of Rita's is a friend of ours. Come sit down and have a drink. I want to know all about *Irlanda*, land of rebels and poets. Atala, liquor for our friend.'

The barmaid appeared with a very long thin glass full of amber brown liquid with a strange straw sticking out of it.

Julio said, 'Drink, my Irish revolutionary.'

Sonny raised the glass. He said, '*Sláinte*,' and swallowed a mouthful, wondering where his title of Irish revolutionary came from.

'Wow,' he said, licking his lips. Never before had he tasted anything so sweet. It was like drinking honey made from marzipan.

'Rum,' said Julio, anticipating Sonny's question. 'With a straw made of sugarcane stick. Drink up. We have to talk.'

'How do you know about Ireland being a land of rebels and writers?'

Julio pointed to his missing legs. 'I do more reading than running these days. Plus, Ernesto ordered all of us to read up on the Irish guerrilla tactics during your war of independence.'

'Who is Ernesto?'

'Ernesto "Che" Guevara Lynch, whose veins are flushed with red Irish blood.'

'Jesus, he was my hero when I was a teenager. Were you actually with him? Wait until I tell them back home about meeting you.'

Julio laughed. 'So, you were another he inspired to become a revolutionary and freedom fighter.'

Sonny sipped his rum. Freedom fighter? Hardly likely! God, this stuff was lovely, like nectar really. Mulligan had to start stocking it.

'Why did you call me an Irish revolutionary?'

'I know that the area you come from is full of revolutionaries.'

'Maybe it is. But I'm not a member. There is a people's army trying to drive the British from Ireland so that the whole of Ireland can become a sovereign independent state.'

'Such lovely words, and so wrong,' said Julio.

Sonny kept sipping the rum. 'Why do you say that? Isn't every country entitled to be free, and to govern itself by the will of its population?'

'There is no such thing,' said Julio. 'That's a fantasy.'

Before Sonny could say more, Atala came over and told Julio that he was wanted on the phone. He excused himself to Sonny. 'Sit back and enjoy the music.'

Sonny found it easy to do so. He wondered if it had anything to do with the rum. As the music throbbed, two couples took to the floor and began to dance. Atala appeared with another long glass of rum and a big cigar on a little saucer. Sonny said he didn't smoke, and she laughed her gleaming laugh. She said a Cuban cigar was not for smoking like a cigarette. It was for experiencing one of the pleasures of the world.

Atala moved away. Sonny watched the two couples on the floor sway to the music. It was hypnotic, like a snake emerging to the charmer's piping.

Julia returned with two more glasses of rum. Sonny felt great. He finished off his second glass and sipped on the sugar straw in the fresh one.

'What did you mean when you said we don't have the right in Ireland to a free and independent republic?'

'That isn't what I said. I said there is no such thing.'

'There has to be,' said Sonny.

'I am Cuban, born and bred.'

'So?'

'You know our history?'

'Fidel Castro. Che Guevara.'

Julio laughed. 'There is more to Cuba than that. But in a way, those two names prove my point. Because just like you, I was also once an active revolutionary.'

Sonny didn't want to interrupt him and correct the "just like you" bit. Anyway, he liked that this guy thought he might be a man of action.

'I was part of Castro's movement,' Julio said. 'It was supposed to be glorious, but it was an illusion like all rebellions. We just moved from one form of dictatorship to another.' He paused to stir his drink. 'Ah, poor Ernesto. He had everything: intellect, courage, charisma. There wasn't one of us who wouldn't have willingly laid down our life for him.'

Sonny was struck by the way Julio spoke of Che Guevara, as if he knew him personally. At one time, Sonny's greatest wish would have been to meet the Cuban legend. Engrossed in Julio's reminiscences, he didn't notice someone approach their booth.

He looked up and managed to whisper, 'My God!'

She was like a vision.

Julio said, 'Meet my kid sister, Camila. This is Sonny, an Irish rebel and freedom fighter.'

Sonny had never seen anyone so beautiful in his whole life, never anyone so exquisite. Dark ebony eyes, ivory smile, lips pink as a rose, skin a dusty sheen, long black flowing hair. Jesus. An angel in the flesh standing right in front of him.

He stood up. His head was light for some reason and he had to steady himself.

'It's nice to meet you,' he managed to utter.

'Are you really an Irish rebel and freedom fighter?' Camila asked in a voice soft and warm, as powdery beach sand on a hot day.

Julio said, 'Camila has heard all the stories of our movement and is obsessed with freedom fighters. Aren't you, my sweet sister?'

Camila had kept her gaze on Sonny. He felt her eyes, dark as coal, imploring, bewitching him. 'Please say you are a freedom fighter,' she begged.

'Rebels don't like to admit it, Camila,' said Julio. 'Too often they are called terrorists.'

'That's right,' said Sonny. 'Rebels must be careful.' Which was true. He wasn't saying he was a rebel.

'Not that it matters,' said Julio. 'Because the army you belong to is fighting for something that doesn't exist.'

Sonny dragged his eyes from Camila. He can say I'm in the IRA if he wants to. I can't stop him.

Camilla placed her forearms on the table. 'Julio has become disillusioned, but I think it's wonderful to be prepared to die for what you believe in, like Che was, and now also yourself in Ireland,' she said.

Sonny drank more of the sweet rum. If he *was* in the IRA, he would be prepared to die so he couldn't contradict her.

Julio said, 'What each of you is fighting for has nothing to do with freedom for the people. It has more to do with self-freedom, something that will fill the hole in your own psyche. So ultimately, it's about yourself and not about your country.'

'That's heavy stuff,' said Sonny. Were his efforts to start a peace movement only about himself as well?

'Not so heavy, my friend. If you and your army achieve what you are fighting for, it won't fill that hole. Something else will take its place. You will think, "Maybe if I can just succeed at that, I will be satisfied." Think of Ernesto. He was driven to always find a new cause, and no matter how many of these were successful, he would always have to find another. That is why all countries are run by people primarily interested in themselves. And without fail, they are opposed by people who believe they are inspired by justice and freedom, but the truth is they are not aware of what is really motivating them. There are no free countries.'

'America,' said Sonny. 'Land of the free.'

'Light your cigar,' said Julio.

He decided to try it. Why not? He was in Cuba . . . or at least a Cuban bar.

Julio struck a match and Sonny lit up and blew out a cloud of blue smoke. Maybe this was how Aristotle Onassis felt.

'America is not free. Ask the blacks in the south. Ask me. I have first-hand knowledge of this so-called freedom.'

'What about the Declaration of Independence, where it says "Life, Liberty and the pursuit of happiness". Is that not everyone's right?'

'Saying it and seeing it happen are two different things.'

'There's a belief that everyone can make it in America.'

'A falsehood perpetuated by the successful,' said Julio. 'A lot of immigrants, although poor, are the brightest and most ambitious of their respective countries, the cream of the crop. It's natural that they do well. Also, the only stories you hear come from big businessmen or politicians, rags to riches stuff. But that's like a gambler or a goldminer hitting pay dirt. You never hear of the vast majority who don't.'

'I have to point something out,' said Sonny.

'Later,' said Camila with some urgency. 'Too much talk! Let's dance, my handsome Irish rebel.'

She took Sonny by the hand and led him onto the dance area. Putting her arms around his neck she pressed her body close to him, causing him to move with her in tandem to the beat of the music. Several other couples surrounded them, everyone swaying in unison, unrestricted, unhindered, daffodils in the wind. This was liberty. No boundaries. Complete freedom. A world without rules. He never knew feelings like these existed.

She whispered in his ear that she would be back soon, disengaged, and slinked her way through the crowd. Sonny kept watching until she disappeared completely. He went back to where Julio was sitting and tried to get his thinking sorted. It wasn't easy.

'God, she is out of this world,' he said, and worried for a second that he might have offended the girl's brother.

But Julio just laughed. 'What does your poet say? "A creature made of clay."'

Again, Sonny shook his head to clear it. This guy knew his stuff. Where did he come across Patrick Kavanagh?

Julio saw that Sonny's glass was empty and waved at the barmaid for more liquor. He asked Sunny if he would he like another cigar. Sonny said no. He felt it was the cigar that was making his head spin. He asked about paying for the drinks, but Julio said rum was cheaper than water in Cuba. He still had contacts with old buddies from the time of the revolution, so he had it smuggled in.

Sonny thought about what Julio had said earlier, how people fight for freedom for themselves as much as any cause. Was his own father not fighting for full Irish freedom, because if he wasn't, then what was pushing him? And what about Rooster and Plank and all the others? Even Julia was very committed to the cause . . . Jesus, he had forgotten all about her. But anyway, he was doing no harm.

Just having a few drinks and learning how to salsa. He would teach her the steps when they got home.

'Where were we?' he said, trying to focus. He'd heard of a trick once that if you stand up quickly it can clear your head. But maybe Julio would think that a bit strange.

The Cuban said, 'A civil war was fought in America supposedly to bring about freedom for the black people. It didn't happen.'

'But that's history. Now in America everyone is equal.' Had he said that earlier? Was he repeating himself? It didn't matter, he was saying it now. 'I felt it myself in Times Square.'

'It is a fallacy that we are all born equal. Karl Marx, one of our glorious leader's heroes, not that he paid much attention to him when he got power, said, "A bird in the air is not free." It must stay in its own environment to survive, just like the downtrodden everywhere. Like the bird, they don't have the means to escape their environment.'

Sonny lifted his glass. This discussion was getting beyond him, and he wasn't thinking as quickly as normal. His head was a bit dizzy. But it was so enlightening. Wasn't he lucky to have landed here?

'Is Camila coming back?' he asked.

Julio smiled a crooked smile and said, 'You are handsome, my friend, like Ernesto was. You are Irish, like he was, and you are a revolutionary like he was. So have no doubts, she will be back.'

Sonny looked around the room but there was no sign of her. Maybe he was a revolutionary. What was a revolutionary anyway? Better focus on Julio to keep his mind less fuzzy. 'In America, everyone is entitled to pursue happiness.'

'Yes, but they define happiness in the dollar. The whole system is built around money and acquiring it, and millions don't have the means. Remember what I said about the bird and its environment – it doesn't have the tools to leave the air. Millions are trapped in their ghettos. Where is the freedom for them?'

Sonny emptied another beaker of rum down his throat, maybe the sixth or seventh, perhaps even more. But what the hell! He could hold his beer. And anyway, this wasn't beer, more like the syrup that his mother used to give him as a child when he was sick. He turned to watch the couples on the floor moving their bodies to the music. The incessant throbbing, the hypnotic hip movements . . . he was in another place. A glorious otherworld he never knew of. Then he saw her. She seemed to glide towards him. Camila, the most beautiful creature in God's creation.

He rose to greet her as she crossed the dance floor, and she melted in his arms. 'My famous Irish freedom fighter,' she whispered. Arms locked around each other, they swayed in time with the music. Maybe he *was* famous, he thought. They were floating on a cloud. Camila purred into his ear, 'Tonight I want to make love to my Irish rebel.' She lifted her face to him. Their lips touched and fused together.

19

When Sonny had suggested they do their own thing for a few days, Julia first felt relieved, and then a flash of fear passed through her. Was he getting tired of being with her all the time? That passed just as quickly. Sonny's love for her wasn't shallow or superficial. He adored the ground she walked on. Sometimes that made her feel guilty, but she would never do anything to really hurt him. The Plank affair was just a way of getting a little bit of excitement. As long as he never found out, it wasn't doing him any real harm. But it would be a relief to be free and on her own while here. She wouldn't have to worry about him hanging around like a wet blanket.

She was met at the entrance to the Hilton in Midtown Manhattan by a Sinn Féin guy. He escorted her into a medium- sized banqueting room, where about a dozen men including Big Mac stood chatting and sipping drinks and smoking cigars. They were all over sixty, with one or two a good deal older. The tobacco smoke drifted hazily overhead, creating an atmosphere of conviviality, or conspiracy, depending on your outlook or maybe your expectations. Being a hairdresser, Julia wondered at how many of them had an abundance of white hair. Maybe it was a prerequisite to success, and these guys oozed success. Waiters, male and female, again in green uniforms, scurried about carrying trays of exotic looking delicacies to set on a table covered in green cloth. Everyone made a fuss over the 'lovely Irish colleen'.

As the afternoon wore on, Julia was introduced to at least one state senator (he had very white hair), and two congressmen (one of whom had white hair). The rest were either members of New York City Hall or had political ambitions. Julia had been told she wouldn't have to make a speech. It was a meet and greet.

Not everyone smoked, and very few bothered with the food. Julia was engrossed in everything. She sipped her goblet like a lady and tried a strange looking morsel from the table. It had a fishy taste. Not unpleasant, but she had no wish to have it stocked in the local supermarket. It was easy to talk with these people. You didn't have to say much to set them off. After that, just show some interest and nod and smile.

One of the congressmen rapped his glass to get attention, the bald one with an expansive belly. He also wore a red bowtie. Three others did as well, and Julia wondered if they were from the same party.

When a hush fell, he said, 'Lady,' and he bowed his head towards Julia, 'and gentlemen. This has been a most interesting evening for me and I am sure for all of you as well. Whether Republican or Democrat, we can unite in our love for the motherland.'

There were shouts of 'Hear, hear.'

The man continued. 'I want to thank our hosts Sinn Féin, the oldest party in Ireland let's not forget, for organising it. I most sincerely want to welcome and thank our visitor, the beautiful and gracious,' and here he raised his glass, 'Julia. A toast to her, and to Ireland, the land of all our forebears.'

Everyone raised their glasses.

The congressman asked Julia to say a few words. She feigned surprise. Even though she'd been told there would be no speeches, she had prepared something just in case.

She left down her glass and let her gaze cover the room. 'Oh, my God,' she began. 'If I had known I would be asked to say something, I wouldn't have had the courage to even come. You people make speeches in front of those who rule the world. It is part of your everyday work. I work at a hair salon. What would be your reaction if you were asked to do my job? To give a lady a hair-dye for example?'

There was laughter at this. Someone shouted could she do anything for O' Rourke. A guy with a head of pure white hair stood up and waved. Another said there was plenty of work in this room colouring hair if she wanted it.

Julia waited for the laughter to die down. 'My excuses made, I want to thank you all for being here, for the interest you have shown in the old country, and for the wonderful reception accorded to my husband and myself. What's happening back home is as bad as the Black and Tan era. Catholics are being shot dead for being Catholic. Young people are tortured, harassed, and blackmailed. There is no low that the so-called forces of law won't sink to. I am here to publicise what's really happening, so that the American people, lovers of justice and purveyors of democracy to the downtrodden, will know the truth. So, it has been a privilege to have the honour and pleasure to meet you all, leaders of the free world. Once again, thank you so very much. Thank you. *Go raibh maith agaibh.*'

Everyone gathered around. She had spoken so beautifully, they said. She was a credit to her country. And they began making jokes about curing baldness and colouring hair.

Julia felt almost dizzy. She was ten. It was her birthday. Her father had Greta on his knee playing horsey. Greta was her younger sister and eight years old. She was far prettier than her. She got all the nice dresses and praise. Greta was going to be famous so she had to learn stuff. If there were people in the house, her sister would sing and perform and everyone would clap. They all ignored Julia. It was like she wasn't there. No one knew how she felt. But she did get prettier as she grew up, and when she snared Sonny because he was so handsome, she thought now I have shown them all. But it wasn't enough that Sonny loved her. She was never the centre of attention like her sister had been. Now here in New York, if only for a little while, an exciting life was there for the taking, with everyone wanting to be in her company.

Glasses were replenished. McDonald raised his saying, 'Here's to Ireland. Here's to the United States of America.' There were a couple of 'yahoos. Everyone chatted for a while more. Eventually, people started shaking hands and saying their goodbyes. McDonald approached Julia. '*Mavourneen*, you cannot possibly be leaving yet. I have two impossible-to-get tickets for the latest hit on Broadway. Would you like to go? You'll not believe your eyes.'

Julia caught her breath. God, it was getting better all the time.

'But what about Sonny? I couldn't go without him.'

'I understand fully, *mo chuisle*.' McDonald furrowed his brow to look worried. 'Let me make some calls. By some miracle, I might be able to get a third ticket. If not, Sonny can have mine.'

He looked at Julia's eager eyes. The bitch was dying to go. Wild horses wouldn't keep her away. As for her husband, he was a pussy. Being reared the youngest of twelve in the badlands of Mayo, "first up, best fed" wasn't just a saying. The lad who won the race at the parish sports got the prize; the rest were there to make up the numbers. This Sonny guy was just a number.

Julia said, 'Wait, don't go to such trouble. I don't even think Sonny would enjoy himself. He's more into ancient classics rather than modern musicals.'

McDonald stopped himself from smiling. She was already on the hook. 'Well, let me take you so. You have to ask yourself two questions: when will I get another opportunity to see a famous show on Broadway? And what would they say back home if I spurned such an opportunity? Do you love your husband? Does your husband love you? Wouldn't he want you to be happy and to experience nice things?'

Big Mac paused. Love her husband? What a joke.

Julia's heart raced. What he was saying was all true. Well, nearly all. Maybe the bit about her loving Sonny wasn't quite right. Anyway, she did love him, in her own way.

Sonny was on his knees, bent over the toilet of his hotel bedroom. He didn't want to disturb Julia by his vomiting. Somehow, she hadn't woken up yet. When he'd come in, he didn't even turn on the lights. He'd tried creeping to the bed as quietly as he could but mustn't have made it. Sometime later he woke up lying on the carpet, and he knew he had to get to the bathroom.

Now clinging to the toilet bowl he'd sobered up a bit. What time was it anyway? There was a sliver of grey in the curtains. Nearly morning. He had to face what had happened. Mick told him once that it was better to take unpleasant things on board and try to accept them rather than ignore them. They'd haunt you if you didn't. God, would his stomach ever recover? Mick was right. Better get his story straight.

All right, he went to a Cuban club. He had drinks there, and a political discussion with the owner. He danced with a very pretty girl. What was her name? It didn't matter. Anyway, he danced with her and then . . . God this was making his stomach even worse . . . he threw up all over the dance floor. He was violently ill. He must have passed out for a minute because the next thing he knew they had him propped up against the wall and were rubbing his face with a wet cloth. Eventually, after throwing up a few more times and thinking he would die, he was well enough for them to put him in a cab and send him back to the hotel. That was it, really. He got drunk and was very sick. Lots of people do that. Camila! That was her name. Now he remembered. Was that Julia moving in the bed? He would slip back in beside her nice and quiet. Jesus, he still felt so sick . . .

Julia awoke with a start. Christ, where was she? Strange bedclothes, strange room. Oh God, where was she? What did she do? Vague memories started flooding her mind. A huge stage, show girls, drinking, laughing, singing, people talking, smoking, cameras flashing. McDonald – he was there all the time. Jesus, she must have slept with him. She muttered, 'Oh my God, what did I do? Jesus, Jesus, Jesus!'

But where was he? What time was it? She looked at her watch. Six o'clock and bright outside. She must have spent the night with him. He had a scar on his leg. Something about falling off a roof when he was a child. She didn't want to remember. What about Sonny? What would he say? What could she tell him? What excuse would make it believable? Where was McDonald? Was this his house?

The shrill sound of the bedside phone interrupted her thoughts. Her hand went to her mouth. Should she answer it? She had to think straight, get her head together.

The phone stopped ringing. Julia jumped out of bed. The clothes she had worn the night before lay in a heap on the ground. Where were her panties? Jesus, they must be somewhere. The bathroom maybe. The bathroom was huge, but there was no sign of them. The phone rang again. She was going to answer it this time. Think straight, think straight.

'Hello, who is this?'

'Hello, my lovely Irish colleen,' said Big Mac. Julia stayed silent, so McDonald continued, 'I'm sorry I had to leave so early. I had an appointment. Couldn't miss it. I know you want to get back to your hotel and get some fresh things to wear. Don't forget the account at Macy's. Use it whenever you wish. Anyway, there will be a taxi waiting for you in ten minutes to take you back to your hotel. It's paid for. I will be in touch later. Is that okay, darling?'

'Yes,' was all Julia could manage.

'Have a good day. Chat later!'

Julia hung up the phone. He didn't know that she couldn't remember much of the night. Maybe it was alright . . . except that she slept with him. But she slept with Plank as well. That was different. Anyway, it couldn't be helped now. It was just a mistake. Everyone made mistakes. Sonny would never know, and she would make it up to him.

She searched again for her panties. She must have lost them in some toilet. God, she must have been pissed. She thought, 'Please God, let me not have made a fool of myself.'

The taxi was waiting for her outside. It was the same hotel the function had been in. She didn't notice anything of New York on the car-ride back. What excuse could she make to Sonny? He would see her come in looking like this. He'd know for sure what had happened.

She took the elevator to their floor, crept along the patterned carpet in the corridor. She opened the door gently. There was a smell of alcohol. Sonny must have been at the beer fridge again. He was in the bed, fast asleep. This was her chance to take a shower and be more presentable before he woke up.

Ten minutes later, all showered and perfumed, she slipped into bed beside him. She closed her eyes and pretended to be asleep, even when she felt Sonny suddenly rise and rush to the bathroom. He must have been drinking more than normal. Maybe because he was on his own. Better to let on she didn't hear him.

Two hours later and Sonny was still asleep. Julia slipped out of bed and went out onto the street to get some air and clear her head. When she returned, he was still in bed but starting to wake up.

'Good afternoon, sleepy head. Are you not getting up for breakfast?'

He gave a long groan. 'I must have eaten something that sickened me.'

'Different food than you're used to can do that,' said Julia. She began to fix her side of the bed clothes. No way was it food that sickened him. Sonny had a stomach like a horse, except for alcohol. He must have been drinking more than room-service beer.

'What time did you get in at?' he asked.

Julia had been waiting for the question. No accusatory tone, which was a good sign. Maybe he had no idea.

'It must have been late. A whole bunch of us from the function went to a Broadway show, and then I was introduced to some of the cast backstage afterwards. And there was a buffet. Oh, it was wonderful, darling. I would have loved you to be there.' Here she took a chance. 'I kept ringing the room to get you to meet us. But you must have been out.'

She waited for a response. Sonny just grunted into his pillow.

'The show was spectacular,' she said. 'You would have loved it. The costumes and colour and singing and music and everything. We have to go to another before we go home. Such a pity you missed it.'

Sonny managed to turn his head. 'I got the feeling you just came back this morning.'

Julia ignored that. 'You may stay in bed until your stomach recovers.'

Sonny shifted over on his side. His stomach did feel awful. He knew from experience it would be a day before he had fully recovered. He felt Julia's fingers rub his temple. Would she tell him lies about when she came in? He couldn't be sure, but something kept nagging at him that she hadn't been here all night. But maybe she'd just had a late one. All the hours were jumbled up in his head. She must be telling the truth. The alternative didn't bear thinking about. He would have to believe her.

20

On her way to the function, once again at the Starry Plough, Julia tried her best to forget about the previous night, but it kept coming back to haunt her. She had slept with McDonald. What else did she do? Jesus, how did she lose her panties? Could she have been drugged? She felt a little shiver. When on holidays one time she saw a drunk woman take off her panties and dance around the floor yahooing and waving them over her head. Would being drugged make you do something like that?

There were a lot of people present. At least five hundred guests had paid $100 a head for tickets. Recently arrived immigrants from Ireland mixed with others who were in America for years. Raffles were held. Objects made by IRA prisoners were sold by auction. Some beautiful handcrafted pieces fetched big money from wealthy bidders. It struck Julia that those in jail wouldn't see a penny. She looked resplendent making her speech and received rapturous applause. Big Mac was nowhere to be seen.

Later, wallowing in the adulation, Julia forgot about him for a little while. She hadn't heard from him since the telephone call that morning. She hoped she'd be on the plane and home without having to meet him again.

But no such luck! She saw him approach wearing a huge grin.

'Hello, everyone,' he said to the group surrounding Julia. 'I am rescuing this lovely lady from your devious clutches.' Everyone laughed. Some were pleased to be recognised by this much talked about guy. Julia smiled and waited with a feeling of trepidation.

'Can I have you alone for a minute?' he said to her. Her uneasiness grew. There was something unpleasant on its way. She could sense it. He guided her towards a corner of the room.

'I'm sorry for not being in touch with you since this morning,' he said. 'I was just so busy and hadn't a minute. This is the situation. A seminar has been arranged in Philadelphia tomorrow night, and we need you to speak at it.'

'I'm going home tomorrow,' said Julia.

'I know, but you're going to have to postpone that and go on Monday. The cost of changing your ticket will be covered. Sonny can go ahead tomorrow as planned. It's just an extra day for you.'

Julia didn't know how to respond, except to say that she wasn't staying an extra day. Sonny would go crazy. 'I cannot. I have to go tomorrow. Sonny would never agree. I'm very sorry.'

'This is important, Julia. The people in Philly are very influential and we need to make a good impression. It's an opportunity we cannot afford to miss. That's what I've been up to all day – setting this thing up.'

'I'm sorry, I just cannot.'

'I thought we had something going after last night.'

Julia cringed. Was this just an excuse for more sex? Well, no way. She had her mind made up. She was going home tomorrow.

'I'll be leaving with Sonny.'

'I really need you to do this. Everything will be paid for. You can do more shopping. It's on me.'

'I would if I could. And thanks for all the lovely clothes. But the answer is no.'

His tone changed. 'The clothes cost a lot of money. I would have thought you owed me something.'

'I will pay you for the clothes, if you like. I am going home tomorrow and that's final.'

Big Mac's eyes became cold. He said, 'I didn't want it to come to this, but I am afraid you have to carry out the engagement.'

He put his hand in his pocket and took out a picture. Julia suddenly felt faint. Cameras flashing. Vague memories sped into her consciousness. She only glanced at the picture, but she had seen enough. She was lying beside him naked in the bed, her arm around his neck.

He whispered in her ear. 'I also have it on tape. How good a time you had. But I am sure you don't need to hear it.'

Julia's mind had stopped working. She had disappeared. She no longer existed. She wasn't even there. She didn't hear herself mumble, 'You wouldn't.'

'It's just an extra night. Sonny can go on tomorrow, and if you want, we can do a repeat in the

Hilton. You didn't want me to leave early this morning. You were having such a good time, if I remember, but that's your choice. So long as you fulfil the speaking engagement.'

She became real again. If she had a gun, she would have shot him.

'Do this,' he said, 'and you can have the picture and tape back, and there won't be another word about your little indiscretion.' He put his hand in his pocket and slowly took out the missing panties. 'But I was hoping you might let me keep these. If you really want them back you can have them once this gig is over.'

The panties didn't make it any worse. It couldn't be any worse. She was trapped. She had no other choice. 'Do you promise?' she said in a shaky voice.

'God, but you're sexy when you're like this. I would love it if we could get together again, but I won't insist. I promise after tomorrow's function, it's on the plane and home to your loving husband. Now go and tell him whatever it is you will tell him, and I will ring you about the pickup time tomorrow. I won't kiss you in front of everyone.' He returned the panties to his pocket. 'Talk later, sweetheart.'

McDonald moved away. He shouted something to an acquaintance with exaggerated good spirits. Julia was left standing there, her mind racing. Was this a nightmare? He had definitely drugged her. Why else could she not remember anything? How was she going to explain this to Sonny?

*

Sonny finally got up. He had phone calls to make. His first was to the Boyne Bar. He asked to speak to Rita but it was her day off. In a way he was glad. Telling her what happened would be difficult. He left word with the girl on duty that he would write to thank her as soon as he got home. Then the difficult call, but he had to make it. It was Atala who answered. As soon as he said hello, she knew who it was.

'Ah, world champion rum drinker,' she said.

'What do you mean?' said Sonny, thinking she was making fun of him.

'You are best drinker of Havana Club Rum in the entire world.'

'I still don't understand.'

'Nobody in this club has ever drunk as many rums as you, so you are the champion. You drank—'

Sonny interrupted. 'No, please don't tell me. I don't want to know. I am sorry for any trouble I caused last night. Is Julio or Camila there? Can I speak to them?'

'No, not here now. But I will tell them you rang.'

'I have to go home tomorrow. Will you tell them I am sorry for being such a fool?'

'It's okay. Once you not die, we are happy. Because you are an Irishman, I gave you so many drinks. The Irish are the best drinkers in the whole world.'

Sonny grimaced into the phone, and his stomach gave another little lurch.

'I think Camila is in love with you because you are a revolutionary hero like Che.'

Sonny was silent. He didn't know what to say. It would be funny if it wasn't so serious and he wasn't so sick. Revolutionary hero like Che Guevara? If they ever found out about this at home, he would have to emigrate.

'I will be in touch with her after I get home,' said Sonny, with no intention of doing so. She will have a new hero by then, he told himself. And anyway, once she found out the truth she would have no interest in him, so he was letting her down easy in a way.

'See you soon, Irishman. You guys always make a great party.'

Sonny hung up. Jesus, Che Guevara! He would have to lie down again and get himself right for travelling tomorrow.

He was still in bed when Julia returned. He sat up when she came in. He could tell by the look on her face that something was up.

She said, 'Oh, are you still not well?'

'Getting there.'

She came to sit on the edge of the bed. 'I have something to tell you, darling. Give me your hand.'

She took his hand in hers and paused for a moment. 'I have to give another talk tomorrow night in Philadelphia so I can't go home tomorrow. All the extra expenses will be paid for,' she added quickly.

'What are you saying?'

Again, Julia paused. 'You know those free clothes McDonald let me buy. Well, I was silly if I thought I would get them for nothing. I have to attend another function in Philadelphia tomorrow, which means I won't get home with you until the next day. You'll have to travel alone, but it's only one day and they are paying for everything. I really wanted to go home with you tomorrow, Sonny.'

'Give him the damn stuff back.'

'I tried, but he won't accept it. He is a ruthless man behind it all. I should never have bought the clothes or have anything to do with him. I didn't know. It was all a mistake.'

'Could you not just ignore him and go home? He can't kidnap you and make you do it.'

'It's not that simple. I took on the trip, and Sinn Féin are involved in this as well. There's no way I can just ignore what he wants. Remember why I'm here. They will say it's only one extra night. It's no big deal. Many people would be happy to spend another free night in New York.

'There's nothing free in this cursed place. These functions are all about raising money for the IRA, not about informing people what it's like in the North.'

'I was doing what I was asked to do, and we did get a holiday out of it.'

Sonny freed his hand from hers. Holiday wasn't the word he'd use. Was she telling the truth? Maybe she just wanted a night with the American with him out of the way? Would she do such a thing? He could wait until the next day as well, but he had to be back in school on Monday. If he disrupted the school curriculum any more than he already had, his job could be on the line. There was something else. If he couldn't trust her to be faithful when he wasn't around, then their marriage was a sham. He would have to go along with it.

'You're very quiet,' said Julia.

'I've heard stories about Big Mac, and the so-called "commissions" he takes from these fundraisers. Are you sure this gangster isn't trying to seduce you?'

Julia shivered. 'If he was the last man in the world, I wouldn't touch him with a hurley stick.'

Her reply was genuine and sincere. Sonny recognised the tone. She didn't like him.

Julia had no twinge of conscience. She was telling the truth. He had used her like a tramp.

'Okay,' said Sonny. 'There's nothing we can do. It's just one more night and then let's get out of here.'

That night Julia wanted to make love to Sonny, but he rejected her advances saying he was still too sick. Julia said she understood. This was the first time this had happened. But then again, he was actually sick. Perhaps it didn't mean anything.

The next day Julia packed Sonny's case and jammed some of her new stuff into it. She said she had earned it and wasn't going to squander it now. Sonny didn't disagree. He was pleased at the anger she had for this guy. When Julia's taxi arrived to take her to Philadelphia, they kissed goodbye in the foyer of the hotel.

21

Kennedy was busy as per usual but there was little fuss and no delays. Bags checked in, a walk - through duty free, a wait of an hour, and onto the Aer Lingus New York to Dublin, six-and-a-half-hour flight. Sonny had a window seat. He was looking out at the airport tarmac waiting for take-off. An American guy in the same row as him sitting by the aisle noticed the empty seat between them. Trying to be friendly, he patted Sonny's arm and said, 'Always nice when the middle seat is free, don't you think? Means more elbow room.'

Sonny ignored him. He turned and looked out the window again.

In Philadelphia, Julia wore one of the new dresses, a little blue satin number with back straps and hopefully not too much above the knee. She had paid a big enough price for it. She admired herself in the mirror. Not too formal, not too sexy, and not too frumpy either. Maybe a little bit sexy on second thoughts, but if that got attention what harm?

The hotel was glitzy and so were the attendees. Men and women all dressed up in evening wear. Julia was glad she wore something sexy. She had to hold her own. Despite the trauma of the previous day, the feelings of exhilaration and excitement at mixing with these people were creeping back. This was really living. South Armagh was so far from here . . . somewhere in another world.

She saw Big Mac mingling, shaking hands, relaying anecdotes to anyone and everybody. Every time she looked at him, she felt a churning in her stomach, an urge to vomit. Somehow, she would get her revenge.

Once in school in a nature study class, a jam-jar of frogspawn had been left sitting on the window. Over time the pupils would see the tadpoles appear. One day she had been told to go out into the yard and put more water in the jam-jar from the tap. When she was in the yard, two older boys from another class dared her to pee in the jam-jar. She went into the toilet and did it. The boys reported her to the teacher.

The teacher made her stand up in front of the class and tell the other children in the room she was a stupid, bad, dirty girl. It was the same feeling as when Big Mac showed her the photograph. She had somehow disappeared. Nobody could see her. She didn't exist.

She got her revenge on those boys. She accused them of pulling off her knickers, which they didn't. They got into trouble and were suspended. Ten years later she heard that the teacher was having an affair with a married man. She wrote to the bishop informing him of this. It all came out.

Big Mac had it coming, some way, somehow. He had stolen a piece of her very being, and the only way it could be restored was through revenge. She understood now the real meaning of getting your own back. You got back the bit of you that was stolen so you could be whole again.

He didn't come near Julia, but he did introduce her to the guests in lavish terms as she waited in the wings.

'To everyone who meets her,' he said, 'she evokes memories of the old land. The lilt in her voice, the laughter in her eyes, a smile as wide as the Shannon, skin soft as a new born lamb in Connemara. She is all this and more, in spite of living in the terrible warzone of South Armagh, where atrocities against the Irish Catholic people are occurring daily. Ladies and Gentlemen . . . Julia Mone.'

'The hateful bastard,' Julia said under her breath as she walked on stage. His time was coming. But in the meantime, she was going to enjoy being the centre of attention. All eyes were glued on her.

Sonny's plane landed in Dublin airport bang on time. The flight had been good. No turbulence, nice food, not too long. He recovered his carry-on bag from the overhead locker, left the aircraft and headed for baggage pick up. He couldn't wait to get home to his own bed. Julia would arrive the next day. Even now, without being outside yet, the air smelled fresher. Maybe it was just his imagination. God, America . . . it was some country.

Sonny's brown case, with the orange Armagh colours tagged to the handle, appeared on the revolving baggage conveyer. He picked it up and headed out past customs. They didn't even nod at him. His car was in the long-term car park. He would have to come back tomorrow to collect Julia. Luckily, her flight got in late in the evening after school hours.

Sonny had left down his suitcase to unlock the car when he felt a hard object sticking into his back. A gruff voice said, 'Don't move. We're taking this. You will find your stuff in a brown case with no label on it still on the baggage conveyer. I hope we didn't soil your pretty dresses. You'll look lovely in them.'

There was sniggering and laughing, and then a strict command. 'Don't move for five minutes, missy. Okay?'

Sonny realised what was happening. He kept calm. It was just like being held up by the Brits, only more sudden. Never argue in these situations. You never know who or what you're dealing with.

'Okay, fine,' he said. 'Just take it easy.'

'Smart cookie,' said the voice.

In a few seconds, Sonny could sense he or they were gone, but he waited a couple of minutes before turning around. No sign of anybody or anything. A couple lugging suitcases and three children, one bawling its head off, were passing fifty yards away. Another car with an elderly couple drove past. Sonny headed back into the terminal. He explained to security that he'd forgotten one of his bags, and he was allowed back to the carousel.

He knew as soon as he'd felt the gun in his back why he was being robbed. It was an inside job in the baggage area of Kennedy. A sympathiser, or maybe just a paid crook, had emptied his suitcase and filled it with money, most likely dollars. They had to do something with his clothes so they had a spare suitcase to make the switch.

Sure enough, when Sonny went back to the baggage conveyer a lone brown suitcase was sitting on the belt going round and round endlessly. It contained his clothes and Julia's dresses jumbled and stuffed into it haphazardly.

Julia was finishing her speech. She knew it almost off by heart. If she was here any longer, she would add bits to it. She knew she could make it better. Maybe more Irish, but she would have to learn how to say it. A pity this was her last appearance.

At the end of her speech, the applause was deafening, and Julia knew what it was like to be famous and to have people give you a standing ovation. She felt intoxicated. She had to force herself into the wings where Big Mac was waiting.

On seeing him, reality came rushing back.

He gushed over her. 'You're the greatest thing since the Empire State Building. I want you to stay in New York. I will make you a star, a film star.'

Julia brushed past him ignoring him totally. She went to mix with the guests. A very handsome man approached her. God, but he was fetching, as her sister would say at a dance. He looked to be about forty, flecks of silver in his hair, with the sexiest smile she had ever seen. He said his name was Ethan, but everyone called him Ed. He used the smile again and asked her if he looked like an Ed. There was something about his smile. It was almost cruel but captivating, and for a moment she thought, 'Is this another Big Mac?' At least this one was handsome. God, she was getting such attention.

'I have to find someone,' she said, and she moved away.

She located one of the Sinn Féin men and asked about a taxi back to New York. He said he would get it organised. Another older man caught her by the arm as she was passing and said he wanted to congratulate her. She thanked him and chatted for a couple of minutes. At the same time, she let her eyes wander over the room. She could see Smiler Ed chatting with three other ladies. None of them was as pretty as her.

The handler said the taxi had arrived and asked if she was ready to go. She wouldn't tell Big Mac she was leaving. She had done what he wanted and that was it. She let her gaze linger over the scene one last time. Such glamour. Such excitement. The three ladies were all laughing at something Smiler had said. The Sinn Féin guy stood waiting patiently.

Finally, she said, 'We have to go.'

Sonny was waiting for her in Dublin Airport. Even from a distance, Julia could see that he was annoyed about something. Was he still sore about the extra day? She was going to have to massage his ego.

They greeted each other, but Sonny gave her a very perfunctory hug. Little more was spoken until they reached the car.

'You are very quiet, darling,' said Julia.

'I have reason to be.'

'Tell me, Sonny, what's the matter? This is not like you.'

'You made a complete fool of me. You, and I don't know who else. Probably Big Mac.'

'You're going to have to explain because you've lost me.'

There was very little traffic on the road. Sonny stared straight ahead through the windscreen.

'First you seduced me into going to the States. Then you left me to go out with Big Mac, who is a mobster. You didn't come back to the hotel that night, I'm sure of it, and I don't know what you were doing with him. You headed off on a trip to Philadelphia, maybe an excuse to be with that hoodlum. Then I was used to smuggle a suitcase of money through Irish customs. If I had been stopped and searched it was the end of my career. Nobody would believe I didn't know what was in that suitcase.'

Julia had her hand up to her mouth. 'Jesus,' she said, 'I had no idea about the money.'

Sonny listened carefully. She only mentioned the money. No word of all the other stuff.

'What's the story then with you and the gangster?'

'God, Sonny, there isn't a story. He used me as well by giving me free clothes and a night at a show. I went to Philadelphia and gave the speech. I came back to our hotel as soon as I had finished. I never spoke to Big Mac. I just wanted to get away from him as far as possible. And I didn't seduce you into coming with me. Well, maybe I did a little bit, but I wanted to have you with me. I wouldn't have enjoyed it otherwise. So maybe I was a little bit selfish in that, but it's because I love you so much.'

Sonny didn't reply. She could be so convincing, and in his heart of hearts he wanted to believe her. That was always his problem.

There was nothing more said between the two. Each stayed with their own thoughts.

Julia tried to take in what Sonny had said about the money. Big Mac was even more ruthless than she could have imagined. He had no respect for anyone. He had used someone who was opposed to the Provo's campaign in order to enhance it, and he didn't care that Sonny might have gotten time over it, along with losing his job. Maybe Big Mac got a kick out of doing this stuff. He had used both of them like they were worth nothing. She would never forget how she felt, and the expression on his face, when he showed her the panties.

In bed that night neither Sonny nor Julia slept well. They hardly spoke for a couple of days. Eventually, Julia decided the ball was in her court. She was the one at fault and she needed to make a big gesture to show her remorse. He deserved that at least. Plus, she missed the chatter and his warm feelings towards her.

When Sonny returned from work that day, Julia took him out into the back garden. There were two full black plastic bags lying in the middle of the garden. Julia took a matchbox from her pocket, lit a match and threw it on top of the bags. In a couple of seconds, they were aflame. Sonny just stood there, silent but curious.

Julia pointed to the blazing bags. 'Those are Big Mac's free dresses, and that's what I think of him. I don't want to be reminded of him anymore by having them in my wardrobe. This is him out of our lives forever.'

The bags burned furiously. Sonny stared at the fire. Julia loved those dresses. It must have been very hard to burn them without ever getting to show them off to her friends. He would have to try and forget the New York episode. Get back to basics.

'Can you forgive me, my darling?' said Julia.

'I forgive you.'

'How about we go for a little siesta?'

The flames were beginning to die down. Julia took Sonny's arm and led him into the house. It nearly broke her heart to burn the dresses, but it had to be done. And she was sincere about it. She kept the little blue satin one. She just couldn't part with it. She remembered the way Smiler had looked at her in it. It could be hidden away, and she could say she bought it locally when she got a chance to wear it. Sonny wouldn't know the difference.

22

A huge crowd had gathered for a meeting of the Community Wanting Change group. Sonny was even more determined to do something having seen some of the machinations that went on first hand. He didn't tell anyone of what happened. What was the point? And it might lead to him getting into even more trouble. Anyway, half the people in the crowd probably had a story they could tell. That's why they were there.

'Order, order, can we have some order?' called Frank Brannigan. He was wearing a red dickie-bow. Sonny thought he looked ridiculous. Frank had been trying to come up with some gimmick that would make him recognisable and set him apart as an individual – his own personal brand. His moustache didn't generate much positive feedback, and a goatee beard generated negative feedback, so he hit on the idea of a bowtie after seeing Robin Day on television. The fact that Robin Day happened to be a famous political commentator and politics was where Frank intended to make his mark was a happy coincidence.

'Settle down everyone, please.' Frank began by stressing to the audience the importance of what they were trying to do – perhaps stopping the country from sliding towards sectarian civil war. 'Do I have to remind you of the terrible events of this past fortnight, not even newsworthy enough to warrant a headline in the papers.'

Frank was referring to Bobby Parley, a Protestant who had been heading home from a whist drive when he was abducted and shot. The whist drive was run by the parish priest for a school upkeep fund, so the attendees were nearly all Catholics. Bobby didn't mind that. He loved whist, and a night out was all he wanted. But rumours began to spread that whist wasn't his only interest. He was a spy in the enemy's camp. That was all it took, as deadly as a formal conviction in a court of law. The sentence soon followed.

Around the fireplace, however, where people felt they could speak freely, it was wondered what a spy would learn at a whist drive. The upshot was that Joe Watters, a Catholic on his way home from a *céilí* a few nights later, had been murdered by way of retaliation.

Frank stood up. 'The last meeting had decided on running a peace candidate in the local election, so this meeting should be short and sweet.'

'Does this candidate have to have a party behind him, or a party name?' asked Sonny's teacher friend Sean Donnelly. Sean was also at the head table next to Pete the Pipe, then Frank, then Alice and Sonny.

'It's better to have a name,' said Frank. 'The name is supposed to say in a word what the party stands for. Like the Labour Party, for example.'

'Labour Party, me arse,' said someone in the crowd, but he didn't expand on what he meant.

'So, can anyone think of a name? said Frank. 'Not the Labour Party,' he added, which got a laugh.

'Why not call ourselves Reliance?' said a young John Lennon lookalike who went to all the meetings.

'I like it,' said the lady with the cultured voice from the last meeting. 'It's ambiguous, and we can't be accused of being political.'

'Any objections?' asked Frank.

No one said anything. 'That's settled. Now, who's going to be the lucky candidate?'

Even as he spoke, he unconsciously fingered his bowtie. There was silence in the room.

'Ask for proposals,' said Alice.

'It's been suggested that I ask for proposals,' said Frank to the room.

Again, there was silence until a voice said, 'I propose yourself, Frank.'

Someone else said he would second that proposal.

Frank pretended to be flustered. 'Wait, wait, I have a lot on just now. I don't know if I'd be free to take it on.'

But Sonny was just relieved that no one had suggested he run. He jumped up and said, 'A round of applause for our unanimous choice of candidate: Frank Brannigan.'

As clapping echoed in the room, Alice dug Sonny in the ribs and said, 'I hate you.'

A small election committee was formed and they met in the same hall, now mostly empty, the next day. Alice and Sonny and his two teacher buddies, Sean Donnelly and Pete the Pipe were on it. So was Blythe Atkinson, the lady with the cultured accent, and the studious boy who looked like John Lennon. His real name was Clint. Alice was delighted when he asked to be involved. There was more depth to him than his youthful image, and she loved his enthusiasm.

'A candidate's primary function is to educate the electorate,' said Pete the Pipe, and since he usually said so little, everyone listened.

Sean Donnelly laughed a throaty laugh. 'Educate them to believe what you're selling. Is that what you mean?'

'Perhaps,' said Pete. 'But don't we all believe that what our man is standing for is a worthy venture.'

'Hitler's election committee believed the same thing.'

'Maybe it was worthy at the start.'

'Let's hope Brannigan doesn't go down the same road,' said Sean, and he stood up giving the Nazi salute.

'Where is Frank anyway?' asked Pete. 'He doesn't seem to have much commitment.'

'He has a lot of irons in the fire according to himself,' said Alice. 'Or maybe he doesn't think he'll win. Being on the losing side wouldn't appeal to him.'

Sonny said, 'Frank wouldn't run if he didn't think he could win. Yeah, he's self-centred, but it might turn out to our benefit.'

'Maybe,' said Alice, unconvinced.

For the next hour or so the committee discussed what kind of slogans and commitments they should put on their leaflets. Alice looked at Clint as the debate wore on. His eyes were shinning with delight at the to and fro. She would love to have a son like him. Maybe there was still time, but it was getting more unlikely every passing day. She wasn't going to marry just anyone. Julia was so lucky to have snaffled Sonny. Why were they not having children? Oh well, it was none of her business.

23

On a Saturday night in Cairnduff you had two options: stay at home watching TV, or head into Mulligan's for a few drinks. Rodney Walsh, Cairnduff's former boxing star, wasn't much into TV, especially on a Saturday night. So, like most other locals, his choice of entertainment was Mulligan's West Wing. Occasionally there might be a well-known singer in attendance, although that was rare for two reasons. The first had to do with their fee. Mulligan couldn't understand how some singers had the nerve to demand huge sums when most people just love to get up and sing for nothing. The other reason was that famous singers weren't keen on playing in South Armagh. Even the showbands that would play anywhere with a stage, or even no stage, were dubious of the area.

By default, therefore, Mulligan's was the in-place on a Saturday night. Rodney liked it there. He was well thought of by the locals, who looked on him as a kind of gentle giant – harmless, as long as you didn't get him riled up. Also, his experiences in the States had taught him a lot. There he was thought of as a commodity who could make ruthless chancers a pile of cash while he got his face battered in. Here he knew the value of being at home in his own community, surrounded by people who cared about him.

Through the door into the bar, Rodney could see Sonny and Julia Mone come in. He felt a bit sorry for Sonny. It was admirable what he was trying to do with the peace initiative, but Rodney knew a thing or two about hopeless fights. And Sonny had his hands full as well with that Julia one. 'Give me ten rounds with a New York slugger,' he thought to himself, 'rather than face a few minutes with her.'

Sonny stuck his head into the West Wing to see who was in. He saw Rodney Walsh sitting at the bar. Rodney raised his glass to him and Sonny waved back. He then went to join Julia at their usual table.

'A few couples are up dancing already,' he said to her. 'They look like undead zombies shuffling around. If you shot them, they would rise up and start staggering about again.'

He turned his attention to the bar. Nearly all the regulars were there, but someone was missing. Where was Rooster? His absence stood out like a car with no driver. Usually, he would arrive at ten precisely, and it was now twenty past. Sonny was reminded of the Sherlock Holmes story about the dogs that didn't bark. It was the absence of something that was remarkable. Could he be sick? It was hard to imagine Rooster being sick, but he was human after all.

Then it struck him that Plank hadn't been in the West Wing, and he wasn't in the bar either. Two missing! How strange. He said, 'Maybe having a night off, could that be it, love?'

'What are you on about?' said Julia.

Sonny laughed and leaned over to give Julia a peck on the cheek. 'It's not important. I was really talking to myself.'

'Jesus, Sonny, you're becoming more absentminded by the day. Albert Einstein wouldn't be as bad.'

'Do you really think I'm as smart as Einstein?'

'Laurel and Hardy, more like.'

'That's two people.'

'Well, you're the silly one.'

Sonny kept it going. 'But they're both silly.'

'Oh my God,' said Julia exasperated. 'Is this the entertainment you get on a night out in this not even one-horse village.'

'Okay, stand by, here she comes,' said Sonny, nodding towards Ruby the English woman who was lifting the mic and filling her lungs as she prepared to sing.

Before she could utter a sound, the doorman ran in shouting, 'Raid! They're surrounding the place.'

In an instant, British soldiers were inside the bar and lounge, rifles pointed menacingly at people, threatening everyone to stay still. Every person complied, except for Ruby, who didn't seem scared of the soldiers at all.

She began to berate them, using the microphone so everyone could hear. 'How dare you come in here and interrupt proceedings.'

A sergeant pointed a rifle at her and yelled for her to be quiet.

'You're Hitler's fucking fascists, that's what you are,' Ruby shouted, shocking the locals with her choice of language, as well as her gall in challenging the soldiers.

'I said be quiet,' roared the sergeant. 'Someone plug out that fucking mic.'

Ruby kept going. 'You're all in a foreign land. Why don't you go home and leave these poor people in peace.'

By now two soldiers had mounted the stage. They grabbed her. The microphone fell and there was a whine of feedback in the speakers.

During all this commotion, Rodney Walsh had kept still. He had his hands high above his head and was staying quiet. But when the soldiers began to haul this slight woman across the floor, something stirred in him. He was sixteen. His young sister was crying again in the hay barn. Their uncle was with her. Rodney beat that man to within an inch of his life. Neighbours never questioned the uncle's punishment. They said he had it coming.

Now in front of Rodney's eyes an innocent woman was being manhandled. He walked over to the soldiers and said, 'Leave the lady alone.'

Everything seemed to stop. Even the soldiers froze. The ones dragging Ruby seemed surprised, even confused. Sonny drew in his breath and Julia put her hands over her eyes.

The sergeant in charge looked Rodney up and down. Was this guy an idiot?

Sonny whispered a prayer to himself. At best, Rodney was in for a hiding, but there was nothing he or anyone could do to help. One false move and a scared soldier could open fire. In a crowded space, with that kind of weaponry, it would be a massacre.

Rodney moved to release the woman, but he was hit in the face by the butt of a rifle. Blood began running from his nose. He was enraged. 'You are a cowardly English bastard hiding behind a gun,' he said to his attacker. 'You are all a band of cowards. Without weapons you're as weak as oul' women.'

'Shut up, shut up,' Sonny said to himself. 'You'll get yourself shot.'

The soldier who struck Rodney was about to hit him again when the sergeant intervened.

'Stand down, corporal,' he said. He came to look closer at Rodney. He was big all right, but just another drunken Irish lout. It was time for a bit of amusement. Give the lads something to talk about, get himself a bit of much needed exercise, and best of all teach these monkeys a thing or two. Sergeant Lighthouse had a cupboard full of trophies and belts won in the ring, and while there were no medals to be won here, it was an opportunity to flex his muscles and show off a little.

'Okay,' he said to Rodney. 'I will lay down my gun. Would you like to take me on man to man? Or in this case, pig to man.'

No one in Mulligan's knew what to think. This guy was challenging Rodney to a fist fight. He couldn't have known of Rodney's history. But then again, Rodney's best fighting days were long behind him.

Rodney figured he had two options: take the guy on or back down. But fighting an English soldier was madness. It could even be fatal. People were shot for nothing by these bastards. Better to walk away.

As Rodney turned his back, Lighthouse gripped him by the shoulder, swung him around and pasted his nose with a straight right.

'Fight, you Irish pussy,' he shouted, loud enough for everyone to hear.

Rodney paused. You could have heard a pin drop in Mulligan's West Wing. Only the noise of beer coolers humming in the background broke the silence. Rodney stood looking at the soldier. Eventually, after what seemed like an age, he put up his fists. The combatants squared up to each other.

There wasn't one Irish person there who didn't realise the significance of this moment. Alone on that little dance floor, Walsh represented six hundred years of the Irish being beaten down by English lords and masters. All those centuries of pain and loss had coalesced into what was happening here and now. The immensity of it was difficult to comprehend.

Right away the omens were bad. As soon as the soldier squared off it was obvious that he was a trained boxer. He had goaded Rodney into a hiding. This was confirmed when he hit Rodney two punches to the face before the Irishman knew anything about it. An audible groan went up in the room. There was to be no changing of history. The inevitable was about to happen again.

Walsh gamely tried to cling to his opponent to prevent more punishment. He attempted to put in to practice what he had learned in dingy basement gyms in the Bronx. But even there, against people who could dance and jig he was playing the role of a punch bag. The soldier's boxing skills were way ahead of anything Rodney had picked up. The guy kept slipping out of his reach like an eel from the poacher's grasp.

Rodney felt a tingling in his fist. He knew what he had to do. It would cost him, but there was no other way. He stood back, his arms hanging loose by his side, as if exhausted.

The Englishman pounced to add to the torture. He would teach this oaf a lesson he would never forget. Bang, bang, bang. His fists struck repeatedly. He stepped back to take a look at his handiwork. Blood streamed from the bastard's nose, and one eye was closed. He would soon close the other one. This idiot was out on his feet. Easy-peasy. Time to finish the job. He rushed forward again.

Rodney shook his head and for a split-second regained clarity. This was it. With one mighty effort he released the Big Clout.

Lighthouse never saw it coming. It exploded on the side of his jaw. With a look of amazement etched on his face, his body went rigid, motionless, as if hung frozen in time and space, before dropping like a stone onto the maple floorboards.

For a few seconds, silence reigned. Nobody moved. Everyone was trying to take in what they just witnessed. Some soldiers ran to the body lying sprawled on the floor with its mouth gaping open. The corporal shouted for water. They tended to their boxing hero and he started to come round, as they carted him out to one of their vehicles.

The rest kept their rifles trained on the punters in case they had any ideas about continuing the fight. An order was barked from somewhere and the soldiers withdrew, taking the English woman with them.

It was as if a spell was broken. The locals of Cairnduff whooped and cheered and gathered around their champion, who was on a seat rubbing his fist. He said he thought it was broken. Someone shouted, 'A broken hand isn't important! You've emulated Cú Chulainn!'

But Rodney was glum. 'They still took poor Ruby away.'

'It's her they came for in the first place,' Sonny said to Julia.

'Yeah, she was bound to get attention singing rebel songs every night. What did she expect?'

Rodney was taken to a doctor. After he had gone, there was talk of putting a plaque up on the wall showing Walsh standing over the prone soldier's body. Mulligan was all in favour. It would be a tourist attraction. People would come from miles around. Someone else suggested that Mulligan give Rodney free liquor for life. At that, the bar owner disappeared.

Mick prophesied that in a few days, when the hullaballoo had settled, all the commemoration plans would die a death and come to naught. Hours later they were still celebrating when Ruby, the English woman, walked in. She told them that once they realised, she couldn't be made talk, they let her go. Sonny couldn't help but smile. Mick said she must have begun singing in the armoured vehicle on the way to barracks. 'I'd say they couldn't wait to get rid of her.'

24

'I can't,' said Julia. 'I have turned a new leaf.' She had decided to stop seeing Plank and was refusing his entreaties. He kept phoning and asking why. 'It's been months,' he argued. She didn't find it easy to refuse, and it seemed to get increasingly difficult the more New York faded from memory. Sometimes when on her own she would take out the satin dress and hold it against herself in front of the mirror and remember the way everyone admired her in it. The guy with the smile, would she ever see him again? There was one guy she didn't want to see. Every time she thought of him, her blood boiled.

Sonny was at work when the phone rang again. She guessed it would be Plank. He'd realise she was on her own and knew her well enough to know she'd be fed up. Could she hold out for much longer?

'Hello, love.'

'Hello, Plank.' He liked to be called Plank. She suspected it made him feel more popular with everybody. She knew what that feeling was like.

'I'm meeting a guy in Belfast on Tuesday. Would you like to come with me for the spin? You never get out of the house.'

'I can't really. I have other things planned for Tuesday.' If only he knew how hard it was for her to say that.

'You might like to meet this guy. He mentioned your name.'

Julia furrowed her brow. What guy in Belfast would know her name?

'I don't know anyone in Belfast.'

'He's flying in from America. I have some business with him.'

Jesus, who was it? Someone who knew her, but she'd met dozens at the functions. She had to keep calm.

'Is he coming from New York?'

'Yeah, you met him over there. He's the top cat.'

'What his name?'

'McDonald. He's Irish but over there a long time.'

Julia went silent. What was she to do? Big Mac the bastard was coming here and had the gall to mention her name. He could blackmail her into doing anything he wanted. But what could she do about it? She needed time to think.

'Are you there, Julia? Were you cut off?'

'Yes, I am still here. But I can't talk now. Can you call me back in an hour?'

'Great, will do. I'm sure you will be pleased to meet this guy again. He had a great word to say about you.'

When she hung up, Julia sat down on the sofa. Big Mac was taking money over, that was for certain. Obviously, Plank was to handle it and transport it on. He never really said it, but she knew about his involvement with the IRA. It was just an understood thing between them. They never spoke of it so she couldn't be accused of having information or be quizzed by security forces. But why was Big Mac transporting money himself? He wouldn't know about Plank and her, but he would know that Plank was in South Armagh. That had to be it. He would shift the money and meet up with her afterwards. She would have no choice but to fall in with whatever he planned.

Plank rang thirty minutes later. 'Is that you, Julia? Are you free now?'

'Yeah, I'm free.'

'Great.'

'Plank, do you really love me?'

'Of course.'

'You sure it's not just sex?'

'No, I really love you. But I like the sex as well. Do you?'

'I miss having your arms around me.'

'That's lovely, Julia. When can we be together?'

'Soon. Very soon, darling. But there's something I want you to do for me first.'

'Anything, honey. You just name it.'

'I want you to get me some things.'

'Fire away, darling. A cruise ship if you want.'

Julia spent a long time in front of the mirror. She wanted to look her best. Even Big Mac would be impressed. She gave herself one last look and wondered if she needed a tablet. The doctor had shown no hesitation in writing out the prescription. He had given her a month's supply. Due to the Troubles half the country was on sedatives, he said, and he knew that Sonny's peace initiative was causing her even more stress. He just warned her not to take more than one at a time as they were strong. She'd hidden them from Sonny. He didn't like medications of any kind, especially tranquilisers. She'd better take one now in case she got too nervous to go through with what had to be done. She swallowed a pill with a little water, lifted her handbag, checked the contents, and headed out the door.

She always parked her car at the back of the safe house so that locals wouldn't notice it. Plank's car was already there. He would have Big Mac with him inside the house. It wasn't easy getting him on board with her plans. She had to tell him what happened in New York. He had tried to be indignant about her cheating on him, but then she told him she was drugged and blackmailed. Seeing himself as a top man in the movement, Plank couldn't allow an outrage against his woman to go unanswered. His pride was at stake. But Big Mac was supplying much-needed money to the cause. That meant complications.

Julia had to convince him. She told him that Big Mac was skimming money off the proceeds and pocketing it himself. McDonald didn't care about the cause. He'd raise money for the Brits if he thought he could take a cut. He had only come to Ireland to blackmail her into having sex with him. But wouldn't it be sweet revenge for both of them if the money he was skimming went to Plank instead?

Plank said that they couldn't take the cash themselves. He'd have to report it to the higher-ups. But

Julia argued that he wasn't taking it from the Provos. He was taking it from McDonald. It was never going to the IRA anyway. The logic of this made sense to Plank. It even appealed to him. In the end, he agreed to go along with Julia's plans.

'Ah, the lovely and beautiful Irish colleen,' gushed Big Mac, getting up from his seat when Julia came in. He was wearing a suit and green tie. Julia took particular note of the tie. Plank was sitting on the edge of a sofa. Julia let Big Mac kiss her on the cheek. She said, '*Céad mile fáilte.* Your tie is crooked at the back and making your shirt bunch. Let me fix it for you. Sit down for a second.'

'How thoughtful of you.'

Big Mac sat in an armchair as Julia went behind him and set her bag on a side table next to a jug of water. She took a small pistol from the bag and brushed the man's ear before pointing it towards the jug.

'Don't make a move, you bastard,' she said and pulled the trigger.

There was a sharp crack. The bullet hit the jug and smashed it, spilling water all over the floor.

Big Mac let out a squeal. 'Jesus, Julia what are you doing?'

'Down on your belly. Hands behind your back, or the next bullet is in your brain.'

She couldn't believe how calm she was. The pistol in her hand felt natural. It seemed to give her a sense of power she had never felt before.

McDonald just kept saying, 'What are you doing? Plank, stop her, for fuck's sake.'

Julia put the gun next to his ear and fired again. It almost deafened him. After the bang all he could hear was a high-pitched whine.

He dropped to his belly, all the time pleading with her to stop the playacting. Julia told Plank to get the rope.

Plank went into the kitchen. He came back with a roll of nylon rope and began to tie Big Mac's hands together.

'I'll have the law on you,' Big Mac hissed, as threatening as he could make it.

Julia said, 'This is South Armagh. We are the law.'

'I'll kill you both,' he said. 'Please let me up.' And he continued to alternate between pleas and threats, occasionally coughing and retching from floor dust.

Julia pressed the pistol to the back of his head and warned him. 'Keep quiet, pig, if you don't want me to blow your brains out.'

When he was bound hand and foot Julia turned him over so he was face up. She went to her bag and took out a cutthroat razor. She crouched down and held it front of Big Mac's face. He stared at it in horror.

'Where are my panties?' she asked him.

'In my suitcase.'

'You brought them all the way over here, you sick bastard? You thought you were going to add to the collection?'

Big Mac shook his head, or maybe nodded, or maybe he was just trembling.

'Do you swear that you will post them to me if we set you free?'

'I swear, I swear. By almighty God, I swear.'

'I know you will. Stop yammering.' Julia ran her finger over the flat of the blade. 'Now I am giving you a choice,' she said. 'Do as we say and lose one testicle. Be difficult and lose two.'

'What are you saying?' Big Mac whispered.

'You heard me first time. Cooperate and lose one ball. Give trouble and lose two.' Julia giggled. 'Or as many as I can find.'

Standing off to the side, Plank stared at her. She didn't tell him anything about this. He thought they were only going to slap him around a little.

'My God, you're mad,' Big Mac shouted, struggling to free himself.

Julia then began to cut his clothes off. Big Mac fought and squirmed. 'Please, please, please,' he said. 'I will send you the panties. Don't do this.' He cried and begged her to stop. He would give her anything she wanted, and do anything she wanted.

Julia felt a twinge of pity for him. He was so frightened. But she kept her face blank. This had to be done. She had to have revenge for her sense of self, to restore her dignity. And she had to do it to save herself. Otherwise, he could blackmail her into doing anything he liked.

'Remember what I told you,' she said. 'Don't cooperate and lose two balls. Cooperate and only lose one. One is sufficient for me as a souvenir. You know the way you like to keep souvenirs of your conquests. I have the same hobby.'

Julia began cutting away a trouser leg, slicing neatly along the crease. 'Before I begin let me explain something. You will be fine. I have watched my father de-ball lambs and little pigs hundreds of times. If it's done right, it doesn't really hurt too much, and there will be very little blood. My advice is to keep the wound clean. I will throw some Dettol over it. It will heal in no time. I have never seen a pig die because of castration, and you're a pig, aren't you?'

Big Mac was hardly listening. He kept promising her everything she wanted if she would just let him go. Julia moved to the other trouser leg. 'Oh, I will let you go, but you will be a little bit lighter.'

Eventually Big Mac was stripped naked. His clothes lay in tatters beside him. Julia took a camera from her bag. She took pictures of him. She told Plank to set up the recording machine.

'Did you bring the whiskey?' she asked him.

'It's in the kitchen,' said Plank, barely able to get the words out. He could do with a drink himself. Big Mac lay on the floor, squirming like a maggot on a fishhook.

Julia fetched the bottle. She unscrewed the cap and poured some whiskey over Big Mac's balls and then ordered him to drink some. 'Just like you drugged me, remember? But this is for your benefit, not that you deserve it. It will do two things: dull the pain and keep the wound from getting infected. We don't want you to die. However, piggy, keep in mind – cooperate delete one jewel, don't cooperate delete two. It's up to you.'

Big Mac was living a nightmare, but some part of him realised that he had to survive. His only chance was to cooperate, no matter how bad it was going to be.

'What do you want me to do?' he managed to croak.

Plank took from his pocket a folded-up piece of paper. He handed it to Julia, who held it in front of Big Mac's eyes. A statement he had to make – that he had drugged and raped Julia, and that he was skimming money from the donations. But it had to be said in a certain way. Like it was part of a normal conversation.

'Plank will help you rehearse.'

As Plank was going over what McDonald had to say, Julia was fitting on a pair of thin plastic gloves for the operation.

Watching her, Plank felt a shiver. God, this was a side to her he had never seen before. She never told him she had this in mind. He would have to watch her in future.

Big Mac knew the score. He had $50,000 in a bag with him for the IRA. He was being made to say he only had $40,000, which meant Plank would keep ten grand for himself, and nobody any the wiser. The whiskey seemed to have given him greater clarity. Julia was getting revenge, Plank was getting $10,000, and he was losing one of his balls. There was nothing he could do except try to stay alive. He asked for more whiskey. This time he drank as much as he could.

He repeated what Plank had instructed him to say as Julia stood by with the razor in her hand. Eventually Plank was satisfied with the recording. He took a swig himself to stop his hands shaking. Don't cross this woman, he reminded himself.

Julia made McDonald drink until he was barely aware of anything. He was only conscious of them helping him into Plank's car. He had no real perception of being dumped naked and very drunk by the side of the road a few miles away.

Later, an RUC barracks received a report of an undressed, obviously inebriated man, who seemed obsessed with his balls. The arresting cops couldn't figure out why he kept checking them and then laughing hysterically, as if in some kind of relief.

25

Sonny was hosting the committee meeting this week. Usually, they went to Blythe's big house a mile from the town, mostly because of the quality of her baking, but Alice said it wasn't fair on her. Blythe insisted that she loved having them. She said it was lovely to be washing six cups instead of just one, the six members being herself, Sonny, Pete, Sean, Alice, and Clint. But Alice insisted they all take turns hosting. Sean was disappointed.

Each of them found places to sit in Sonny's living room. Sean sniffed at one of the buns that Sonny had bought from the local shop and returned it to the plate with a grimace. Alice said she had a letter from Frank Brannigan that he wanted her to read out.

It was brief. '*A Chairde*, I want to inform the committee that I am standing down as your candidate in the upcoming local elections. I thank you all for your faith in me but, because of other commitments I couldn't give the canvass the necessary time or put in the work required. I will of course always be willing to help out in any way I can, time permitting. I wish every success to the person picked to succeed me. *Is mise le meas*, Frank.'

'Time permitting,' said Sean scathingly. 'How much time do you have if you lie in bed till one in the afternoon?'

'It's the best news I've heard this week,' said Alice. 'He never had his heart in it. He didn't show for meetings, and all because he knew he wouldn't win. Why would we need a guy like that?'

'Agreed,' said Sean. 'And since that's settled, thanks be to God, Mr Sonny, you're next in line.'

Sonny looked around the room. 'No way. I don't have the skills to be a politician.'

'The only skill you need is an ability to bluff, lie, bluster, and not answer questions,' said Sean. 'Cheat a few times on your wife and you're a shoo-in.'

Sonny had a flashback to New York and felt a shiver go through him. Every time he saw the word America, he was back in the Havana Club. A few nights ago, when he and Julia were watching TV, an ad set in Cuba came on. It had salsa music and beautiful girls as a backdrop. Watching it, a feeling of excitement coursed through his body, and then just as quickly a feeling of guilt. He had to jump up and tell Julia he was putting on the kettle.

'Are you speaking from experience about cheating?' Alice asked Sean innocently.

'Enough messing,' said Sonny. 'I don't want to be a politician.'

Pete clacked his pipe on his teeth. 'If you think about it, Sonny, you have no option. Either you become the candidate or the entire project folds ignominiously. There is no one else suitable. It's up to you.'

'There were hundreds at the last meeting. Don't they have a say?'

'The reality is this little group is the meeting. If we were to never call another public meeting, no one would be surprised. All the previous talking would be so much wind, which means it's up to us. At this stage it's your baby.'

'Can I think about it?'

'There isn't anything to think about. You started this. Are you going to follow through, or are you going to march your men to the top of hill, *à la* the Rev Ian, and march them down again?'

Sonny knew Pete was appealing to his pride, and that both of them knew what his answer would be. Even if it was just for pride in himself, he had no choice.

'Okay, I will take it on, assuming no one here objects.'

'Object?' said Alice. 'Why would any of us object?'

Pete said, 'Now that that's solved, the question is how do we best get our message across?'

The others started making suggestions, few that hadn't been heard before. Alice let her thoughts wander as she gazed around the room. Julia kept a nice house, but why wouldn't she? Hadn't she Sonny for a husband? Any woman would be house proud having such a partner.

'You're very quiet, Alice,' Sonny said.

'Just thinking.'

'What are you thinking?'

Alice pulled her skirt over her knees with both hands. If they only knew what she was thinking.

'I think we need a slogan, something that sums you up in a few words,' she said.

Sonny turned to her. She always looked so attractive in an open, kindly way. It was amazing some guy hadn't snaffled her yet. It couldn't be from lack of offers.

'Have you one in mind?' he asked.

'What about, "Make love not war,"' said Sean.

'Originality isn't your strong point, Sean,' said Pete.

'It's just that I like the sentiment.'

'I'm sure you do. Well Alice, what have you got?'

Alice frowned and said, 'Give me a minute to mull it over.'

There was a knock on the sitting-room door. 'Can I come in?' called Julia.

Sonny got up and opened the door. Julia had a trolley laden with a teapot, cups and saucers, sugar, milk and biscuits. 'Hello, everyone,' she said. 'Tea's up. Politics is thirsty work.'

'You're very kind,' said Blythe, relieved that Julia's spread wasn't a patch on hers. 'Would you not get involved with us, Julia?'

'I'm not politically minded. I see them on TV talk, talk, talk. Negotiate this, negotiate that. It never gets anywhere.'

Sonny cleared his throat. 'Darling, Brannigan has resigned. He isn't going to be the candidate so I am running in his place.'

Julia paused while pouring a cup. The tea nearly brimmed over. 'You're what?'

'I'm going to be the candidate instead of Brannigan.'

Her mind began to race. Would there be functions and the like if he won? It would never compare to New York, but it would be a start. But he wouldn't win. But then again, he might. You could never know.

'That's wonderful, darling. You'll get my vote for sure.'

Even Alice smiled at that.

Peter said, 'I know you can say that politics is all talk, Julia, but nobody ever died from talking.'

Alice almost snapped her fingers. She had the one-liner.

'I just love the décor of this room, Julia,' she said.

'My husband has impeccable taste. Don't you, honey? And he's a dab hand at the home decorating. It's good to have a man around the house.'

'It must be,' said Alice.

'Aw, well you have more freedom on your own, I guess.'

Alice smiled. 'I suppose you picked up the habit of saying "I guess" in the States.'

Julia glanced at her. Why did she mention America? For a second, she thought of Big Mac hogtied on the floor.

'I just thought it was important to let the world know what we are suffering over here. If we had no one prepared to resist, where would we be?'

No one in the room replied to that.

'Thanks for the tea,' Sonny said. 'You're a darling.'

'No problem. And if you become famous, you're not to leave me for a young one, do you hear?'

'If Sonny becomes famous then so will you,' said Blythe.

'If only,' said Julia. 'And me without a stitch to wear. Oh well, I will have to do with what I have. And since you're all working to make me first lady, I'll leave you to it. Aren't I lucky to have such a wonderful husband?'

In the kitchen, Julia wondered if she had been too bitchy with Alice. Alice liked Sonny; a blind horse could see that. And she would be better for him than lots of other trollops out there. God, imagine if he won the election. It would open doors to all kinds of functions, conferences, trips abroad . . . Jesus!

Back in the sitting-room, the sugar bowl was passed around and the committee sipped their tea. Sean asked, 'Where were we?' and Clint said, 'The slogan,' and Sonny said, 'So, Alice. Get any brainwaves?'

'As a matter of fact, I did. Thanks to something Pete said.'

She paused deliberately just to annoy them.

'Come on, come on, out with it,' said Sean.

She looked at each one of them in turn and smiled. 'Talking Hurts No One.'

26

After the meeting broke up, Sonny said he'd drop Alice home. They'd barely made it to the nearest crossroads when they were stopped at a British Army checkpoint. Even though most people in Cairnduff were used to the hold-ups, it was still always nerve-racking. You never knew if you'd be ordered from the car and searched. Mostly, it was young men travelling alone or in pairs who were hassled, but no one was immune. It was thought locally that it really depended on the mood of the soldiers, and you could never tell in advance who they were or what they were like.

'Play it cool,' said Sonny.

He approached the checkpoint cautiously. It was the Paras. No sudden movements. He rolled down the window.

'Driving licence,' said the soldier.

Sonny handed him the licence. The soldier hardly glanced at it. He moved back from the car and Sonny could hear him talk to his base over the radio.

The soldier came back to the open window again and said, 'Okay, out. Both of you are being taken in for questioning.'

'On what grounds?' Sonny demanded to know.

'On the grounds that I am ordering you. Now out of the fucking car.'

Sonny reached his hand over and touched Alice's knee. 'Don't be scared. It's a mix-up. They're just trying to frighten us, or they're digging for information. Cooperate as best you can and try not to lose your cool. They have nothing on us.'

'Out, I said! On the double,' barked the soldier.

Sonny and Alice were bundled into an army Saracen and guarded by two soldiers. Their car would be left abandoned by the roadside, which wasn't a bad thing from Sonny's perspective. Neighbours would recognise it and know what had happened. Julia could be informed of his whereabouts. Alice's family would be told as well. Protests could be launched. The protests would fall on deaf ears, but they would put the security forces on alert that people knew there were two locals in custody. Anything to lessen the chance of being subject to abuse.

Sonny and Alice were made to sit opposite each other. They were told not to speak. Sonny glanced at Alice. She was very pale and had her head down staring at the floor. She was clearly very frightened. He wanted to put his arms around her and reassure her. But he couldn't move.

'*Ná bí buartha, mo ghrá,*' he said to her. In the North, school' kids weren't taught Irish, but there were lots of common words that most people knew. Alice understood he had told her not to be afraid, and despite her predicament, she felt something stir in her when he said, '*mo ghrá*'. My love. It was only a term of endearment, she told herself.

The soldiers weren't happy not knowing what had been spoken. One shoved Sonny and said, 'Shut the fuck up!'

Sonny's mind was racing. This was no usual roadblock. It had been prearranged. He'd never seen one so close to his house before. The plates on his car would have told them who was inside. The soldier didn't need to examine his licence because he already knew who it was. But why were they being taken in for questioning? Alice was as clean as he was, even the authorities knew that. He could just pray that there wasn't something worse in store.

They were led into the barracks and separated. The room Sonny was taken to had a mirror on one wall, which he immediately realised was a two-way pane of glass so people on the other side could watch and hear everything that was being said. They were probably observing him right now. Better just to sit and pretend to be unconcerned and not let them see his anxiety.

Alice was led into a room similar to Sonny's. It was bare except for a table and three chairs. She could see a big mirror on the wall and wondered why it was there. She was left alone for what seemed like hours. Remember what Sonny said. They were just trying to scare her. Well, if that was the case it was working. The longer she sat there the more she worried about what was going to happen.

Sonny knew they were watching him. They hadn't searched either of them, which he found strange, but then again maybe not so strange. They knew neither of them would be carrying anything illegal. He had a pen and a sheet of paper with headings to be discussed at the meeting in his pocket. These guys would read it, but there was nothing incriminating. The topics they discussed would come up at any political meeting. If he started writing on it maybe they'd think he was confessing something. What could he write that would annoy them?

Alice flinched when the door to her room burst open. A soldier strode in with a bundle of papers under his arm. He sat behind the table and glared at her. He was big and imposing and angry looking. His stare made Alice feel like she was sitting there naked.

'Okay, ducky,' he said. 'Let's get this over with. My friends call me Hitler. They are being kind. You don't want to know what my enemies call me. Spill it all out . . . now!'

He almost shouted the 'now' which made Alice jump. She tried to speak but no words came. Eventually, she manged to say, 'Spill what out?'

'Everything you know about the terrorists.'

'I don't know anything.'

'Listen, ducky, you work behind the bar among that den of criminals. And you consort with, and sleep with, known IRA members. And you say you don't know anything? Are you trying to make a fool of me?'

'That's not true. I don't sleep with anyone.'

'What about Mickey Beatty? He has emigrated recently. Very suspicious. Probably lying low as a sleeper. Wasn't he one of your lovers?' What about Sonny? How often do you bed him and he a married man?'

'That's lies. I don't go to bed with him, and I don't have any lovers. I only went out with Beatty three times years ago. Anyway, how did you know that?'

'Listen, missy, I ask the questions.'

Just then then another guy came into the room. He seemed surprised to see the room occupied. Then he shook his head as if exasperated.

'Are you at it again, Hitler?' he said.

'At what, for Christ's sake?'

'Giving people a hard time. I know your methods.'

'I haven't even begun to employ my methods. She says she doesn't know anything, but they all say that until I get working on them.'

'She looks like a nice respectable girl. Why don't you leave us for a few minutes and let me talk to her? I am sure she wants to cooperate.'

'You're a fucking softie, and softness doesn't get anywhere with these people. It takes the big stick at the end of the day.'

'Please, leave us for a couple of minutes.'

'Fine. But I know what works and what doesn't.'

Alice was relieved when Hitler left. He had petrified her. This new one didn't seem as bad.

He said, 'He's a fucking sadist that guy. I'm sorry about the language, but he drives me nuts. My advice to you is to try and give him some information. Even a little, just to calm him down. He takes this job very seriously. He's a fanatic really.'

'I can't give him anything because I don't know anything.'

'What about Mickey Beatty?'

Alice pricked up her ears. He knew about Mickey also? Jesus, they were doing good-cop bad-cop. She had heard about it loads of times. They were treating her like an idiot. Well, she wasn't an idiot. Her fear subsided. Just keep telling the truth and say she knew nothing. They could good-cop bad-cop her all they wanted.

Sonny was thirsty and he was still afraid, but he wasn't going to ask for anything or let them see his fear. There was movement in the hallway and the door opened. A tall man dressed in a suit and tie and carrying a briefcase came in.

'Hello, Mr Mone,' he said as he sat down. His face was pale, long and thin. Everything about him was thin, even the fair hair across his scalp. He kept nodding his head up and down every few seconds. It was like a toy dog Sonny had one time. When you put a penny into it, it would nod its head as if saying thanks.

'We had an argument about what it was you were writing,' said the man. 'We knew that you knew we were watching. My colleague said you were describing your surroundings. I said no, it was something about us, because you knew we would read it. Who was nearest?'

Sonny sat back in his chair. He slid the sheet of paper across the table. 'See for yourself.'

The man lifted the page and read out loud:

'The British army, they are best,
Have no fear, I speak in jest,
Maybe they'll all soon go home,
And leave us happy here alone.'

He smiled a strange humourless smile. 'Ah, I was right. I was right,' he said, obviously pleased with himself. Or maybe he was pleased with Sonny.

'Where is Alice? What have you done with her? I demand to see her now,' said Sonny.

'Be calm. Trust me she will come to no harm. It's amazing that anyone could be so clean in the world we live in today.'

'If she's so clean, why have you arrested her? And what am I here for? I have done nothing wrong.'

The man laughed a sort of wry laugh. It didn't seem real. There was something unreal about his whole being, and the continuous nodding didn't help.

'Yes. We don't have anything on you. You even behaved admirably in the New York salsa club. As regards Alice, her arrest is just her part in the play. Or more to the point, giving those members of the cast who are interrogating her a chance to play their role.'

Sonny made sure to stay still. Had they been following him? Or was someone giving them information? Maybe Julio wasn't all he seemed. Hadn't he been plying him with drink all night? And when it came to it, how much did he really know about Rita? Sonny stopped himself from speculating. This was what this guy wanted, to have him doubting everything.

'Did you imagine we would let your wife go to the United States and not be interested? Of course, you came into the picture also.'

Did he know about him taking the money back? If he did, he wouldn't be here talking about a salsa club. And even if they had guys tailing him in America, they couldn't know about the money exchange.

'My name is Potts by the way. Believe me when I say it is a pleasure to make your acquaintance.'

'Why have you got me here?' Sonny said trying to gain his composure. 'And I want Alice let go now.'

Potts leaned back in his chair. With his eyes fixed on Sonny, he said, 'Give the lady a cup of coffee and tell her that Mr Mone will be with her very soon.'

It took Sonny a moment to realise that he was speaking to the observers beyond the mirror. There was no response. No sound of footsteps or doors opening. Sonny could only hope the order was being followed.

Potts spoke again. 'The bit part players have finished their roles. Alice will be fine. All of this will just become a scary anecdote to tell her friends. And I won't keep you long.' His head bobbed again as if he was nodding to himself. 'Okay, now to business. I want you to think of a play. A play has actors, a director, and a producer. What is going on in Northern Ireland is a play.'

'Where people die,' said Sonny.

'My father kept greyhounds. In the evening, when I was a child, he would take me to blood them. They would follow their instinct, catching hares and rabbits and so on. Did you ever see greyhounds tear apart its prey?'

Sonny sat staring at the guy. He shook his head.

'The dogs are in a state of ecstasy. My father explained that was the natural order of things. The strong must devour the weak to maintain stability. There is always a class of animal, or human, and we are mere animals after all, that is the strongest. Should that class not rule?' Potts picked some lint from his sleeve and let it drop to the floor. 'Let me elucidate further.'

Sonny was struck by the word 'elucidate'. He could have just said 'explain'. This guy was certainly mad but also precise in everything. Precise people were dangerous.

'I am going to give you a history lesson and hopefully at the end you will understand. The man's head bobbed up and down.

'Following its defeat,' he began, 'at the Battle of Hastings on the 14th of October 1066, a battle that began and ended on the same day, England structured herself as a nation at war. Since that time, she has fought wars on every continent and in every century. In the long reign of Queen Victoria, some 64 years, there wasn't one year in which Britain was not at war with someone.'

A fly flitting around the room briefly landed on the table in front of Potts. It struck Sonny that had it landed on the man's throat, he might have trapped it with his jaw.

'Most of the European countries who were adversaries are now allies. The United States, Canada, Russia, Japan, and China are no longer interested in having conflict with us. The same can be said of countries in Africa and South America. But England needs wars. Her whole sense of self is built on war. It is intertwined with all her institutions. Go to any church in England and what will you see? War! Battles standards! Plaques lauding heroes who died for England. Even the children of royals must serve their time in the armed services. England's psyche is bound up with war, and more importantly, being at war. We are a martial people. It doesn't matter who the enemy is. We must have heroes coming home in body bags.'

Sonny sat rigid in his chair forgetting his initial fears. Why was he being told this load of bullshit?

'Have you heard the phrase, "An acceptable level of violence"?' asked Potts.

Sonny nodded.

'It really should be, "The desired level of violence." Why desire such a thing, you may ask. After all, violence means death. It means grief. It means loss.' He paused and looked at Sonny closely. 'Remember the greyhound? It will only run after the mechanical hare so many times. Every so often it needs the real thing. Blood, Mr Mone. Blood, or it will lose enthusiasm, and when that happens it wins no races. An army needs conflict. It needs to lose soldiers or it goes soft. England was founded on its armed forces. They are what constitutes its essence, its soul, just as the pursuit of the dollar constitutes the beating heart of America, or the work ethic in Germany, or the artistic impulse of Italy.'

'What about France or Spain? What are the souls of those nations,' said Sonny, forgetting for a moment his situation.

'France has this notion of "Liberty, Equality Fraternity" as its soul. And what has that led to? Proletariat unrest, strikes, student protests. As for Spain, the reason it is not a unified country is because it doesn't have a soul. It's a collection of regions that want to do their own thing . . . but I digress. What would happen if England's armed services went soft like the greyhound?'

Sonny didn't answer.

'Are you starting to see why I am telling you all this?'

Sonny shook his head.

'We need the Northern Ireland conflict, the so-called Troubles. We need to lose a few soldiers every so often. We need the taste of blood. Are you getting the picture now?'

'Who are you?'

'I am one of the directors of the play. There are others. As for the producer, there are many of those as well. They are the ones who put on the show. They pay for it, and they take the profits. The City of London, the bankers, newspaper barons, the old universities, the leading members of the Privy Council, not forgetting the royal family.'

'The establishment,' said Sonny.

'Yes, you could call the producers that.'

'Why are you telling me all this? And do you expect me to believe it?'

'I took you to be an aware young man.'

'Make me more aware,' said Sonny, 'and then let me out of here.'

'Very well. It has to do with this movement you are trying to start up. A peace movement of all things.'

'Jesus,' said Sonny. 'Now I have it, but I don't believe it.' He stood up. 'I just don't believe it. You don't want peace. You need soldiers killed to keep your armed services on their toes, and the troubles here does that.'

'Soldiers need to experience real combat. Officers need combat to gain promotion. Generals need combat to study tactics. Do you know that when there is a war on, young men rush to join up. What's the point of a soldier in peace time?'

Sonny sat down and looked at Potts nodding his head. He still couldn't believe he was real, or that he meant what he said.

'The little thing you are doing is miniscule in the grand scheme of things. In all likelihood it would peter out on its own. However, it's easier to squash it now and take no chances.'

'What do you mean squash it?'

'What I mean is that you forget about the whole idea and go back to your books, which I know you love.'

Sonny tried to tell if he was bluffing. Not a flicker on his face. He was deadly serious.

'What if I don't?'

Again, the fly landed on the table. Potts lifted his head and stretched his chin, as if to rest it from the nodding. 'If that fly was in your kitchen, presumably you would squash it just to be rid of it. In our play, you have the same relevance as a fly in your kitchen. And you would be just as easy to remove.'

The man unfolded himself from the chair, lanky and sparse like reeds in a swamp. He picked up his briefcase with long bony fingers. 'Our meeting has concluded. There is no record of this conversation ever having happened. Goodbye. You won't ever see me again. I will go first. You can let yourself out in one minute. Your friend will be waiting for you.'

'You didn't answer me. What if I don't drop the idea?'

The man walked towards the door without speaking or looking at Sonny. He opened it and slipped out into the hallway, closing the door again with a gentle click.

When Sonny left the room a minute later, Alice was waiting in the corridor. She threw her arms around him in relief. It was the first time she had ever held him.

Sonny didn't tell Alice about the threat. Nor did he tell Julia when he got home. What was the point in scaring them? But he let Julia know about the tail in New York. That affected her as well and she deserved to know. If he was paying attention, he would have seen her freeze, then breathe, then blink slowly.

She was thinking, did the Brits know about her and Big Mac? How much had they told Sonny? What did he know? But she had learned a few things dealing with Big Mac, in New York, in Philadelphia, and in a South Armagh safe-house. Stay in control. Sonny's tone of voice would be different if he suspected her. She knew him backwards. He hadn't been told anything.

'My God, in what's supposed to be the freest country in the world we were being followed? And now poor Alice was lifted. Is she okay? Are you okay, darling?'

'Yeah, Alice is fine. And it will take more than that to worry me.'

'Oh, you poor thing. Here give me a hug.'

While in Julia's arms, Sonny said, 'They were keeping an eye on us because we live here. We're under their control. When you think about it, this Potts guy wouldn't dare cross Big Mac and his connections. Remember all the big noise politicians at the functions? They're a layer of protection that even the Brits can't penetrate.'

Julia released him. She said, 'And who's protecting you? This country is getting worse all the time, so please be careful, darling.'

That same evening, Sonny called unannounced to Pete. Even before his friend had shown him into the sitting-room, he could smell the pipe smoke. Pete was unmarried. He told Sonny one time that he was about to get engaged when his intended put it to him squarely that it was either her or the pipe. He had mused on the ultimatum. Marital bliss or the loss of his pipe? He broke the news to her as diplomatically as he could 'The pipe,' he told her.

Sonny didn't know if the story was true but he liked the pipe smell. A kind of homely aroma. Besides the smell, the room was a mess. Papers, books, and journals lay scattered everywhere. Exercise books taken home from school to be marked were piled up on a desk in the corner.

'Shovel some of that junk off a chair and sit down,' said Pete, 'and reveal the secret of your mission.'

Sonny told him the whole story. When he was done, Pete didn't say anything and sucked on his pipe reflectively. Sonny leaned forward, eager for what he had to say.

'So, what is the soul of Ireland?' Pete said. 'What is its essence?'

'Jesus, forget that,' said Sonny, exasperated. 'What about the other stuff?'

'The notion that the Brits use Northern Ireland as a training ground for soldiers has been around since they were first deployed. So that's not new. It has a certain gruesome logic. What I don't know is whether the threat to you is real. It may be a scare tactic, or . . .'

Pete shrugged his shoulders.

'If they wanted me dead, Jesus, what am I saying? Wouldn't they just do it?'

'Maybe. We have no way of knowing. What do you intend to do?'

'Don't think I haven't thought about it . . . a lot.'

'Who wouldn't? And?'

'I couldn't live with myself if I backed down. Years from now wondering if the guy was bluffing or not.'

'I have to admire your courage, but there is one thing, as your friend, I need to say to you.'

'Yeah?'

'You say if you back down, you will never know if the guy was bluffing or not. This means you are always going to be curious. But at least you would still be alive to be curious.'

Sonny tried to adopt a lighter air. 'You're supposed to be my mentor. Is that the only positive thing you can say?'

'The truth is, if I were really your mentor, I would be even more negative.'

'I can take it. Hit me, counsellor.'

'Now you're acting all heroic and pretending you are not afraid. The only person who isn't afraid when confronting danger is an idiot.'

'All right, Pete. I'm sorry.'

'Sonny, for generals and people who prosecute wars, anyone who gets in the way is, as our friend Mr Potts said, as worthless as a fly, and as easy to kill. Why don't you get in touch with your policeman friend.'

'Eric?'

'He might know how real this Potts guy is. Or maybe he could give you tips on personal protection. He'll have learned a thing or two about that after his wife got shot.'

'Good idea.'

'And I have just one more question to ask,' said Pete, adding more tobacco to his pipe.

'Oh, aye, what's that?'

'Have you made a will?'

27

In an unused wing of a dilapidated hotel deep in rural county Cavan, seven men ranging in ages from thirty to seventy-five sat around a magnificent old oak table in the centre of a huge room. A chandelier with only some of the bulbs lit hung over the table. Highly decorative cornices on the ceiling, now going black in places because of damp, had coats of arms with Latin inscriptions that nobody in the room understood. The rich velvet paper covering the walls had become tattered around the edges. Once upon a time, the polished hardwood floor would have had handmade rugs from the Far East laid on top, but not anymore.

None of this was noticed by the group of men. All of them had serious looks on their faces. The one thing they all had in common was a sense of awareness, or uneasiness, in their countenance and posture. For some, this fox-like guardedness was innate. For others it had developed over time. They didn't seem particularly friendly or hostile to each other. At the moment no one was speaking. Clearly the atmosphere was tense, as if things had come to a head.

One of the younger men in the room stood up. 'Comrades, it's resolution time. The decision we have to make today is one of the most profound in our history. If we make a particular judgement, it will have consequences that none of us can know. Before we decide, I want to once more clarify the reason I am promoting it. It is simple and can be put into a few words: lose South Armagh and we lose the war.

'I know some of you have argued it's not just South Armagh. We have Tyrone, Belfast, Derry, and so on, and it's not the whole of South Armagh, you say. It's just a bit of it.

'That is all true. We can resist and take on the enemy in these other areas as well, but it is only in South Armagh where we cannot be defeated militarily. I don't need to rehash the history for you. Going back centuries, almost to prehistory and the time of Cú Chulainn, South Armagh has always been bandit country. South Armagh has never allowed itself to be dictated to by government or state laws.

'But now a small bit of it is up for grabs, and if it's taken from us, and taken by the son of one of our most revered patriots, then we have lost South Armagh and we have lost the war. It is ironic that the person who has caused this trouble should be who he is. But he must be dealt with. His popularity is more dangerous than the entire British Army. I ask you to vote in favour of doing what must be done. He represents too big a threat. And the clock is ticking. We have four weeks to spare.'

The man sat down again. Every other person in the room sat quietly, lost in their own thoughts.

A voice said, 'My God, his father and I were like brothers.'

Another voice said, '*Sin a bhfuil.*'

The vote was four to three in favour.

28

Sonny rang Eric several times but there was no reply. He drove to his home and knocked on the door. Again, there was no answer. He went to two of his neighbours' houses, also Protestant families. Even here they wouldn't answer the door, though it was clear there were people in the houses. Sonny knew it was just an indication of fear. They would have seen him and surely realised he wasn't there to do them harm, but they were taking no chances. Who could blame them?

Two days later while Sonny was having breakfast, the phone rang. It was Eric Johnson.

'Can you be at the Vic in an hour?'

Sonny, still half-asleep and confused at the suddenness, blurted out, 'Yeah, sure. The Vic in Castlehill?'

'Back bar. See you there.' The phone went dead.

Sonny parked his car a good distance away from the Vic. The pub was situated in what was once the Protestant end of the town. Nowadays it had a more mixed population. Once it had been called the Victorian Bar but now was known to everyone as the Vic. It still had the old style rich mahogany interior, including brass fittings on the mirrors behind the bar. When Sonny walked in, he caught that austere Protestant smell. There'd be no knees-up on these tables. Drunkenness and making a fool of yourself was for Catholics, who would rather sing and dance than work. In this establishment the patrons would leave on time without being asked. Early to bed meant you rose early to do the work of the Lord.

But he was imagining things. If any of that was ever true, it had long since passed. There was a cigarette machine in the corner and speakers for playing piped music, most likely Led Zeppelin or The Who. The guys sitting at the bar were just as likely to get drunk and mess around as any of their Catholic peers. It was good they were young, though. They were most likely focused on other things – girls or Glasgow Rangers – and not the stranger who had just walked in for a morning drink.

Sonny ordered a bottle of beer, because it would be even more strange to be sitting drinking a mineral. Eric was late. He turned when he heard the door open, but it was just some guy in an expensive looking coat. The man paused and looked around the room. Then he approached the bar and asked for a pack of ten Woodbines. The barman pointed to the machine and said it only dispensed packs of twenty. The guy said he wouldn't bother and left. A minute later, Eric came in.

Sonny rose to greet him. 'Did your scout give you the nod?'

'How did you know he was a scout?' asked Eric.

'A guy dressed like that wouldn't be smoking Woodbine cigarette. And he wouldn't be wanting a pack of ten. And he certainly wouldn't leave without buying any. I bet you he doesn't even smoke. Then there was the way he let his eyes rove around the place, like he was an estate agent valuing the property.'

'Why wouldn't he be buying Woodbines?'

'Woodbines are a working man or woman's smoke, and he didn't look like he was in that bracket.'

'Wow, you should be in my profession, Sherlock Holmes. But you will forgive me if I have to be ultra-cautious after what they did to my wife. You know it was me they were after.'

'How is she?'

'Fine now, thank the good Lord.'

'That's good,' said Sonny.

'My neighbours said you were at my house, which is why I rang you. Sorry I didn't give you much time to be here. It's not that I suspect you would tell anyone of my whereabouts. It's just that I don't trust telephones.'

'Thank you for meeting me.'

'So, what's up?'

Sonny told Eric about being picked up and his meeting with Potts. He told him what Potts had said and described the threats he'd made. Eric listened in silence. When Sonny was finished, he leaned back in his seat.

'I have heard rumours about the guy you call Potts for years but never really believed them. It was generally thought that these kinds of myths were yarns to scare young cops for the fun of it. "Don't go prying into other people's affairs or you'll end up disappeared." That kind of thing. Nobody really thought it was true. Now you have confirmed it for me.'

'Can you do anything about it?'

Eric looked at him. 'Could *you* take down Rooster if you wanted?'

They both sat in silence for a moment.

Eric said, 'It's bad, Sonny. Nobody knows what's going on. Nobody trusts anyone. Take my wife for instance. It's assumed the IRA shot her intending to get me, but I have my doubts. She was shot with a small-bore pistol that's not the sort the Provos use.'

'Did she get a look at him?' asked Sonny.

'It all happened so fast. He was a small fellow, she said. But there was one strange thing that I cannot fathom. She remembers a smell of aftershave lotion. Something really sweet. She was adamant because she was sure it was something the detectives could follow up. But why a guy going to murder someone would be wearing aftershave beats me.'

'Maybe a decoy. To throw the cops off the scent . . . literally.'

'I don't buy it. That's not the IRA's modus operandi. It's not how they think. A so-called freedom fighter wearing aftershave as protection would hardly go down well.'

'I agree,' said Sonny.

'Nobody is safe. You can't be sure who the enemy is. I know of at least one Catholic policeman who was set up by guys in his own barracks and murdered. Some policemen are dirty, and I mean really dirty. There are some really bad apples.'

Sonny wanted to ask why Eric didn't just quit. But then he realised, if all the decent cops gave up the whole barrel would rot. It would be bad for everyone. In his own way, Eric was taking a stand against bullies, something Sonny could appreciate.

Sonny said, 'Is there any advice you can give me?'

'Keep a low profile. Vary your movements. But the reality is if someone wants to get you, they can. You could apply to get a handgun for self-protection, though I doubt they would give you a licence.'

Sonny smiled to himself. Imagine going home and showing a gun to Julia. She'd think he'd joined up. What would her reaction be? She was always on to him about not doing his bit. But if faced with the reality, would she welcome it? Maybe yes, but maybe no.

'I don't think that would be any good,' said Sonny. 'I'd probably shoot myself by accident.'

'It gives little protection anyway. If they want you gone you won't see them coming.'

Just then Eric's scout came in the door and stood waiting. Eric pointed to him. 'That's how much protection I get. My superiors know I'm a target, and its bad publicity to lose members. That guy reckons I have been in here long enough, so I have to go. It's been good seeing you again, and I hope you stay safe. Someday this will all end, and there will be some terrible stories that come out you can be sure, but it will also mean that old friends can meet for a drink without fear.'

After Eric had gone, Sonny sat musing for a couple of minutes. Could he cope with the constant sense of dread that Eric lived under? Could he ask Julia to do so as well, when she'd never wanted any part in politics to begin with?

29

'You're away from me again,' said Julia.

'I'm not,' said Sonny. '*Panorama* is always interesting.'

'You can't fool me. Your mind isn't on the TV. Where is it?'

Julia was right. Sonny's mind wasn't on the current affairs programme. He was thinking of the warning he had been given. He couldn't tell anyone about it except Pete, which meant having to keep it bottled up.

'Electioneering is tiring,' he said.

'You aren't doing as much canvassing as you were.'

'I don't want to come to the boil too soon.'

This was only half true. The campaign was getting great feedback, and he had a fair chance of winning as long as there were no slip ups between now and polling day. But he had for all intents and purposes abandoned the so-called peace movement. No more meetings. No more canvassing. His excuse was that it had served its purpose as he was now in the political arena. Alice was disappointed, but she said nothing. It wasn't her place to tell him what to do. The others on the committee went back to their day-to-day lives. Hopefully his withdrawal from campaigning would be enough to satisfy Potts. But he just couldn't bring himself to drop out as a candidate. If he had any chance to make a difference by being elected, he couldn't give that up. He might be afraid, maybe even a coward, but he had pride, and he wasn't going to be bullied by faceless people . . . that is if they even existed.

'Let's go to Mulligan's tonight,' said Julia. 'It will be a change of scenery if little else.'

She thought it would be good for Sonny if there was something troubling him, but there would also be an opportunity of seeing Plank. No harm keeping an eye on him. The English woman was no angel and if she offered herself to him, he'd be like a child offered ice-cream. She had to accept that was just the way he was. But she could see what body language, if any, there was between them, or if the bitch had her claws set in someone else.

'Why do you always want to sit out in the bar instead of the lounge?' Julia asked Sonny after they arrived.

'You can see more. You can see into the lounge from the bar, and you can have a conversation without the band and the English woman blowing the ears of you.'

'Whatever there is to talk about here puzzles me.'

Sonny put his arm around her and tickled her chin. 'You can whisper sweet nothings into my ear.'

Julia shrugged his arm away. 'Quit the messing.'

Alice came into the bar and on seeing them walked over to say hello.

She said to Julia, 'Are you ready for your husband to become a famous politician?'

'Stop,' said Sonny. 'One, I am not elected yet, and two, even if I was, and that's a big if, it's hardly Downing Street or the White House to be a councillor in Cairnduff.'

'What was the thing you quoted at one of the meetings?' said Alice. 'Mighty oaks from little acorns grow.'

'You have a wonderful memory, Alice,' said Julia, half rolling her eyes to the heavens.

'Well, you won't be elected at all unless you get back out there canvassing,' Alice said to Sonny with a hint of reproach.

'God, you're both at me now. There're still months before the count.'

'Would you not get involved, Julia? They say you were a huge hit in New York. We could do with such talent.'

'Who said that?' asked Julia.

'I don't know. I heard it somewhere.'

'I am very busy just now with the hairdressing, and I am sure you and Sonny and the rest don't need me butting into your plans, whatever they are.'

'We have huge plans, don't we Sonny?' said Alice.

'I'm sure you do,' said Julia.

'Do you want to hear another quote?' said Sonny.

'Oh please, yes,' said Julia. 'And Alice will always remember it.'

'If you want to make God laugh, tell him your plans.'

'That's why I married Sonny,' said Julia to Alice, putting her arm around him. 'He knows so much, don't you honey? Aren't I the lucky girl?'

'Yes, it must be lovely to be so much in love,' said Alice. 'Oh my God, I better get going. Do you see the time? I will see you two love doves later.'

After she walked away, Sonny said, 'Why are you always sniping at her?'

'I never snipe at anyone,' said Julia. 'Any sniping that's done she does it.'

'It sounds like sniping to me.'

'She's just jealous because I have you and she has no man.'

'I don't think she would have any trouble getting a man.'

'Not the one she wants.'

'It's never easy getting the thing you want,' said Sonny.

Julia just looked at him but said nothing.

By now the crowd had started to come in, the usual regulars but not Rooster. It wasn't his time yet. The English woman sang a couple of songs and then went back to the table where she was sitting on her own.

'You'd imagine she'd have some company,' said Sonny to Julia.

'She'll be in company soon enough; you can be sure. She is just waiting like those flowers that attract insects and devour them. They are all gaudy just like her, and when they lure their victims, they suck them in and that's the last you'll see of them, which serves them right.'

Sonny laughed. 'My God, Julia, you are a scream. You should be a poet or a writer or something with an imagination like that. The poor woman!'

'You think I'm joking? Just you watch.'

Mick Ryan came over and sat beside the couple. 'I hear great things about both of you,' he said.

'What do you hear?' asked Sonny.

'You are becoming a politician, and Julia here took Broadway by storm.'

'I am not a politician yet, but you are right about Julia. She was a big hit in the States. I was surprised you never joined our project, Mick. I know you aren't a man of violence.'

'I was on board,' said Mick. 'You just didn't see me.'

'You're the only man I know that can ride two horses at the same time,' said Julia.

'Because we are all friends here, I can answer that by saying you never know which horse is going to win and you wouldn't want to end up on the wrong nag.'

'You're something else, Mick,' said Sonny. 'But what you're saying has some truth in it. It's not easy for people to take sides in the times that are in it, when you don't know who the next victim is going to be.'

'You hit the nail on the head, Sonny. But I have to go and look for Scotty in case he starts throwing money around buying drink for everyone.'

Sonny saw that their glasses were almost empty and said he was going up to the bar to buy another round. Julia got up to go to the ladies.

While Sonny was waiting to be served, Gerry Callaghan, a farmer from nearby Willisburg, approached him and said he heard he was going to stand for election. He wanted to wish Sonny luck, and said he would be getting both his and his wife's vote. Sonny thanked him, and Gerry moved away. Sonny studied his face in the mirror behind the bar. Had he what it took to be a politician, no matter how insignificant? And what about Potts? Even without campaigning, it seemed that word of mouth was going to propel Sonny into the seat. Surely that wouldn't go unnoticed.

He had just sat down when Julia returned all flustered.

'What's wrong?' he said. 'You look like you've seen a ghost.'

'Sonny, the English woman was in a cubicle, and Lucy Dorian picked up a piece of paper that had fallen out of the English woman's bag. It was like a pass with a picture of her on it. Lucy read out loud what it said. It said she was a colonel.'

'A what?' said Sonny.

'I can't remember the name on it. It was something like Winifred Butterfield, but I'm not sure. I think it was Colonel Winifred Butterfield, and below that it said, "Special Assignment Officer – Category One Clearance". But it was her photo for definite, and the word "Colonel" was in front of her name, I'm sure of that.'

'Jesus,' said Sonny. 'What happened?'

'The English woman came out of the cubicle and grabbed the paper out of Lucy's hand, and Lucy shouted at her, "You're a spy, I'm going to tell Rooster."'

'Jesus,' said Sonny again. 'Lucy's brother was shot by the Brits. There she is sitting over there waiting on Rooster to arrive. Where is the woman now?'

'I don't know. I think she must have never left the toilet.'

'Jesus!' said Sonny.

'Will you quit saying "Jesus" and say something sensible.'

'If she's still in there that means she's afraid to come out. She knows if she tries to leave Lucy would shout out that she's a spy, and she'd never make the front door. She'd be mauled. But that also means she must be a spy . . . Jesus!'

'What will happen, Sonny? What will Rooster do when he comes in?'

'She hasn't a chance in hell of getting out of here without being interrogated by the IRA.'

Julia put her hand to her mouth. 'Oh my God.'

'Rooster won't mess around. People will be sent for right away.'

Julia shook her head as if to clear it. 'I never liked her anyway.'

'How could you not like her? You didn't know her.'

'I knew enough about her standing up there on the stage every chance she got and painted up like a flamingo so as to get all the men to ogle her . . . including yourself I suppose.'

'I never ogled her.'

'Well, she's in trouble now when Rooster comes in.' Julia paused and looked around. 'Where did I put my handbag?'

'It's probably at your feet under the table.'

Julia bent down and looked under the table. Then it struck her. 'Jesus, I must have left it in the toilet when I rushed out.'

'You may go back and get it.'

'I can't.'

'Why not?'

'She's in there.'

'She won't bite you.'

'My purse is in it. I have to get it back. Will you go?'

'Into the ladies? No way!'

'Please, Sonny, I'm afraid to go in.'

'What if someone saw me? There are people who would just love to be able to say they caught me snooping in the ladies. It wouldn't be great for my election hopes.'

'I can't ask anyone else, or they will wonder why I don't want to go myself.'

'Go in, grab the bag and leave. Don't look at her. Don't say anything.'

'If I'm not back in a couple of minutes raise the alarm.'

'Now that is funny. Don't be silly.'

'Okay, I'm going to chance it.'

Sonny watched Julia trying to put on a determined stride as she headed for the toilets. He thought about the strange English woman coming to live here and getting all the attention from the guys. The more he thought about it the more it all fitted together. Who would ever suspect a woman spy in Cairnduff? It was the perfect cover.

Julia returned, bag in hand.

'You got your bag, Julia.'

'Yeah.'

'Was she there? Did you see her? What did she say?'

'I saw her.'

'Did she say anything? What was she doing?'

'If I tell you, will you promise not to do it?'

'Do what?'

'Promise me?'

'I don't know what you are talking about. How can I promise not to do something when I don't know what that something is?'

'She wants you to go into her.'

'What?'

'She wants you to go into her.'

'Sit down, darling, and calm yourself. Here, take a drink.'

Julia took a sip from the glass.

'Now slow down and start at the beginning,' said Sonny.

'I got my bag where I had left it. She wasn't there. When I was coming down the little corridor that connects the gents and ladies, the little broom cupboard opened, and she came out. She must have been peeking. She stepped in front of me and said she wanted you to come to her. I rushed on past.'

'Me?'

'You wouldn't have recognised her as the woman who was up on stage singing an hour ago.'

'Why?'

'Her face was white, her make-up smeared, her dyed hair all bedraggled. I can tell you; you wouldn't be saying she's sexy looking now.'

'Trust a woman to notice so much.'

'It's not funny.'

'I know it's not funny.'

'I'm afraid of what will happen.'

'Nothing will happen.'

Julia looked at Sonny's expression. 'You're going to go in to her, aren't you?'

'Let me think.'

'If you do, I'm leaving. I can't bear to be here if something happens.'

'I didn't say I was going in to her.'

'You're going all right. You never could resist a lame duck, the lamer the better as far as you're concerned.'

'Why me, I wonder?'

'Who else here is going to help her?'

'No one, that's for sure.'

'She must know you're not in the IRA, which goes to show how much she knows about everybody.'

'I might go in and talk to her just for two seconds and see what she wants.'

'God almighty, Sonny, you know what she wants is for you to help her get out of here.'

'Maybe she's entirely innocent.'

'If she is innocent, why has she a document saying she's a colonel?'

'Maybe it's nothing, you don't know.'

'If she was innocent, she wouldn't have looked so guilty.'

Sonny nodded. That was true anyway.

'A woman can tell things about another woman,' said Julia. She had often wondered if Alice suspected anything about her and Plank.

'I will have to check it out,' said Sonny. 'I will be less than a minute.'

'Why do you have to go to her?'

'You know I couldn't live with myself if I didn't even try and find out the truth.'

'You already know the truth.'

'I will know for definite. And I feel I have a duty to be definite.'

'Duty? Everyone says you won't do your duty for your country, and now you're doing the opposite, taking sides and getting us all into trouble.'

Julia stood up to leave. She had to go. She couldn't be here if Sonny was going to help this woman. What about Plank? Him in the IRA and this woman a spy. He would need to know. If he let anything slip around her it would be a disaster for him, for the both of them.

'I have to go,' she said. 'I couldn't bear to be here if anything happens.'

'Nothing will happen.'

'You don't know that.'

'Julia, for Christ's sake. I just can't leave her there all alone.'

'That's up to you.'

'Don't go. How are you going to get home?'

'Mick or someone will give me a lift, or I can get Gabby's taxi. I'll be all right. I might call to see my sister so don't wait up for me.'

'Please wait. I won't get into trouble.'

'I'll see you later.'

Sonny watched her move away. Maybe she was right. It was scary. What was he getting himself into?

'I'll be home very soon, darling,' he called after her.

On her way out, Julia made sure she accidentally passed Plank. Nobody heard her tell him to meet her at the usual place later. He was also to make sure that Sonny saw him still here after she had gone so as not to arouse suspicion.

30

The toilets were situated in such a way that patrons in both the bar and the lounge could use them. As he walked through the bar, Sonny glanced around to see if anyone was taking any notice of him. Why should they? Everyone uses the toilet in a pub. The ladies and gents were on either end of a corridor with another room in the middle used for storing cleaning materials. It wasn't unknown for guys on the run to spend a night concealed in the cupboard. Unfortunately, if you were detected there was no escape from it. Sonny knocked gently on the door. 'This is Sonny,' he said quietly. 'Are you in there?'

The door opened. Ruby stood there, if that was even her name. Julia was right. This wasn't like the lady on stage just a short time ago. Remnants of make-up created tiny brown rivulets on an ashen face. The once alluring eye mascara now only served to make her look like a circus clown. Something had taken its toll . . . fear, obviously.

'Quick, come in,' she said. 'Did anyone see you?'

Sonny entered the room. It was cramped. A single wire with a bare bulb hanging from the ceiling was the only light. He could smell the alcohol on her breath. He had heard people talk about the smell of fear, and for a second, he imagined he could smell it – a kind of sweet, sickly smell. Maybe it was the dirty wet rags lying in a corner. He would have to be firm, harsh even. If this woman was a spy, he was leaving himself open to all kinds of trouble by even going to her.

'What do you want with me?' he asked.

'You have to help me,' said Ruby.

'Who are you anyway? Why are you in Cairnduff?'

'I'm a historian.'

'Why are you hiding if you are a historian?'

'Lucy Dorian saw a piece of paper with my picture on it and she thinks I'm a spy.'

'What was the paper she saw?'

'I was at the funfair with my nieces, and there was a machine that would take your picture and print out a certificate saying whatever you wanted to put on it. It was only fun. You could say you were the prime minister or anything, and we all printed out things. I think one of my nieces said she was a famous film star. I said I was a colonel in the army, stuff like that. I kept it as a reminder of the lovely day we had.'

'Let me see it.'

'It got me into enough trouble. I tore it up and flushed it down the toilet.'

'If it was such an obvious fake so what if Lucy saw it?'

'I know she's an IRA sympathiser, and she might think I'm an informer. If I go to leave, she'll tell others and get them to stop me.'

'How do you know so much about Lucy?'

'I hear things.'

'Maybe you want to hear them. Maybe that's your real job.'

The woman didn't answer this. She moved towards Sonny in a seductive manner. 'If you help me, I could be very friendly with you.'

Sonny was amazed more than anything and managed to blurt, 'What are you at?'

'I know your wife isn't very good to you, but I can be.'

'How do you know anything about my wife?'

'Let me show you what a real woman can be like,' said Ruby, and she moved to put her arms around him.

Sonny was disconcerted for a second. But he recovered his poise. He took her wrists and gently pushed her back. 'What do you take me for? I'm not that stupid.'

Ruby seemed to realise that Sonny wasn't going to succumb, and in a pleading tone she said, 'Will you help me?'

'Why are you so desperate?'

'Is there a back way out of here?'

'No.'

'Could a hole be made in the ceiling?'

'You're crazy. Even if you got out onto the roof and down into the yard, it's completely closed in.'

'What can I do?'

'There's one way out of here and that's through the lounge and out the front door. Even it has security to prevent drive-by attacks.'

'You must help me then.'

'Why did you pick on me to ask for help?'

'Because everyone knows you are trying to start an organisation to get the troubles stopped, and you're not in the IRA like all the rest of them.'

'Who told you all this?'

'Jesus, it's common knowledge. Everyone knows, not just me.'

'You're an undercover agent. You scare me.'

'Please, I beg you.'

In spite of his determination to be harsh, Sonny couldn't help but be touched by the terror in the woman's voice.

'All the females around here are jealous of me. They think I'm trying to seduce their husbands and boyfriends away from them, and some of them are throwing stones in a glass house.'

'I don't believe a word of what you are telling me.'

'It's the truth, I swear it. How can I convince you?'

Again, she tried putting on some sort of sexy voice. 'I'm a very loving woman.'

Sonny gave that short shrift. 'You're a spy, and because you're a spy, you know everything about everyone.'

'I only know about things because I overhear them.'

'How do you hear these things?'

'I told you, I'm a very loving woman. People like my company, and it's only natural to gossip.'

Sonny put his two hands over the top of his head and closed his eyes tight. God, it was so frustrating. This woman was a ringer, a spy and a British agent if ever there was one, but she was a human being. And he had formed a movement that advocated respect for all and an end to stuff like this. He couldn't be a hypocrite and ignore her plight, even though she was the worst kind of enemy to his own people.

'Say you will help me, please,' she said.

'How can I help you?'

'If you escort me out, I will be all right.'

'You're really crazy if you believe that. If Lucy shouted out, you're a spy the Pope of Rome walking beside you couldn't save you.'

'You have to help me.'

'There's no way I can.'

'Please, on bended knee, I beg you to help me.'

Sonny took a deep breath. He had to do something. The fear in her face was too hard to ignore.

'All right. I will do something, but it could have serious repercussions for me.'

'If you do, you won't regret it, I promise.'

'Give me your contact's number. I will ring your people and tell them of your predicament.'

'I cannot do that.'

'Why not?'

The woman threw her arms in the air as if frustrated. 'Because I don't have a contact number.'

Sonny was angry. 'Listen, lady, you don't want help.'

'Oh God, I do.'

'Then give me the number.'

Ruby became angry, almost accusing. 'Do you think help would come? Maybe in a week's time they might arrive in strength, and check out the place.'

Sonny let himself lean back against the wall. She was right. No way would they take the risk of being set up in an ambush.

'Anyway, I'm not an agent.'

'I don't understand why you keep denying it at this stage. Is it the way you have been trained?'

'I'm a historian.'

'The fact you know so much proves what you really are. What drove you to become what you are?'

'What reasons have you for not being in the IRA?'

'How do you know I'm not?'

'You have to help me get out of here.'

'There isn't any more I can do.'

'Please, think of something.'

'I have to go,' said Sonny. He was telling her the truth. There was nothing he could do, nothing anyone in this whole building could, or would, do for her.

'Is Rooster Riley in the lounge?' she asked.

'Why?'

'He carries out all the executions.'

'I don't believe you.'

'Christ, you're so naïve. He gets a kick out of putting a gun to people's heads and pulling the trigger. He never shows mercy, no matter who it is.'

'You are an English spy who would accuse anyone of anything,' said Sonny. 'I'm wasting my time with you. I have to go.'

'Don't leave me. I beseech you.'

'Is there any message you'd like me to deliver to someone. A relative maybe?'

Ruby slumped her back against the wall and said almost to herself, 'I always knew this day would come.'

Sonny took a deep breath. 'Good luck, Ruby.'

She lifted her head. 'Before you go, I want you to know that my dad was blown to pieces by an IRA bomb in London. I was just four at the time.'

Sonny had his hand on the handle of the door. 'I'm very sorry. Goodbye. May God help you.'

He pressed down the handle but didn't open the door. Jesus, there was nothing more he could do. He'd have to leave her to her fate. God almighty, why hadn't she been more careful?

'I can tell you something if you can think of a way to help me,' said Ruby quickly.

Sonny hesitated. 'What can you tell me?'

'Something very important.'

'Okay, tell me.'

'What will you do to help?'

'Jesus, woman, what can I do?'

'Something, anything, for Christ's sake.'

'What do you know that's so important?'

'Promise me you will help me in some way.'

'What do you know?'

'Your wife . . .'

Sonny glared at her. 'What about my wife?'

'She's having an affair.'

Sonny had the door opened. 'Jesus Christ. You would say anything that suits you. I'm going.'

Sonny left and closed the door behind him. In the dim light of the storage room, Ruby whispered almost to herself. 'You know that already, don't you?'

31

Sonny headed straight over to the bar where Rooster was sitting huddled with Lucy. He caught Mulligan's eye and ordered a pint. While waiting for the beer he went over to Rooster and said into his ear, 'Can I have a word with you?'

Rooster, staring into the mirror behind the bar at Sonny, nodded and said, 'I will be with you in a couple of minutes.'

Sonny returned to his usual seat. He kept an eye on Rooster, who was still in deep conversation with Lucy and sipping from his mug of black tea. Why was he making him wait?

People were going in and out of the toilet but no one suspected the woman was in the broom cupboard. They would have no reason to open the door to look inside and would probably think it was locked anyway.

Eventually, Rooster got up and approached Sonny, saying, 'You wanted to see me?'

'Yeah.'

'Before you say anything, you were being watched going in to the English woman.'

'You saw me.'

'You were seen. Let's leave it at that.'

'Can you do anything, Rooster?'

'What do you mean?'

'You know what I mean?'

'Tell me.'

'Can you make sure she gets out of here safely?'

'God, you look so much like your father. Where does the time go?'

'You're avoiding the question.'

'What question?'

'Will you intervene to save the English woman?'

'Hopefully she will stay there until closing time, and then she can be picked up without any fuss.'

'She says she isn't guilty of anything.'

'We've had our suspicions about her for some time. Now this pass she carries is a giveaway.'

'She says it's a joke thing.'

'She will have to be interrogated.'

'We all know what that means.'

'It means her being interrogated, and if necessary, tried as a spy.'

'Didn't the Brits pick her up for interrogation on the night Walsh and the soldier fought. They wouldn't do that if she was a spy.'

'A bluff to give her more cover,' said Rooster. 'They probably gave her tea and biscuits and a taxi home after being de-briefed on all she'd found out.'

'Rooster, you give the word and I will personally have her on a plane to England tonight, and that will be the last you ever hear of her.'

'That's not possible.'

'Why isn't it?'

'I don't have the power to allow that.'

'How come?'

'Fucking spies and touts are always dealt with in a particular way. In every uprising the bastard touts were always our downfall.'

'You are assuming she's guilty.'

'She will have a trial. Did you consider your own position since we spoke? I hear lots of talk about this peace movement you are involved in.'

'Why are you so keen on me?'

'Many of our lads only think of the excitement of it all. We need people who can think strategically. You have the intelligence. Just think what we could achieve if we worked as a team. And you never know, you might like the other side of it as well. Holding a powerful rifle can give a tremendous buzz to a young fellow.'

'What about you? Does it give you a buzz?'

'My days of holding a rifle are long past.'

'Rifles are not used in executions.'

Sonny knew he was sailing close to the wind on this one but he couldn't resist. There was a pause between the two men. Rooster took a sip of tea and turned his one eye on Sonny.

'What are you suggesting? What did that woman tell you? Because remember, she was trying to snare you into helping her. Did she tell you anything else about me?'

'She didn't tell me anything,' said Sonny.

'She's a cunning bitch,' said Rooster. 'She'd say anything to save her hide.'

Sonny racked his brain. Rooster had already decided about the woman. What other approach could he use to change his mind?

'Ruby also has a story. Please, Rooster.'

'Blood, Sonny. The warm blood of true patriots. We must keep feeding our sacred earth with it, else we are doomed as a nation.'

Just at that moment, Mick approached the table where Sonny and Rooster were seated. He had a curious look on his face.

'Hi, Rooster. Hi, Sonny,' he said.

Sonny said nothing. Rooster said, 'Hello, Mick.'

'Is it my imagination, or is there something going on?'

'What do you think would be going on?'

'There's something, I can sense it. Where has the English woman disappeared to?'

'Is anyone saying anything?'

'I don't think so, but I haven't seen Ruby leave.'

'We will have to tell you, so you don't go spreading rumours. The English woman is hiding in the closet in the corridor leading to the toilets.'

'Why?'

'She is going to be picked up and questioned when the place clears.'

'My God. I knew it. I knew it!'

'What did you know?'

'I said it to Scotty. What is an English tourist doing here? It smells funny to me and now I'm proved right.'

'I'm warning you, not a word about this to anyone now or later. Am I getting through to you?'

'Loud and clear,' said Mick.

'I hope so. Loose mouths can't be tolerated.'

'Don't you worry,' said Mick. 'I'm out of here and home to my bed. If Scotty is looking for me, tell him the arthritis is at me.'

Mick walked away with his head down in case he might see something he didn't want to see.

Sonny looked Rooster in his good eye. This was his last chance. 'Rooster, the English woman's father was killed by an IRA bomb. For the last time, will you let her go?'

'I have no responsibility in the matter if she is guilty. What has to be done has to be done.'

'It's a human life we are talking about.'

Rooster stood up. 'No matter. I am going into her to tell her the situation.'

'Listen to her story, please, Rooster,' said Sonny.

He watched Rooster make his way to the toilets, and then kept his eye on the closed door. His quiet vigil was interrupted by Plank, who had come to stand over Sonny's table.

He greeted Sonny warmly. 'Ah, how's it going, my old friend? You and Rooster were socialising there like old army buddies.'

Plank looked all around him, making himself as visible as possible before sitting down.

'Hardly army buddies,' said Sonny.

He took a drink from his pint. Better not mention the English woman to Plank. There was no way of knowing his reaction.

'You don't usually come out on your own without Julia,' Plank said.

'Julia was here. She has gone to visit her sister. Poor Mary can do with the company with Rory in jail. He's been there almost two years now, and no court appearance or anything.'

'It's a way of keeping us off the scene,' said Plank. 'Legal internment it's called.'

'Yeah.'

'And these are the people who are supposed to dispense justice.'

Sonny remembered Donal's so-called hearing. The guy in the mask sitting on the right. Stones in glass houses.

'The cops call it finishing school,' said Plank.

'What does that mean?'

'It's in jail they learn from one another, all the different strategies to do with carrying out a campaign of resistance. Mostly they discover how to make bombs and stuff.'

'I bet,' said Sonny.

'I have managed to escape the finishing school; thanks be to God. Do you remember when we were at real school? You sat beside me in fourth class and everyone said you were the smartest in the whole year.'

'It didn't get me very far.'

'It's not easy to get anywhere when you come from our side of the ditch.'

'At least we are not in jail like several of our classmates. If I'm not mistaken, Rafferty and McKenna were also in that fourth class.'

'They were unlucky really. But that's not much comfort to their families . . . Then again, maybe it is.' Plank picked up one of Julia's empty glasses. There was still lipstick on the rim. He knew the taste of it. 'To think they have joined the rollcall of those who gave their lives for their country,' he said. 'They are up there with the best of them. We have to be proud that they were our schoolmates.'

'Joe McKenna had a champion conker. One time I offered him ten marbles for it, but he wouldn't part with it.'

'None of us knew what was ahead of us,' said Plank.

'Do you have no fear of what might happen to you?' said Sonny. 'From all accounts you operate in a high-risk zone at times.'

'What do you mean high risk - zone?'

'If, for example, you were a member of a certain organisation, and I don't know if you are or not, would you not be scared? At best you could end up in jail for years. At worst you could be killed on some manoeuvre. If you stand close to the fire there is always a chance you'll get burned.'

'No way. I don't intend to take chances. That's for dead heroes. What's the point in being a hero and you're dead. You may as well be a coward. It won't matter once you're feeding the daisies.'

'That is true, but there are people who do things because, in the back of their minds, they will always be called heroes.'

'Those are the crazies. Believe me I'm not one of them. I intend to do my own thing. *You* do your own thing. I've always admired you for standing up for what you believe in, despite your background.'

'You don't have a republican background like me, yet you still got involved.'

Plank glanced around. He said, 'I know how genuine you are so I will let you into a secret. Something my uncle taught me. He was a committed socialist, and hated the wealthy and privileged who he said fed themselves on the labours of the poor. He told me these privileged people used laws, and made laws, to suit their pursuit of riches. He argued that if you were reared in one of those American ghettos that are always on the news for drugs and stuff, and you wanted to be successful, there was only way. You had to be involved in the drug trade, and fair play to them.'

'Wow, he was outside the box on that.'

'He said it was legitimate because it was using your environment to better yourself. Those who would condemn it were the privileged. But they had used *their* environment to get rich.'

'But there's a contradiction,' said Sonny. 'That's capitalism. If your uncle was a socialist, why was he promoting capitalism.'

'Well, I have to admit my uncle was inclined to change his position when arguing stuff. But I think he was saying this: beat them at their own game.'

'Aren't the IRA supposed to be a socialist movement?'

'You must be joking. How many socialists are there in this area, in this so-called republican hotbed? Do you mean to tell me the small farmers of South Armagh are socialists.? The IRA was never socialist.'

'What about James Connolly. Wasn't he a socialist?'

'Maybe, but his Citizen Army was separate to Pearse and the others. Connolly only came on board for the Rising. Pearse a socialist? He was a barrister for Christ's sake. Even today do you ever see a socialist barrister? Collins? An English civil servant! None of them were poor. Don't talk to me about socialism. De Valera and Fianna Fáil socialist? Bullshit! Is the pope a prod?'

'Well, it can't be right to feed people drugs to get rich.'

'It's funny, you know, I said the exact same thing to my uncle. Do you know what he said? He said there are thousands of highly respected people getting rich feeding people drugs in this country, meaning publicans. He said alcohol caused more misery than any other drug going, and yet because it's the elite who run the pubs, the auctioneers, the big farmers, they are accepted. He said look at how many TDs are publicans. And he was right. Our man Mulligan here has over a hundred acres. I gathered spuds for him when I was a lad. He gave us ten shillings a day with a penny deducted for every potato we missed. My hands were so cold and my fingers frozen so stiff, I couldn't even eat my dinner, such as it was. I wonder how much he pays Alice behind the bar?'

All the time Plank and Sonny were chatting, Sonny was keeping an eye on the toilet door watching for Rooster to appear. Whatever he was saying to the English woman was taking a while.

'So, you think being involved in the IRA is your way of improving yourself? That's not very patriotic,' said Sonny.

'You were the smartest at school, and you said yourself it didn't get you very far.'

'Maybe you don't have to go very far to get what you want. Seeing as we are talking, I will tell you a secret. My dream is to live in a peaceful land and to be able to go to the library every day and read all the wonderful books that have ever been written. To be in a position to do that without having to work, to earn a living for Julia and myself, would be my way of bettering myself.'

'When are you going to be rich enough to retire and live like that?'

'Well, I can dream.'

'I don't intend to dream, and I don't intend to end up in prison, or have my name on Ireland's roll of honour. You are the only one I would ever say this to.'

'Thanks for your confidence,' said Sonny, draining the last of his pint. What was keeping Rooster?

Plank said, 'You know I wasn't very smart at school and the others called me Plank because they thought I was thick. I didn't get picked on the team. Nobody would play conkers or marbles or any other game with me. They taunted me and called me names, and I don't know how many times I went home after being beaten up and bullied.'

'I was never involved in any of that.'

'You were always inside the classroom reading something.'

'I'm sorry. Schoolboys can be cruel.'

'Well, they don't bully me now, the bastards. I see them around the place. Now they show me respect. I have to tell you, Sonny, I never had anything against you and never will. It can't be easy doing what you do, trying to get a peace thing going and everything. I know what it's like when people no longer want to be your friend. Maybe you don't need them.'

'Everybody needs friends.'

'You would not believe it, but there are people now who want to be friends with me who used to bully me at school. I let them buy me a drink and smile inside to myself.'

The toilet door opened. Rooster appeared and came over to their table. Sonny was brought back to his present problem with a bang. He would have liked to continue his talk with Plank, but not now.

'Hi, Rooster,' said Plank.

'Hello, Plank.'

'Well, I gotta go, Sonny,' said Plank. 'I enjoyed our little chat. You know I always liked you.'

'See you, Plank.'

When Rooster sat down in the vacant seat, he said, 'What was that little *tête-à-tête* with our dashing friend about?'

'Nothing really. Just passing the time of day.'

'Plank is a showman. I'm not sure if his heart is really in what we are trying to do.'

'Do you ever really know anyone and what motivates them?'

'Why? Did Plank tell you his reasons for being involved?'

Sonny was dying to hear what had transpired between Rooster and the English woman, but he knew he was walking a thin line. She was a spy, and Rooster was her arch-enemy. Sonny wasn't involved, and as such he couldn't be seen to be up to his neck in the outcome and maybe dragged into the whole affair. He would bide his time and let Rooster dictate the terms of their discussion.

'We talked about our time at school. He sat beside me for one year. Benny McKenna and Riser Rafferty were in the same class as us.'

'Ah, poor Riser and McKenna. So young, but at least they had the honour of joining the long list of Irish martyrs. Your father would read the roll call of local heroes every year at the Easter commemorations.'

'I know. I was taken to them as a child.'

'It's important to instil into the youngsters the importance of their heritage. Some genius said, "Give me the child and I will give you the man."'

'You could call that brainwashing.'

'Look at the Catholic Church. It's pretty successful. They get them from the word go with baptism, and right through the years after that with communion, confirmation, and even getting married. If you marry someone who is not a Catholic you must agree to have the children brought up as Catholics.'

'Can I ask, do you believe in God?'

'You're just asking that to hear what I'll say. But I don't mind. Most people know my devotion to my religion. I am proud of my faith and try to get holy communion every morning. We must all account for our time here when we go. I don't want to be found wanting.'

'Does that fit into the psychical force stuff?'

'Jesus taught us about the blood sacrifice. He shed his blood so that we might be saved. Patrick Pearce followed on from that. To his understanding, bloodshed is a cleansing and sanctifying thing. I can't comprehend why there isn't a movement to have Pearse canonised and made a saint.'

Sonny was still scared to bring up the Ruby situation but felt it was time to bite the bullet.

'Saints,' he said, 'are often people who die for their beliefs, but then the problem is people at war have different beliefs. So, who is right? For example, the English woman has her own beliefs. By the way, what did you tell her?'

'She will have to be questioned fully. I didn't have time to go into her story at length,' said Rooster.

'Just let her go,' said Sonny, 'and in no time she will be forgotten about.'

Rooster smiled. Sonny could never remember seeing Rooster smile before. This was a first, but what did it mean? It wasn't really a smile more like a smirk or sneer.

'There is a protocol that has to be followed.'

'Yeah, questioning and execution.'

'You're out of your league, Sonny. Get your own act together and then maybe you will have more influence on events, instead of running around trying to organise hippy, peace-loving loonies. Just think of it. If you join up, I will guarantee you will be my eyes and ears, under my supervision as it were. Everything, Sonny, isn't as clear as it seems sometimes. And there is something else I heard on the grapevine.'

'Oh yeah? What's that?'

'There are people who are concerned at the way you are wrestling control from them in the locality. Very high up people, I might add.'

'What do you mean?'

'That's all I am going to say. Just be careful.'

Sonny looked at him. Was that supposed to be a threat or a warning? Maybe a bit of both. But he knew he wasn't going to get any more out of Rooster on this subject, and there was something else he was curious about. He took a drink, and in a conversational tone said, 'You missed the big fight. Walsh did us proud.'

'Yes, he did indeed.'

Sonny listened carefully to his answer. No comment on why he wasn't there. 'You would have been enthralled. It's always the way. You go somewhere all the time, and then the one time you don't, something exciting happens.'

'I was sorry I missed it. The Brits know they can't get anything on me so they give me plenty of hassle. When I went out that evening every tyre on my Land Rover had been slashed. I was grounded for the night. Had to get four new tyres.'

'It's not nice always being harassed,' said Sonny. 'Never mind the expense.'

'Tell me about it, but I have to go.'

'What about the English woman?'

'She will be taken care of. My advice to you, Sonny, is to let the protocol run its course and don't stand in its way. Goodbye.'

Sonny sat staring at his glass. What was Rooster on about when he said not everything was clear, and that people weren't happy with his peace initiative? Surely, he was talking about the republican movement, which meant he now had serious enemies on both sides. He didn't want to be another causality of the damn troubles, forgotten about in a week's time. And there was his responsibility to Julia. He had no right putting his life at such risk. Was he a coward? He could admit he was a coward. But he wanted to father children and leave his trace in the world. What was wrong with that? And there were a million books he hadn't read. Maybe nothing would happen. Maybe Potts was bluffing. Maybe Rooster was as well. But it would only take one word from any of these people and he'd be dead. And what would people say? Ah, wasn't it a terrible thing to happen, and he'd be put in a grave with some flowers over it and that would be it.

On his way home through the car park, Sonny passed Rooster's Land Rover. He thought of him having to buy four new tyres and without thinking glanced at the wheels. Those weren't new tyres or even nearly new. He was lying about why wasn't he there the night the Brits raided Mulligan's. And what did he mean about being under his supervision if he joined up? Did he mean supervision or control? The whole thing was a mess, and it was *his* life at stake. His life . . . God, he didn't want to die.

Julia was still out when he got home. Probably still at her sister's. He rang Pete, who was surprised to get the call. Phone conversations were thought to be recorded, and important stuff was usually said face to face. But in this instance, Sonny was hoping it *was* being recorded.

'I am not putting myself up for election,' he said.

A moment's silence on the other end. 'This is a surprise,' said Pete. 'Can I ask why?'

'You know how I told you I had become a thorn in the side of certain powerful people? Turns out I'm a thorn in the other side as well. I'm going to keep a low profile until everything dies down. No meetings or anything. You can explain to the others what's happening. The truth is, Pete, I'm very scared. I don't want to be a martyr.'

'I agree with you. You have every right to be afraid. Who wouldn't be? In reality, you have little option. You have my full support in your decision, Sonny.'

Sonny hung up. If the security forces were listening in, Potts would get to hear of his withdrawal and so get off his back. And once Pete started spreading the word, the locals would know inside a day or two. He felt a sense of relief, and Pete's support made him feel better about himself. He would have to tell Julia as well. He glanced out the hall window into the dark driveway. What was keeping her?

32

Julia sat on the sofa in the safe house. She was scared. Scared because of the English woman. She knew Plank. He was susceptible and weak behind it all. He could easily be led the wrong way, and this Ruby one was capable of anything. With her seductive charms, she could get him to confide in her, and walls have ears. Stolen money, the torture of Big Mac, it could all come out, and her up to her neck in it as well. And on top of everything, Sonny was getting suspicious, she could tell. Was there any way she and Plank could get away from it all and start a new life? Did she even love him enough to do that? Did that matter if they needed to escape?

A car pulled up outside. It was Plank. Julia rushed to open the front door.

'I was driving like Sterling Moss to get here,' he said. 'Let me hold you, darling.'

Julia extracted herself from Plank's arms and sat down.

'Tell me about the English woman.'

Plank had taken off his jacket and was parading around showing off a new jumper. 'This again? There's nothing to tell. Do you like my new jumper?'

Julia ignored his strutting around. 'Mick said you were eyeing her up.'

'Mick is like Markey's oul' dog, going a bit of the road with everyone. Why in the name of God would I be eyeing up the English woman when I have you?'

'I would be a fool to think you wouldn't go with someone else behind my back.'

'I could say the same about you.'

'That's different.'

'Why?'

'Because Sonny and me aren't really suited. That's why I'm here.'

'Why did you marry him in the first place?'

'I just wanted to love someone and feel loved. My sister always got the limelight. And Sonny was so handsome. But sometimes he's like a child living in cloud cuckoo land with his peace movement.'

'You shouldn't be saying things like that about your husband.'

'Why not?'

'It's not respectful to Sonny.'

'My God, you are sleeping with Sonny's wife – me – in case you don't know it, and you want to be respectful towards him?'

'I have no quarrel with Sonny.'

'Well, if the two you want to be best buddies go ahead.'

'What are we quarrelling about, Julia?'

'I'm not quarrelling. I just want to know when are we going to get away together.'

'As soon as possible.'

'What does that mean?'

'It means when we have things worked out. I have a business deal that I'm waiting on to be finished, and then I want to get far away from this place and be with you. Does Sonny suspect anything?'

'You should know, being so respectful to him and all.'

'*Does* he suspect anything?'

'I don't know. Sometimes I think he does, sometimes I think he doesn't.'

'Rooster is putting pressure on him to join up.'

'He's not going to join up now, that's for sure. I used to wonder was it because he was afraid.'

'It's certainly not fear. Not too many would have the courage to try and start a peace movement in South Armagh.'

'What's going on? You don't like me criticising him all of a sudden.'

'Let's not talk about Sonny. Come to the bedroom. I want you so much.'

'You didn't say how long it will be before we can get away for good.'

'I don't know, I keep telling you.'

'When will you know?'

'Soon, darling. Very soon.'

'Tell me again why we can't get away right now.'

'I have already explained to you. I have money coming and have to be around to see the deal concluded.'

'What deal?'

'It's better you don't know.'

'Do you think I'd let it out or tell someone?'

'Why do you always think the worst of me? Me that worships the ground you walk on.'

'Maybe you just say that.'

'We are wasting good loving time,' said Plank.

'Tell me again you don't fancy the English woman and have had no dealings with her.'

'I swear the same sacred oath I took when I joined up. I've only seen her around the bar the same as everyone else. Now will you come to the bedroom?'

Julia relaxed a little. Maybe he was telling the truth. 'I should tell you I think she is in serious trouble.'

'What are you on about?'

'I was in the ladies tonight along with Lucy Dorian and we both saw a certificate fall out of the English woman's bag saying she was an army colonel.'

Plank looked at her almost speechless. 'Say that again.'

'She had an identity pass thing with her picture on it saying she was a colonel.'

Plank slumped onto a chair. 'Oh my God.'

'Why are you so anxious?'

Plank spoke in a quiet voice like he was almost afraid to ask. 'What did Lucy do when she saw it?'

'She told Rooster.'

Plank closed his eyes and put his hands over his face. 'Oh my God. Oh, God.'

'What's wrong with you? What's going on?' asked Julia.

'Why didn't you tell me right away?' said Plank accusingly.

'Aren't I after telling you?'

Plank jumped up from the chair and began pacing the floor like a caged tiger. 'Fuck, fuck, fuck! What am I going to do?'

Julia was taken aback. She stood looking at him helplessly. 'Why do you have to do anything? You said you had nothing to do with her.'

It was as if Plank hadn't heard her. 'Fucking think, think, think!'

Julia shook her head. 'You knew about her. You knew she was a spy, didn't you?'

'No, no, no, I didn't.'

'If she knows about McDonald and the IRA money, she will tell them everything. Was she also arranging this money you are supposed to be getting?'

'No, that's not it. Rooster will be looking for me. I didn't tell him I was leaving Mulligan's. He will have to round up some of the other boys.'

'So, let them take care of it.'

'I should have been there.'

'You're here now. Let's go to the bedroom.'

'I can't. I have to be getting fucking back.'

'What?'

'I have to go.' Plank was talking to himself more than to Julia.

Julia rushed to him and put her arms around him. 'Please, don't go. I love you.'

Plank tried to extricate himself from her embrace. 'I must!'

'Please, please,' said Julia. 'We can go to the bedroom. I want you.'

Plank struggled loose and made for the door. 'Are you coming?' he said. 'I will drop you close to your house.'

Julia just planted herself in a chair. 'I'm not going. I'm staying.'

'Please yourself,' said Plank opening the door.

He was halfway to the car when Julia ran after him. 'Wait, wait, I'm coming. Don't leave me here. I'm coming.'

Sonny was asleep on the sofa when Julia let herself in. She checked her watch. Not too late. She nudged Sonny awake. 'Don't be sleeping on the sofa all night.'

He scrunched his eyes and looked around. 'Sorry, I tried waiting up for you. How did you get on?'

'Mick left me with my sister. And she just dropped me off. She's still in a bad way about Rory.'

'I was speaking to Mick before I left. He never mentioned giving you a lift.'

'Oh, you know Mick. Too busy nosing into other people's business. What about the English woman? What did she say to you?'

'She said she was innocent. Rooster is going to have her lifted for interrogation.'

Sonny didn't want to say that Julia's suspicions were right. He didn't want to tell her what kind of woman Ruby was with her attempts at seducing him, because they were heartbreaking in a way. A desperation born of fear.

And he certainly didn't want to mention the accusation Ruby made against her.

'Innocent! That one would do or say anything. I know just to look at her. She was smart enough to look for you to come to her aid.'

'I'm not so stupid to believe everything she said. Though I believed her when she said the IRA killed her father.'

'Did she tell you that?'

'He was killed by an IRA bomb left in a mailbox. She was only four.'

'Jesus, you couldn't be up to the things they come out with. She was playing on your sympathy. Don't you believe for one second anything she told you . . . do you hear?'

'I won't. I'm not stupid. Anyway, it's all none of our business.'

'I'm wrecked,' Julia said. 'Come to bed. You'll freeze out here. I want you beside me.'

33

Ruby felt cold. She couldn't stop shivering. It wasn't because of a lack of clothes or heat. This was a deathlike chill that enveloped her in an all-embracing blanket of fear.

If she looked around from where she sat tied to a chair, she would see she was in a hay barn similar to hundreds of others in farmyards around the country. At one end of the barn there were bales of hay piled to the roof. A baler and other farm machinery were stored at another end of the building. High in the steel structures, pigeons and swallows nested happily together. A single rope with no obvious purpose dangled three feet from the ground from one of the crossbeams. It was maybe the only feature of the place that Ruby noticed.

Outside, a lone figure kept guard. He was armed with a revolver concealed inside his zip-up jacket. He had never fired the gun in anger, though Ruby couldn't have known that. He had been part of a group of volunteers who abducted her from Mulligan's when the last of the punters had left at closing time. The other volunteers had dispersed. The fewer people involved in what was going to happen the better. He had been designated to be a lookout while someone higher up questioned the captive. Secretly, even to himself, he hoped he wouldn't be ordered to shoot her. But he also hoped he wasn't a coward at heart. The Brits had no compunction about killing people.

Ruby stopped trying to loosen the ropes that had her tied to the chair. For a few seconds, she tried to practice what they had told her in training. Never give up hope. Keep conscious of your situation. The enemy may not hold all the cards. But it was useless. All she could hope for was that it would be quick. The rope hanging from the beam filled her with dread. 'God forgive me my sins. I am sorry for all the wrong things I have done. Please, please help me, Lord. Please.'

'All quiet, Volunteer Callan?' she heard a male voice outside say to her guard.

She knew the voice of her executioner. It was Rooster. He was merciless. 'Jesus, please help me. Please, please.'

'All quiet sir.'

'Good. Keep your eyes peeled.'

Rooster entered the barn and surveyed his surroundings. This kind of thing gave him a ripple of excitement. What must it have been like to be Caesar?

'Please, please, Rooster, don't kill me,' begged the woman in the chair.

'Let's get this done,' said Rooster. 'We went over some of this in Mulligan's, but I want you now to fill me in on everything you know. It's your last chance of getting out of here alive. You have nothing to lose except a chance to live.'

'If I tell you everything, will you let me go?'

'Yes.'

'Swear it.'

'I swear.'

She didn't believe him, but she remembered her training. Every minute you live in a situation like this increases your chance of survival. If you are dead nothing can happen. Her superiors wouldn't approve of her confessing, but they weren't here, and anyway, Roster knew nearly all there was to know.

'Please loosen these ropes first,' said Ruby.

Rooster pointed a gun at her forehead. 'Talk, bitch, if you want to live.'

Ruby started to speak. Her voice felt strange. 'I was recruited by the Foreign Office and served in various embassies as a staffer, but my job was always to get information that couldn't be obtained by the usual means ambassadors employ.'

'A honey trap merchant, you slut.' His face twisted in a grimace. The thought of ensnaring people through sex enraged him.

'I did what had to be done,' she said.

'So, Plank was easy meat for you, the dirty bastard. He would tell you everything.'

'You promised you wouldn't kill me if I confessed.'

'Keep talking, whore.'

'Plank likes money and girls. He is a fool. He is involved with the Mone woman.'

'Is she a traitor also?'

'Plank and her took money from John McDonald which he intended to keep for himself the last time he made a delivery.'

'Keep talking.'

'Plank said McDonald wasn't going to hand over the money anyway, so they took it.'

'Was she involved?'

'I think she is obsessed with Plank. She just wants the high life. A good time. She didn't believe they were stealing it from the movement. They were just taking it from McDonald.'

'Anything else?'

'That's all I know. I never really found out anything that people don't know about already. Will you let me go?'

'Did you ever hear your handlers use the word Wolfhound?'

'Just a couple of times. I know nothing about it, only that Wolfhound is supposed to be an agent deep inside the Republican movement.'

'What else did you hear about him?'

'Nothing else, I swear. Please let me go.'

'If he was an agent then you and him are both on the same side. Have you heard of someone called Potts?'

Even in her terrified state, it flashed across Ruby's mind that Rooster shouldn't know about Wolfhound and Potts. She stammered, 'Only . . . only, that he's someone at the very top of the bureau.'

'I heard he is a very strict taskmaster, with his own as much as the enemy.'

'Everyone says that. They are afraid of him. I've never seen him.'

'Is there anything else you have to tell me?'

'No, that's everything. Please let me go. Please, please, you promised you would.'

Rooster didn't answer. He walked over to the door and whispered to Callan, 'You live up by White Rocks. Is Rourke's quarry hole accessible?'

'Yes, sir. As far as I know, a jeep or four-wheeler like yours would get to it.'

'That's fine. Now I want you to clear off. I will take care of business from here on in.'

The young IRA man stood to attention, relieved he would not have to be involved in what was about to happen. When he was a child, everyone said Rourke's quarry hole was bottomless. Rooster would dump the woman into it. There would be no witnesses to her disappearance. If it ever came out where the body was, Rooster would know who had squealed. From now on, best to keep out of his company as much as possible. It was that one eye. When he looked at you, it made you want to shiver or something.

Rooster watched while the volunteer sped off in his car before going back into the barn.

'Please, please, you promised you would let me go if I talked,' moaned Ruby.

'Shut the fuck up, whore,' said Rooster, and he dragged her, chair and all, out to his jeep. Behind the vehicle he untied her from the chair, but he made sure her hands and feet were still bound. He dumped her into the back of the wagon.

As the car made its way through dark twisting roads, the woman begged Rooster to let her go, but she knew he wasn't listening. Eventually she felt the jeep grind to a halt. Rooster came around to the back seat. He pulled her out and undid the ropes. They were parked in a derelict entry on a backstreet somewhere.

'Two streets up are the army barracks where your handlers are based,' he told her. 'Get back to England as soon as fuck, for if I hear, even hear, your name mentioned again, never mind see you, next time you won't be so lucky.'

Ruby staggered against the wall hardly believing it. Was she still alive? Oh, thank God, thank God.

Rooster jumped into his jeep and roared away.

She tried to take in what was happening. She really was still alive. Why hadn't he shot her? How did he know about Potts? And Wolfhound . . . Jesus, that had to be it. What did he say? Wolfhound and her were on the same side.

Rooster was Wolfhound. And he was afraid of Potts . . . Jesus!

34

Sonny was sitting alone in Mulligan's drinking tea and trying to get his head around all that was going on. The lies Rooster told him about the tyres, his warning about what might happen to him, plus his insistence that he come under his wing. It was all a mess and he was scared. Then what about Julia? Would the English woman make up lies about her having an affair? It made him sick just to let it enter his head.

Mick Ryan walked in to the bar and came over to sit beside him.

'Can I join you? You seem down in yourself, as the saying goes.'

'Who wouldn't be depressed and the way things are?'

'Tell me about it.'

He had a lot to be depressed about, Julia most of all. But he couldn't talk about her. Just bluff that it's other things.

'The troubles. They never end. So much killing and damage from bombs. Not to mention the everyday hassle. Last week James Kenny's wedding was delayed for four hours. He was held on the road by the soldiers just to annoy him. All the guests and wedding plans, everything disrupted. Should the Provos not call a halt, just for a bit of normality?'

'This is a war of resistance, Sonny,' said Mick. 'While the union flag is the official flag of this state, there will always be those who are driven to take up arms, and that's no matter how hopeless or futile it may seem. The incessant drumbeat of history, especially in our area, will see to that. And it's impossible to change history.'

'We can change the present.'

'Our history is what makes us the way we are.'

'Can we not create a new history?'

'Every uprising was an attempt to create a new history.'

'Does the other side not have a different history's drumbeat urging them on?'

'Their drumbeat has always been stirred up and fuelled by ambitious politicians, and is therefore inauthentic. Ruthless men who would do anything in pursuit of power teach religious hatred towards their fellow countrymen. They exploit dormant fears, false though those fears are. It was their forefathers who were planted here to eradicate the native Irish.'

'How long do they have to be here before they can say they are Irish?'

'They can say it today, but they choose not to. They say they are British.'

'Wasn't Wolfe Tone, the so called first Irish republican, leading an army of Presbyterians, also a product of the plantation?'

'That proves my point. If the Protestant people weren't always deceived and led astray by the demagoguery of evil men masquerading as patriotic politicians, they would by now be just like the Norman invaders before them. "More Irish than the Irish themselves." The problem lies not here but in London.'

'So, nothing changes until the Brits leave.'

'In truth, it looks like that. Really, I don't see any other way.'

'What about talking. Negotiation?'

'Many people, Sonny, will see that as naïve. The Brits will always renege on their promises. Every new generation of Irish politicians has to learn that fact anew.'

'You make it sound impossible.'

'If it were easy the solution would have been discovered long ago,' said Mick.

Just then Rooster came in. He narrowed his good eye when he saw Sonny. Maybe he hadn't expected to see him here. Or maybe he'd been looking for him. He came over and greeted both men.

Mick stood up to go. 'I have to leave you to it. I have an appointment with my GP. The oul' arthritis is playing hell with me. I was arguing the Irish perspective with Sonny, Rooster. You can continue where I left off.'

Mick sauntered off towards the door.

'Don't bother,' Sonny said to Rooster. 'I'm heading as well.'

'Before you go, Sonny,' said Rooster, setting down a hawthorn stick he had been carrying on the table. Sonny wondered if the stick was a substitute for a rifle. Maybe it made him feel more comfortable, although it could also be a sign of unconscious fear and a way of coping with it.

'I want to say,' continued Rooster, 'in our situation at present there is no black and white, no matter how vehemently it is sometimes claimed. I know you disagree with how certain matters are handled, but if you would just open your mind, you would see the logic behind it all. Throw your lot in with me and we can achieve great things together.'

Sonny lifted his tea and took a sip. He placed the cup down again without saying a word.

Rooster shook his head. 'Let me tell you something that very few people know, just to get you into the loop. Do you remember Mrs Johnson, the RUC man's wife, shot when she opened her front door to a masked gunman?'

'Yeah, another IRA hit gone wrong.'

'The IRA never claimed responsibility.'

'They never claimed responsibility because there was so much local anger.'

'We never claimed responsibility because we didn't do it. The gun used in that attack was a small-bore pistol. It wasn't the type used by volunteers.'

'What are you saying?'

'This is very a dirty war. No one knows what's going on.'

Sonny didn't speak for a moment.

'You are very quiet,' said Rooster.

Sonny drank the last of his tea and said, 'I don't know what to say. Anyway, I have to go. I will see you later.'

'Sonny, remember that not everyone is as good or bad as how they portray themselves. Sometimes people will put down false trails so others will have the wrong opinion about them. They're the ones you have to watch out for.' Rooster leaned down so his face was next to Sonny's. 'I am just saying it would be unfortunate if something bad happened to you.'

Rooster straightened again and began to don his coat. 'Sonny, throw your lot in with me.' He took up his hawthorn stick and turned to walk away. 'Take care, my boy.'

Sonny stayed in the bar for several more minutes. He swirled the cold dregs of his tea and thought of the threat Rooster had just made. It seemed everyone was out to get him. But there was something else Rooster said that struck him as odd. The attack on Eric's wife. Rooster was right about the small-bore gun. Eric had told him that in the Vic pub. So how did Rooster know about it? It wasn't exactly common knowledge. Perhaps he knew because he pulled the trigger. But no, Rooster didn't wear aftershave . . .

Jesus, maybe that was it! Cheap perfume might smell like aftershave. And what about the sweet, sickly smell he thought was fear or dirty rags when he was talking to Ruby in the broom cupboard? That might come across as aftershave in the panic of the moment. It would also make Mrs Johnson automatically think her attacker was male.

Sonny shook his head. It was the type of small gun a woman like Ruby might use. And Rooster knew about it. What was all that talk about false trails? And what about the English woman? For sure she had been shot, but it would be days, even weeks, before rumours about her sudden disappearance could be openly discussed.

35

Julia answered the door to Plank. He looked both excited and anxious.

'God, what are you doing here?' she said. 'Sonny will soon be back.'

'I had to come. I have a business opportunity in Spain. A contact there needs a guy like me. I'm heading out tomorrow, and I want you to come with me.'

Julia pulled him in by the arm so he wasn't standing in the porch. 'What are you saying to me?'

'That money I was waiting on has fallen through. But I still have the money we got from Big Mac in the bank, and this new gig will see us living the good life. Sun, sand, and piña coladas.'

'I don't know what you're on about. You want me to run away to Spain with you tomorrow?'

'Isn't that what we had planned all along? To get away somewhere and be together?'

'Yes, but—'

'No buts! This is what you always wanted. I will quit the IRA and stay over there.'

'Can you do that?'

'Of course, I can. Anyway, I could always act as a sleeper and be activated when required.'

'It's a crazy idea. What is this job?'

'Nightclub security. For a string of places. Real high-end stuff. You'll love it. And weren't you always on to me to take you away?'

'I know.'

'We will be so happy together.'

'I don't know.'

'What don't you know?'

'What to do.'

'Do what we both want.'

Julia tried to play for time a little. 'Was Rooster looking for you about the English woman?'

'I made an excuse that I had a sick stomach over something I ate, and that's why I couldn't be contacted. It was no big deal. As far as I know she is out of the picture.'

Julia sat on the sofa. Head down, she stared at the floor. Her mind was racing. Something wasn't right. The English woman was dead for sure, and coincidently Plank was offered a job abroad. Ruby would have been interrogated and confessed everything she knew.

'Will you promise me not to come back here if I don't go?' said Julia without lifting her head.

'Why not? I don't understand.'

'I'm afraid something will happen to you if you come back.'

'Why are you afraid?'

'You know how strict they are. What if Ruby knew about us taking the money McDonald was skimming? What if she told them?'

'How would she know about that? Who would tell her? Nothing will happen. Say you will come.'

'I so much want to, but . . .'

'Okay, I promise I won't come back here. Please, Julia.'

'What about Sonny?'

'You don't love Sonny. You love me.'

'I know that I don't love him. But he is very kind and good-natured. I should never have married him.'

'Everyone makes mistakes.'

'Why did all this have to happen?'

'Isn't going away what you always wanted?'

'Give me a moment to think,' said Julia. Something was wrong. Plank was in serious trouble. He was running, and she was involved too, just as deep as him. Convincing Plank to take the Big Mac money was her idea. Maybe if they got away it could all be put behind them in a different country.

'We have to hurry,' said Plank.

'Tell me truthfully. Are they after you?'

'I will keep a low profile, because you never know what the English woman told Rooster. Maybe a pack of lies.'

'They have people everywhere watching everything. They will get you.'

'No way! I can outsmart them. Anyway, we don't even know if they *are* looking for me. Come with me. It's what we dreamed about, you and I.'

'I know,' said Julia. 'But it's so sudden. I'm not ready. Nothing is packed. God, I can't think.'

'Don't think, just do.'

'What about clothes and stuff?'

'You won't need to take much. It's warm in Spain.'

'I will need *some* things.'

'Take as little as possible.'

'I can't leave if Sonny is here.'

'Think of some excuse to get him out of the house.'

'Then what?'

'I can't get the money from the bank until twelve, but I will pick you up at one. We can get a boat to England, and from there to Spain. We can travel incognito.'

'Hold me, darling, and tell me I am doing the right thing.'

Plank took Julia in his arms and squeezed her tightly. 'Yes, my love. We are doing the right thing.'

'Do you love me?' said Julia.

'Of course, I love you. We will have a wonderful life together and be so happy.'

'Oh God, I hope so, darling.'

'I have to go now before Sonny gets here.'

'Promise to watch yourself until tomorrow.'

'Don't be worried, darling.'

'I have such a bad feeling. If anything happened, I couldn't live without you.'

'Nothing is going to happen to me.'

'I would die if it did, you know that?'

'Don't think like that. Just think of how wonderful it will be, us together.'

'Are you really, really sure?'

'Yes, I'm really, really sure. Now be in bed when Sonny comes home.'

'Are you sure you love me?'

'Of course, I love you.'

'Oh, I hope so, darling.'

Plank looked Julia in the eye. He kissed her. 'It's going to be great. I'm going now. Until tomorrow, darling.'

Julia clung to him for a few seconds not wanting to let go. Finally, she released him.

'At one tomorrow, darling,' she said. 'Bye, my love.'

36

Julia didn't sleep much. She heard Sonny come in but he didn't come to bed. He must be sleeping on the sofa again. She thought about going out to him. To tell him to come to bed, even just to lie beside him for one last night. He really was a good man. And he loved her so much. Why couldn't that be enough? Because she couldn't love him, not the same way he loved her. It was her selfishness, but she couldn't help it. He'd be better off without her.

Next morning, Sonny was still lying on the sofa with a coat for a blanket when Julia entered the sitting-room. His eyes were closed but she could tell he wasn't sleeping. Why did he always think he could fool her?

'Did you sleep on the sofa again?' she said. 'I didn't hear you come in.'

He stirred. 'I didn't want to wake you. I cannot get to sleep this last while.'

'Why not?'

Sonny didn't want to say the real reason had to do with her. 'All that's going on. The poor English woman.'

'Yeah. Maybe she had her reasons. Like how you told me her father was blown up by a bomb when she was a child.'

Sonny squinted at Julia in the morning light. 'You've changed your tune about her.'

'I'm just saying sometimes people do things. Maybe because they're desperate, or in love, or something. There are millions of reasons.'

'It's funny. Plank said something similar to me a few nights ago.'

Julia froze. What did he know? Why mention Plank's name?

But Sonny didn't give any sign of being concerned and was wiping the sleep from his eyes. 'He said people joined the IRA for all sorts of reasons. Patriotism, socialism. He himself pretty much admitted that he just wanted to get back at the guys who bullied him at school. But don't go saying that to anyone either. He told me in confidence.'

Julia said, 'My lips are sealed. Do you want some tea and toast?' She filled the kettle and pretended to be interested in what Sonny was saying. 'I suppose everyone's background influences their life's journey and where it takes them.' She poured the tea and left the toast on the table. Then, all of a sudden, she felt a shiver, as if someone had walked on her grave. Where did that come from?

'What's the suitcase doing under the stairs?' Sonny asked.

Julia had her answer ready. 'I'm spring cleaning.'

Sonny was picking at his breakfast. His mind was in turmoil. The ache in the pit of his stomach at the thought of her having an affair was almost unbearable. If she would only make love to him maybe it would make him feel better.

'Will you come back to bed with me for an hour after breakfast?' he asked her.

'I can't this morning. I have to go shopping.'

'Please, Julia. I need you to hold me.'

Oh God, why was he making this so hard? 'I would like to, but not now, darling. And I meant to say, will you pick up a dress in the pub from Alice? She wants me to shorten it for her. I told her you would be there at half-twelve because she is off in the afternoon.'

Sonny gave in. 'Well, tonight will you come to bed then?'

Julia said, 'Be on time with Alice in case you miss her.'

'Promise me you will come to bed with me tonight,' pleaded Sonny.

Julia brought the dishes to the sink. Why did he have to keep on about this now, making her feel so guilty? But it had to be done. There was no turning back. He would get over her eventually.

'Okay,' she said. 'I am running into town now. Be sure and don't forget to pick up the dress from Alice. Don't miss her, darling.'

'I won't. I will be home early, love. And I just want to say to you that I know you don't love me with the same intensity that I love you. But that's okay. Love is not supposed to be selfish, so I have to be aware of that and understand where you are coming from.'

He could say more but this wasn't the time. He never could understand what it was about her that he found so bewitching. It wasn't just her looks. It had more to do with her personality. Underneath a tough exterior, she was basically unhappy and vulnerable in some way. It was part of who she was and maybe that was what he wanted to fix. Even though in his heart of hearts he knew it was unfixable.

Julia hid her head in a cupboard and pretended to look for something. 'Remember about the dress,' was all she could say.

37

Rainwater dripped through rusty cracks in the galvanised roof of the barn, the same barn in which the English woman had been interrogated. The drops fell on the figure of Plank who was tied to a chair. His eyes and ears were covered, so he couldn't hear Rooster's familiar voice commenting on the weather, and another voice saying, 'You wouldn't put your mother-in-law out on a night like that.'

'I don't have a mother-in-law, Volunteer Carney,' said Rooster.

'Sorry, sir.'

'Okay,' said Rooster, 'let's get this over with. You stay outside and keep your eyes peeled while I question this fucking tout.'

'Do you need me with you?'

'No, you stay here.'

Rooster went inside the barn and laid his umbrella on a bale of straw before removing his overcoat and a flat cap he had been wearing. He placed them carefully beside the umbrella. This kind of thing usually evoked flashbacks. There were pigs being slaughtered. A strange almost erotic tingle coursed through his body at the memories. He glanced at his captive. Better get this done and dusted. The guard outside wouldn't hear anything that was said. He bent over Plank and removed the mouth gag.

Plank immediately began pleading. 'Please, please let me go. Who's that there? Is that you, Rooster? Rooster, is that you?' he beseeched.

Rooster listened, wondering if there was anything more, he didn't know about. Anything the English woman hadn't already mentioned.

'I know it's you, Rooster. Please, please, don't shoot me! Please, Rooster! I didn't know she was a spy. I was just having sex with her, not doing anything else.'

Rooster removed the ear muffs. 'Who told you she was a spy?'

'No one. I just guessed. I'm sorry, I'm sorry!'

'She was going to give you money for information, wasn't she?'

'No, no, I didn't know she was a spy. I swear.'

'You're a lying bastard. Why did you tell her about the money you and the Mone bitch stole off the Yank?'

'I was just trying to impress on her how rich I was.'

'Why did you mention the Mone woman to her?'

'I was bragging about the way I could get women.'

Rooster checked that the lookout was still outside. 'Have you ever heard anyone in the movement use the word Wolfhound?'

'No, please, Rooster.'

'You never heard anyone say that name.'

'No, I swear I didn't.'

'What about the name Potts?'

'No, never. Please, Rooster. I have arranged to go away with Mone's wife and that will be the end of it. Please, please, Rooster.'

Plank was no longer aware of the water dripping on his head. 'I'll do anything. Please, Rooster, oh please, don't shoot me!'

Rooster, satisfied there was no leakage, and only barely conscious of a feeling of excitement, removed a revolver from his overcoat, stepped behind his victim, and shot him in the back of the head.

Birds burst from the rafters and flapped around the barn. Plank and the chair to which he was tied crashed to the floor. Blood dripped from the wound and mixed with a little puddle of water. Rooster stared at the swirling pattern for a second. Water and blood to nourish the land.

From outside, Carney yelled in, 'Is he nutted?' His head came around the door, and he approached Rooster.

'He was going to do a runner with Sonny Mone's woman,' said Rooster. 'She was in on it as well.'

'A cracked egg wouldn't be safe around that hoor,' said Carney. 'What will I do with him?'

'Disappear the bastard. He doesn't deserve a fucking grave.'

'Only I have poison laid down for them the rats would eat him'

'You have done what?' asked Rooster, sharply.

'I put down poison to kill the rats. The place is overrun with them.'

'Volunteer Carney, lift those traps at once or you will be eating the poison. What right have you to be killing living creatures? If God didn't want there to be rats on earth, he wouldn't have put them there.'

'Yes, sir. At once, sir.'

Rooster picked up his overcoat, cap and umbrella and walked out of the barn. It was still raining. What now? The Mone tramp. The stolen money. Sonny's peace movement. There were still loose ends.

38

Julia looked up at the clock for the tenth time in as many minutes. It had been a wedding present from one of her aunts. They were given four clocks as presents. Sonny had said there was something not right about gifting things that measured time. Time was always the enemy, he said. Julia had never wondered why he thought that, but for some reason it came into her head now. Sonny was right, as usual. The clock was her enemy. Plank was supposed to pick her up at one. It was now almost half past. If only the hands had stopped Plank wouldn't be late. But he was, and something was terribly wrong. She could feel it in the pit of her stomach. Please God let him come, she prayed. She looked again at the cursed clock. She got up and went to the window. No sign of anything, only a single magpie picking at the grass on the lawn. One for sorrow . . .

'Please come, Plank,' she said under her breath. What would she do if he didn't come? What could have happened to him? Why didn't he ring if he was held up in some way? The phone was definitely on its hook. She had checked it twice to make sure.

It had to be something really bad to prevent him from being here by now. But better not dwell on it. Prayer, her mother argued, was the only answer when in trouble.

Julia got down on her knees by the couch in the sitting-room. What prayers did she know? None would come to her. The only prayers she could think of were ones she learned as a child. Her mind was too crazy and mixed up.

Suddenly, she was standing on a makeshift stage in the school classroom. She was six years old. The room had been converted into a hall for the evening. Chairs for the audience to sit on were placed in front of the stage. She was wearing a blue bonnet and matching blue dress . . . the same blue colour as the New York dress she kept and didn't burn. On her feet she had black shoes and white socks, and she knew she looked beautiful. She knew she looked beautiful because she could see the adoration in her father's eyes sitting in the front row. She was reciting a poem. All the children were told to ask their parents to help them write a poem and then recite it on stage at the school concert. She remembered every word of it, even the cute gestures she made when performing it.

I am a little girl of six, and sometimes I play tricks

On my mammy and daddy, and granddad and granny.

My granny being old said I was bold, and she'd put me out in the cold.

But my daddy just grinned, tickled my chin, and said he'd hide me away in a bin.

Her father was so proud of her, and everyone loved her because she could recite so well. When he took her in his arms afterwards, he told her that one day she would be on the stage, a famous actress known all over the world. But she didn't care about everyone else loving her.

Her daddy loved her, and she loved him. He called her a pixie. 'A wee blue pixie,' he would say.

He never would tell her what a pixie was, but she loved being one anyway. In bed at night, she would say to herself, 'I am a pixie.'

Then her sister came along, and gradually her daddy's love was transferred. It wasn't fair. She loved her daddy more than her spoiled sister did. Even after his heart attack and sudden death, she mourned for him far more than her sister. She wished he could be alive and know how much she missed him. But he couldn't be alive and dead at the same time. Sometimes, when she caught Sonny looking at her, she would see the same love for her in his eyes as her father had that night on the stage. And for a fleeting moment she would feel happy. Plank never had that look in his eyes. God, why was she such a bad selfish person? Sonny loved her like her father did, yet she betrayed him to be with Plank only because it was more exciting. She was always like that, wanting attention from everyone and making them jealous – like she did with her friends when she captured Sonny. And she was still at it, because she knew Alice loved Sonny, even though he didn't realise it. Why couldn't she tell Sonny about Plank and let him maybe be more content with Alice? She was like the dog in a manger. She deserved all she got. She wanted to be admired and loved, and make people envious of her. But deep down she was just a liar, an unfaithful wife, a jealous stuck-up bitch who continued to hurt a man who adored her. If she could get away with Plank maybe Sonny would have a chance to build a new life without her. Even if she didn't get away, he deserved that, and she deserved whatever was going to happen to her. She had made her bed . . .

Was that a car she heard pulling up outside?

Julia jumped up and ran to the window. There was no car. She turned away in dismay. Then there were two loud bangs on the door, like someone hitting it with a fist.

Who was that? Plank would have his car. And he wouldn't knock like that. She wasn't expecting anyone else.

She peeked out the window to try and see the edge of the porch. Two more thuds rapped against the door. Would it be soldiers? She had a very bad feeling. A terrible dread had come over her. But she would have to answer it. She whispered to herself, 'Please let it be Plank.' She turned the lock and opened the door.

Rooster was standing on the doorstep facing her. He looked past her to the suitcase sitting in the hallway. 'Are you going somewhere?' he said.

39

Sonny was mulling over a pint of beer in Mulligan's when Mick came in and went over to where he was sitting. 'You're like someone who knows they won the lotto and can't find the winning ticket.'

'I'm fed up,' said Sonny.

'My oul' uncle Mick used to say things will look better in the morning.'

'If anything, they are getting worse.'

'Sometimes talking about a problem takes the sting out of it.'

'What can talking do?'

'You have to try it.'

'It's not easy.'

'Which is it, the money or the honey?'

'What do you mean?'

'Most problems relate to matters of finance or matters of love.'

'I have been reading about the nature of love, for all the good it has done me.'

Mick took out his pipe and started to suck on it without lighting it. 'What's written in books and what happens in reality are usually the opposite of each other.'

'Do you ever light that damn thing?'

'I'm trying to cut down. Everybody says nowadays that smoking is bad for you, but let's not talk about that. What's the problem, Sonny?'

'Julia.'

'Ah, the lovely Julia.'

'It's not easy, Mick.'

'I know.'

'She asked me to come here at half-twelve to pick up a dress from Alice behind the bar, and now I discover Alice isn't even working today. I'm afraid, Mick.'

'Get it off your chest.'

'There's no intimacy between us.'

'That's not good.'

'She says I sit around reading all day and not getting anything done.'

'And is this true?'

'I can't deny I find it hard to leave a book out of my hands.'

'But you think there is more to it than that.'

Sonny hesitated before answering. 'I think so.'

'Do you love her?'

'Of course, I love her. I give into everything she wants. I can't help it.'

'Does she love you?'

'I don't know.'

'She knew what you were like before she married you.'

'Maybe she thought she could change me.'

Mick tapped the pipe's bowl on the palm of his hand. 'A common mistake made by brides.'

Sonny lifted his beer and stared into the glass. As if speaking to it, he said, 'Sometimes I think she might be cheating on me.'

Mick placed his pipe on the table with a click. 'Have you evidence?'

'More a feeling. I don't know what to think.'

'You think maybe she wanted you out of the way today and sent you on a fool's errand? That she has a rendezvous with someone else?'

'That's hard for me to even think about.'

'You might have to face it, Sonny. Any notion who this Romeo might be?'

'I hate to say this.'

'Spit it out.'

Sonny said nothing for a few seconds, and then in a low voice, 'Plank.'

'Oh, yes, Plank.'

Sonny looked at Mick accusingly. 'The way you said that, did you know about him and her already?'

'I really like you, Sonny. And I admire what you were trying to do with the peace project. But I told you before there were things you might have to face, not nice things.'

'What are you getting at?'

It was Mick's turn to pause. 'I don't want to be the one who has to tell you, but Julia and Plank are having an affair.'

'No, I don't believe you,' said Sonny.

'Wrong. You don't want to believe me.'

'What evidence do you have?'

'If you are honest with yourself, you have all the evidence you need.'

'Tell me the evidence,' Sonny demanded.

'Sonny, you have known about it for some time. Remember when we said that people know in their hearts what others think of them, even if they don't want to?

This is the same thing. You have known in your heart about this for a long time but were afraid to face it. I get it. It's very hard. Don't forget I went through the same thing with my wife, so I know all about it. It's devastating.'

'I can't believe it.'

'Time is the answer. You will get over it. I did.'

'I won't. I can't, I can't,' said Sonny, despairingly.

The door opened. A breeze whistled through the bar. Rooster came in and looked around. He spotted the two men and came over.

He said, 'Ye all seem very serious looking.'

Mick said, 'Will I tell him?'

Sonny shrugged his shoulders. 'You may as well. It seems everyone knows except me.'

'Knows what?' said Rooster, sharply.

'I told Sonny about Julia and Plank having an affair.'

Rooster relaxed. 'Oh, that. You must have known already.'

'It's not easy taking these things on board, Rooster,' said Mick.

'Ah, I forgot you have first-hand knowledge of what it's like.'

'You can scorn all you want, Rooster,' said Mick.

Rooster caught Mulligan's eye and gestured for his usual. He wondered if he should tell Mick to clear off for a few minutes. No, it was good he was here as well.

'From the way you're both going on, ye haven't heard the news, I take it?'

'What news?' asked Mick.

'Plank has disappeared.'

Sonny's jaw dropped. 'What did you say?'

'The rumours have already started. It seems he was fiddling the movement and has done a runner. Sonny, the word is Julia was due to go with him.'

Sonny jumped out of his seat. 'Oh, Christ, no.' He knew exactly what Rooster was saying. Plank had *been* disappeared. He wasn't simply missing. The Provos had already found him and taken care of him; otherwise, Rooster wouldn't even mention his name. Sonny closed his eyes tight. He had to find Julia. Maybe she didn't know the danger she was in. Rooster was his only hope of protecting her.

'I have to get home,' he said frantically. He pleaded with Rooster, 'Will you come with me?'

'You don't need me.'

'I want you to come and reassure her. Please!' said Sonny.

'Have you forgotten already? She was going to do a runner with Plank who was fucking her behind your back. She's a slut.'

'She's not a slut. Don't you dare say those things about her,' shouted Sonny.

'It's what everybody else will say about her.'

'I don't care what everybody says.'

Mick wished he was anywhere else, but he saw that Sonny was sailing close to the wind by standing up to Rooster. He said, 'I feel for you, Sonny, but pull yourself together. If Julia was involved with Plank, then prepare for her maybe being told to leave the area.'

'Say something, Rooster,' beseeched Sonny. 'What's going to happen to her?'

'I have no idea. Mick is correct. She could be told to leave. It will all depend on the committee's report.'

'Please, please, come home with me,' begged Sonny.

'You don't need me.'

'Please, Rooster.'

'I will go with you, Sonny,' said Mick.

'You, see?' said Rooster. 'Mick will go.'

'No, I need you, Rooster. If you come, I'll agree to join up like you wanted me to.'

Rooster hesitated for a second, and then said, 'Okay.'

The three men piled into Sonny's car. No one spoke during the short journey. Sonny drove as fast as he could. He couldn't think. Plank was dead, he was sure of it. Had Julia planned to run away with him? Why didn't he say something to her? He could have said something? Jesus, why didn't he? What was going to happen now?

Sonny jammed on the brakes at the front door and jumped out of the car. He didn't have a key with him as he was expecting Julia to be home. He rang the bell impatiently. He held his finger on it. What was she doing? He banged on the door with his fist.

He didn't hear Mick say that she might be in the back garden. Sonny ran around the side of the house to the back door, but it was locked also. Her car was there. Where could she be?

'Julia, it's me, let me in,' he shouted in the side window, but there was only silence from inside the house. 'I'm not waiting any longer,' he said, as much to himself as to the others. He put his shoulder to the back door and burst it open. He ran into the house, but there was no sign of anyone in the kitchen or sitting-room. The suitcase was still there. Where was she, for God's sake?

He left the others and ran to the bedroom. Mick heard Sonny let out a shriek that might have come from the depths of hell.

'Julia, Julia,' Sonny cried. 'What have you done?'

She was lying sprawled on the bed, her eyes glassy, with an empty pill bottle lying beside her.

Sonny lifted her and cradled her in his arms, rocking her like a baby he was putting to sleep. 'Julia, Julia, Julia,' he sobbed. 'What have you done, darling? What have you done? God, what have you done? Where did you get the damn tablets?'

For minutes, Rooster and Mick stood watching him not saying anything.

Then Mick noticed something. 'She left a note on the dresser.'

'What does it say?' asked Rooster.

Mick read it slowly, as if he had trouble making out the writing. 'Rooster was here. I'm sorry, Sonny, for hurting you so much. Please forgive me.'

'Oh God, Julia, why did you have to do it?' wailed Sonny, still cradling her in his arms.

Mick attempted to give him some small comfort. 'You have her body, Sonny. She wasn't sent away or disappeared into some wild lonely bog. You can give her a nice funeral. All the relatives will be there, and then you will have a lovely grave to visit where you can pray for her soul.'

Sonny looked up beseechingly at Rooster. 'Why, Rooster? Why?'

Rooster shrugged his shoulders. 'It's just the way things are.'

Mick knew in his heart he shouldn't agree with Rooster, but he wasn't able to stop himself. God forgave him, it was just the way he was. 'It's the way things are,' he repeated.

'Nobody is responsible,' said Rooster.

'That's definitely right,' said Mick.

'She's just another victim,' said Rooster.

'Another victim,' said Mick.

'It's our history.'

'Just our history,' said Mick.

'Plank.'

'Yeah, Plank.'

'Now Julia.'

'Poor Julia.'

'The history of South Armagh is to blame.'

'South Armagh is to blame.'

40

The little church on the hill overlooking Cairnduff was packed for Julia's month's mind mass. This simple chapel was a focal point in local people's lives. Sonny and Julia had been christened in it. Both had celebrated their first communion, their confirmation, and took their wedding vows here. Now, in Julia's case, the mass was in her memory. In the fullness of time, Sonny's requiem mass would most likely be celebrated in the same church.

Fr Brady was the celebrant. Many thought that after years of ministration, he would surely be hardened to people's anguish. But the truth was that as he got older, he found it more difficult. It was his job to share the pain, and recently he felt overwhelmed with the suffering of his congregation. Also, the older he got the more disillusioned he became with his dreams of a united Ireland. He was tired. He had witnessed enough grief. Today's month's mind mass for Julia Mone was just a reminder of the tragedy of it all. She died by her own hand, but it was the troubles that had been the ultimate cause of her demise. Sonny had asked if he might give a little eulogy at the end of the mass, and the priest readily agreed. Sonny Mone was a peacemaker. It was to be pitied that he had given up the notion of running in the local election.

Fr Brady didn't give a sermon after the distribution of holy communion. He would give that time over to Sonny. Rooster was sitting in the front pew. He was always one of the first up to receive the sacrament. Fr Brady was his confessor. Sonny made his way up to the steps of the altar. He carried a little piece of paper with things written on it that he wanted to say. He could feel his heart pound. He wasn't a public speaker. As he bent the knee at the altar, a thousand memories flooded his mind. He had served in this church as an altar boy, and the last time he stood on these steps was the day he married Julia.

Sonny turned to face the congregation. Females on the left side of the aisle and males on the right. Cousins and relatives from both his and Julia's family occupied the front seats. Rooster had no right to be among them, but there was no law as to where anyone sat, just tradition. Sonny could see Alice and Blythe sitting together near the back, both clutching hankies. Pete the Pipe and Sean Donnelly were also present, Sean struggling to fit in the narrow pew. Even young Clint had come. It was good of him. He would have barely known Julia.

Sonny drew breath to speak but no words came out. He cleared his throat and began again.

'I won't detain you too long,' he said. 'I just have a few words to say. First, I want to thank you all for being here to honour Julia's memory and pray for her soul. She would be humbled by the numbers here today. She had the very human trait of wanting to be liked, and I know that she is pleased looking down on us all. I also want to thank

Fr Brady for all he has done since the time of her death, and for allowing me to say these words.'

Sonny glanced at what he had written down. 'Julia was the love of my life,' he said before tears filled his eyes and his voice broke. He couldn't get the words out. He took a couple of deep breaths. He had to get through this.

'I know she had her faults, but I have faults. We all have weaknesses. Perhaps you did not know the Julia I knew.' His voice broke again but he continued. 'The Julia I knew was kind and forgiving and generous. Any woman for miles around knew that if they were hard up but had something important on, a job interview or a wedding, they could come to Julia for a haircut and styling, and not a penny would be asked for. She would say to them, "Of course you have to look your best for your big day." She knew how important that feeling was for people. I could tell of another thousand little acts of kindness.'

Again, Sonny paused. Sunlight from a stained-glass window fell across the pulpit. His hands were bathed in yellow and green. 'Julia loved life. She was born in the wrong place at the wrong time. Broadway or London's West End may have been her true home. She had a talent for the stage that was never nurtured. Thomas Gray said the words, "Full many a flower is born to blush unseen." In a way, Julia was one of those flowers. Her talents never got to see the light of day. Perhaps when these present dark times end, our leaders will make a point of helping all our children to pursue their dreams.'

Sonny drew a breath and looked at his paper again, though he was no longer reading from it. 'Most of you here have lost loved ones and know the emptiness it brings. Some of those losses are due to the ongoing situation in our country. This brings me to something I wish to announce. As many of you know, I had intended to stand in the local elections next month on a platform that advocated talking instead of shooting. I don't wish to say why I had withdrawn from doing so. However, following the circumstances of Julia's death, I feel it's my duty to do something, to try anything I can to stop the violence, from whatever quarter it comes from. I feel Julia is giving me the courage to take this step.'

There was absolute silence in the congregation. Alice looked up at Sonny with round eyes, perhaps filled with hope, or perhaps fear. Pete the Pipe had straightened his mouth. He looked determined, resolute. He caught Sonny's eye and nodded once.

'Therefore,' continued Sonny, 'a week from today, and in remembrance of my wife, I intend to put in nomination papers for a seat on the local council. Thank you all again for attending Julia's month's mind mass. I ask you to remember her in your prayers.'

As Sonny stepped down from the altar he glanced at Rooster's face. It was impassive.

41

'And now for the last item on our agenda, gentleman,' said Mr Potts, who was chairing the intelligence committee meeting. 'South Armagh again. God, but this tiny piece of rock and bog populated by mentally deficient savages takes up a lot of our time. But we must persist. Today's problem involves one of our assets. We simply don't know its true allegiance. Is it ours or is it working on the double? Recent events there have clouded the picture. Another of our assets has returned, and when debriefed, claimed of having been sent back to us lucky to be alive. Gentlemen, we need to be one hundred per cent sure of our people. Something will have to be done to clear up what's going on.'

At these meetings the gender of an operative was never referred to. A human asset was just as disposable as any of the other countless mechanical devices at the disposal of the committee. Why give it a he or a she?

Potts, his head bobbing up and down, looked at the other three men for a response. The room they were in was small, the only furniture a table and four chairs. An hour before the committee arrived, the room had been electronically swept. No bugs or recording apparatus had been found. None of the men carried briefcases or files. Only a pen and blank piece of paper each. Having hard evidence relating to their work in anyone's hands was beyond contemplation. No one here was in the business of trusting anyone. Potts in particular had no faith in his fellow committee members, even though, much like himself, they were all handpicked for their special talents.

Take Mr Richard for example. If Potts was hanging from a rope, he wouldn't want to be waiting on Mr Richard to cut him down. But he did come up with some excellent ideas. It was he who put forward the ingenious notion of getting the head honchos of the UVF to instruct their local heroes to do their patriotic duty and end the conflict in a matter of months. Like all good ideas it was simple. All they had to do was plant a bomb in a soft target such as a primary school and cause a massacre. The death toll of children, not even counting teachers and staff, would surely spark a full-scale civil war. Westminster would then have the power to flood the country with the British Army and crush the Provos like the bugs they were. Richard's proposal was at present in the out-tray.

Sitting to the right of Potts, Mr Beddingham drew a doodle on his sheet of paper. A little house with a man looking out the window. He loved to draw and doodle, and wondered about his present drawing. It was coming from his subconscious for sure, but what did it mean? Like his three companions, part of their training included a degree in psychology. Mostly the psychology had to do with how to break a resource to gain information. Any resource could be broken eventually. For some, old fashioned torture methods were effective. Even the simple ones such as the lighted cigarette held against the eyelid were found to work.

The religious fanatics needed more time to be convinced, and time wasn't always available. In those circumstances psychology was used. Beddingham recalled one instance when a resource was putting up a lot of resistance. Someone suggested that if he didn't talk, he would be injected with the virus *Yersinia Pestis*, the black death, and sent home to his family. For whatever reason, this terrified him so much that he sang like a bird. The interesting thing was the same threat had no impact on his companion. Traditional methods had to be employed on that particular resource.

Mr Richard nudged Mr Beddingham and whispered, 'What is the asset's codename, do you remember?'

Mr Potts glared at him. 'It's better, Mr Richard, if we all concentrate on the subject at hand. However, just as an aside – it's not on today's agenda – on the subject of codenames, our assets in the Republic that we know as the brothers Long Johns have both been arrested, and have squealed about their activities. Their orders, as you know, were to generate such mayhem in the South that the Dublin government would be forced to introduce internment. Unfortunately, they were unsuccessful. We have of course denied all knowledge of them. Also, I have received a report concerning the loss of a high ranking operative. Coming from our own stock he was obviously exhaustively trained and had been very effective in the field. It is not unlikely that due to his daring undercover work, much of which will always have to remain secret, he will be honoured with some military medal in the future. As to how his real identity became known, it seems he was in some drinking den, again in this infernal area, when his cover was blown.

Mr Potts paused for a moment, clearly as a mark of respect, while the other three looked sufficiently solemn.

Mr Potts spoke again. 'So, we have had disappointments, which is only to be expected when dealing with such a barbaric and cruel enemy. But on the other hand, the loyalists have created a certain amount of terror with their bombing campaign in Dublin and Monaghan, so we should be thankful for small mercies. How fruitful their efforts would be without our input is an open question.'

Mr Turner wasn't concentrating, despite Mr Potts' rebuke to Mr Richard. His test results were due on Monday. He was a doctor, not that his skills had ever been used to keep anyone alive, not since joining this committee. But being a doctor, he already knew the results by his symptoms. The only question was how long would he have. He wouldn't be missed by anyone here, nor any other member of the department. They were few in number, a handful at best. Only the department heads of the various intelligence agencies, the prime minister, the home secretary, the foreign secretary, and the top civil servants in each of those offices even knew of the committee's existence, and none of them could define exactly its role in the defence of the realm. At times the prime minister, whoever he or she was, it didn't matter, would suggest that the world would be a better place if a certain person was not around. Word would be sent to the committee, and whatever action was subsequently taken, no one could be held responsible. No one could even be accused of knowing anything about it.

This would be Turner's last committee meeting. He shouldn't have come. Whatever they decided he would go along with it. He might be dead himself before the asset was deleted.

Mr Richard said, 'It's not the first time we were unsure of an asset. I don't think it's a big problem.'

He was rubbing his forehead with thumb and index finger, hoping to give the impression that he was concentrating on the situation at hand, but his thoughts were elsewhere. Better get this meeting finished. Lisa's first communion ceremony started at five. He'd have plenty of time to get to it if this was over and done with. Her mother told him the previous evening that the little one would wear a white veil just to please him, even though she wasn't keen on it herself. He couldn't wait to see his little darling all dressed up. Potts loved making a mountain out of a molehill. If he proposed just deleting the asset that would speed the things up.

'Suggestions please, gentlemen,' said Potts. He was sticking to protocol. He and the rest of them already knew what the decision would be. He loved this part of it. Big game hunting, like killing an elephant or lion, didn't compare with taking a decision to delete either a resource or an asset. He could never be the greyhound and carry out the actual kill. Much better to be the greyhound handler. That was where the true power resided.

'We have come up against this before,' said Beddingham, turning his page over and beginning a new doodle. 'I propose we do the same again. We leak the name of the asset we aren't sure about. That way we soon find out. If its own crowd don't delete it then it has gone rogue, and we can do the deletion ourselves. If it isn't rogue, they will delete it and save us the bother.'

'I go along with that,' said Mr Richard.

'I also,' said Mr Turner. Likely his last contribution to this committee. Damn this insidious cancer.

Mr Potts looked around the table. Everyone first had to say "agreed" which the others all did. It fell to him now to say the word, and the asset's fate would be decided. Few people in the world had such power. He'd be on a high tonight. Maybe he would take his wife and the in-laws out for a meal.

'Agreed.'

The others began moving about as if preparing to leave. Potts held up his hand. 'Before we finish,' he said. 'Just for the record, in this same cursed place there is another little matter that I have touched on myself personally. A do-gooder, bringing peace to the world. I warned him off, and suggested the consequences should he persist in his fantasies. Unfortunately, word has reached us that he has not heeded my caution.'

The other three men shifted in their seats. Deleting civilians was always trickier.

But Potts quelled them. 'I have decided for now that it is something we can keep an eye on. Deletion is always an option if he persists and is showing signs of success. So, no decision is necessary just yet. As for the present, I declare this meeting over.'

Before they got up, Beddingham nudged Richard. Earlier he has asked the name of the asset who was the subject of discussion. Beddingham pointed to the new doodle he'd made. It was a huge snarling wolfhound.

Rooster's bedroom was sparse, just like the rest of his living quarters. There was a damp spot in the corner of a once-white ceiling. A huge picture of a woodland scene hung on one wall. The other walls were bare. A trunk holding long-forgotten American clothes rested beside a dressing table with a mirror that had a hairline crack running down the middle. An old armchair with a broken armrest and a brown dining-room chair, were placed adjacent to the bed. The bed was a single divan covered in copious blankets and an old overcoat. At the far end of the room, completely out of place, a child's rocking-horse with one hoof missing lay turned over on the floor. Once painted bright blue and yellow, the colours were now flaked and faded. It silently spoke of a joyful time, perhaps a Christmas morning when the frost made magical patterns on the windows, when icicles hung from the eaves, when a six-year-old boy jumped out of bed and looked in wonder at the horse Santa had left – when being alive meant everything was possible.

Rooster was thinking of death. The death of little pigs. He lay watching the first light shine through the crack where the curtains were closed. Soon he would be able to sleep for a few hours. From the time his stepfather would leave him locked in the cupboard under the stairs, he could never fall asleep when it was dark. He often thought of his stepfather and how he taught him to become a man. When he made him kill his pet pig, Little Lucky, and how he found it so hard to do. 'You are acting like a boy now, but you have to become a man,' his stepfather told him. 'You cannot be both. Try and ride two horses at the same time and you will come crashing down.'

Rooster turned in the bed and hoped for sleep. He hadn't listened to that advice.

42

'Please go over it again, Pete,' said Alice.

Pete the Pipe, Sean Donnelly, and Alice sat around the big table in Blythe Atkinson's drawing-room. They were waiting on Sonny and young Clint to arrive before starting the meeting. Sonny was due to hand in his nomination papers before joining them. In the past week things had gone extremely well. The feedback on the door-to-door canvass was hugely positive. Even known opposition voters mentioned Julia's tragic end. Sonny was going to win for sure.

'Okay, for the second time,' said Pete. 'As you know I ring Sonny a few times a day just to check in with him. This morning, he answered the phone and when I asked if everything was all right, he just said: "Can't talk. Something has happened. See you later."'

'How did he sound?' asked Alice, with concern in her voice.

'I don't know. Maybe excited. I'm not sure.'

'Did he sound scared?'

'We only spoke ten words, so I have no way of knowing.'

Sean said, 'I think the positive thing is him saying, "See you later." That's a good sign.'

'But why is he so late?' said Alice. 'What's keeping him?'

'He may be held up at a road block or something,' said Pete the Pipe.

'Exactly! What if they hauled him in for questioning?' said Alice, constantly twisting a handkerchief in her hands. 'He should have been here by now.'

In the kitchen, Blythe was making the tea. With the exception of Julia's death, the last few months had been so exciting and rewarding for her. Ever since her husband died in a hunting accident in Africa, her life had been boring. Not that it was great beforehand, because he was usually away, and not always on business. Born in India, South Armagh held little appeal for him. Gambling and partying, which she wasn't invited to, occupied a lot of his time. Now the meetings, canvassing, and making new friends had given her a whole new perspective. In fact, she dreaded the thoughts of the election being over and having to go back to her previous existence. After Sonny was elected, she might volunteer to be his secretary or something.

When Blythe rolled in the trolley with the tea and delicacies, Sean's eyes lit up. 'When we win this one,' he said, 'Sonny's next move is either the Dáil or Westminster, and this has to be the official committee meeting room.'

'I'm all in favour of that,' said Blythe. 'We can have tea while we're waiting. Hold out your cup Alice.'

'For God's sake, I don't want tea. I want Sonny to walk through that door.'

'Calm down, Alice,' said Sean. 'He'll be here soon. Don't be worried.'

'He will of course,' said Blythe. 'I'm so excited that we are going to win the election.'

'Yeah,' said Sean.

Pete fiddled with his pipe. He knew Alice was just expressing what they all felt. He'd better try and lift the mood. 'Who would have given us any chance back when we first started out?'

'We have come a long way in a short time,' said Sean. 'It's awful to say it, but Julia's death really swung it, big time.'

'Well, it was her death that made Sonny decide to run again and try to do something positive in the midst of all this suffering,' said Blythe.

Alice threw up her hands. 'Why on earth are you all saying things we already know? Wait, I hear a car. That's him now.' She jumped up and ran to the window, but then her shoulders drooped in disappointment. 'It's only Clint.'

After a moment, Clint came into the room and cheerfully said, 'Hello all.'

'Any sign of Sonny? What kept you?' said Alice.

'Is he not here yet? We were to meet when he was handing in his papers. I thought I must have missed him.'

'Are there any checkpoints on the road?' asked Pete.

'Not that I've seen,' said Clint.

'Jesus God, where is he?' said Alice.

Nobody answered. Alice began pacing the floor. 'Pete, ring the council offices and see if Sonny handed in his papers.'

'Are you allowed to do that?' asked Sean.

Alice turned on him. 'Christ, what does it matter if you can do it or not? I will do it if you don't, Pete.'

Sean shrank back in his chair, 'Sorry, Alice.'

'There's no harm in trying,' said Pete, going out to the hall where the phone was kept.

Everyone waited in silence. Outside, Blythe's donkey brayed. It put a chill through her. Sally always knew when something was wrong and would bray her concern. Better keep her fingers crossed and not mention it to the others. Sometimes Sally was just looking for male company.

None of the others paid any heed to the donkey. They listened to Pete asking if Sonny had handed in his papers. A click when he hung up the phone. He came back into the room shaking his head. 'He didn't hand them in. And he wasn't seen by the returning officer. That's all they would tell me.'

No one spoke for a few seconds. A fly buzzed around the teacakes on the trolley.

'Is there nothing we can do?' said Alice. 'We have to do something. Anything.'

'Ring the police,' said Blythe.

'And say what?' asked Sean. 'That Sonny didn't hand in nomination papers? They wouldn't care. And even if they did, they wouldn't do anything. At the moment, all we can say is that he's late for a meeting.'

'We can go look for him,' said Alice. 'Ask around if anyone has seen him.'

But Pete knew that if Sonny had been picked up, by either side, there would be no trace. He said, 'All we can do is wait, Alice.'

Another rumble of tyres on the gravel drive made everyone in the room sit still. An engine cut out. A car door opened and closed. Moments later, footsteps approached in the hallway. The door to the drawing-room burst open, and Sonny came in breathlessly.

'Have you heard the news?' he said.

'Thank God,' said Alice, so relieved that she forgot to be angry with him.

But Pete was angry. 'What news?' he demanded to know. 'And why in hell's name did you not tell us you weren't going to hand in your papers and have us all worried sick?'

'You haven't heard?' said Sonny.

'Heard what, for F's sake? You're making me curse now,' said Pete.

Sonny paused and ran his fingers through his hair. 'Frank Brannigan put in nomination papers and is being backed by the Provos.'

Pete took the pipe from his mouth. 'What did you say?'

'Brannigan put in nomination papers and is, to all intents and purposes, the Provo candidate.'

For a long moment there was silence except for the ticking of the mantle clock.

'Wow!' said Pete.

'That snake!' said Clint.

Sean stood up and paced the room. 'First, he was our candidate, and when he thought we wouldn't win he resigned. Now, he's taking the opportunity to represent a side he thinks will win.'

'Can he do that?' asked Blythe, seeing her hopes of a new life crumble. 'Surely we can stop him.'

'He can do what he likes,' said Pete. 'He can represent anyone he wants.'

But Alice had been watching Sonny since he came in. Finally, she said, 'Why do you seem so happy about all this?'

He looked at her. His smile widened. 'Don't you all know what this means?' he said. 'We've won!'

Sean frowned. 'What are you talking about? We don't have a chance now.'

Sonny shook his head. 'Alice, what was that slogan we've been using all along, the one you thought of so brilliantly?'

'Talking hurts no one.'

'Exactly! We have forced the Provos into talking. We have made them break the ice, even if it's only in our little pond. But once the ice is broken, it can't be unbroken. The demand for politics instead of bombs and bullets will grow. It's beyond everything we started out looking for.'

Alice realised that what he was saying was true, and now she was smiling as well.

Pete sucked on his pipe in disbelief. 'Sonny's right. We made them do it. Because if they lost this tiny bit of control in South Armagh, they might lose it everywhere.'

'That's what Rooster meant when he warned me about the IRA,' said Sonny. 'His exact words were: "There are people concerned with the way you are wresting control from them." They were discussing having to go political because of me, not killing me, thanks be to God.'

'But did Rooster know that?' said Pete. 'And if so, why would he let you think you were in such danger?

'Maybe he thought I would fall in with his plans, whatever they were. But I can bow out now without regret, thank you very much.'

'I still think Brannigan will let us down,' said Sean.

'I'm not so sure,' said Pete. 'For a start, he wants to be a professional politician, and politics is about winning. Plus, he is very articulate, and he isn't a man of violence. He will be able to argue with the best of them for the value of peaceful means.'

'It's just that I think winning at all costs is disregarding principles,' said Sean. 'I mean, will you vote for him?'

'Interesting question,' said Pete. 'I dislike the man intensely on a personal level. But he represents politics over violence, so I have no choice.'

As everyone discussed whether they could trust or even vote for Brannigan, Sonny drifted over to the big bay window. He gazed out at the huge garden, now largely grown wild and uncared for. The laurel hedges needed clipping. The rhododendrons that lined the driveway had spread unchecked over the paths. Once manicured lawns could now fatten Friesian bullocks. The old sun dial seemed forlorn. Green moss on the hour-lines would soon render its measurement of the sun and the passing of the days meaningless. Somewhere in the old walled garden, a woodpigeon cooed for a mate. In the distance the lake was choked with weeds. Sonny imagined pleasure boats drifting across its surface, back when the entire estate was revelling in pomp and splendour.

He felt Alice come and stand by his side. She put her arm around his waist. The others were still debating back and forth. 'Why are you not joining us, Sonny?' she asked quietly. 'What are you thinking about? Our success ?'

Sonny paused before answering. 'No, I'm thinking that time causes change, no matter what.'

'Yes, it does,' said Alice.

'Julia,' said Sonny.

'Yes, Julia,' said Alice softly.

'She helped bring about change in her time also,' said Sonny.

43

After the ceremony, Sonny visited Julia's grave to lay the altar flowers upon it. Others had also recently left blossoms. The summer sun glistened on the marble headstone, making it glint and sparkle like moonbeams on a rippling stream. The soft sacred silence hanging over the cemetery was made more noticeable by the humming of a lone bee. A few other people stood by their own relatives' graves, praying, or just silently communicating with loved ones. Just as Sonny was kneeling down, a robin swooped down and alighted on a bush growing behind Julia's grave.

'Wow,' he muttered. His mother believed that when a robin appeared it was to tell you a deceased person was happy and in harmony with nature. She knew things. This was a message from Julia. Her discontented soul was finally at peace.

He knelt at the graveside. There was nobody nearby.

'It's been over a year, my dearest, since you left us. A lot has happened in that time. Frank of course won the election, but we had already achieved what we had been fighting for, far beyond our dreams. Now that they see they can win at the ballot box, the Provos are talking about combining politics along with the gun. Each on different hands. It will never be recorded, but the reaction people had to your death will help save many lives in the future. Some people say I'm a fool, but I forgive you, Julia. I know in your heart of hearts you never meant to hurt me. I know that all you wanted was a little bit of excitement.'

He plucked a weed from the side of her grave and tossed it into the verge.

'Oh, and Rooster has disappeared. There are rumours he was a double agent for the Brits and that the Provos shot him. Others say he was a double agent for the Provos and the Brits shot him. Some even say he is holed up somewhere in South America, so who knows?'

Sonny finished speaking. He sat back on his hunkers. Somehow, he felt in touch with Julia. She was happy, he could feel it. He lifted his head and observed the robin. It cocked its head sideways to look at him, beautiful and unafraid.

It was time to leave. He arranged the bouquet nicely among the rest of the flowers on top of the grave.

'I know you will understand, Julia, that life must go on for the living. But rest easy, my darling. A part of me will always belong to you.'

Sonny rose to leave causing the robin to take off and swoop away over the meadows beyond. 'Talk to you later, love,' he said under his breath and began to make his way back to the waiting taxi. He got into the rear seat where Alice was waiting.

She pressed her lips to his cheek. 'I understand you needed to talk to her.' After a few seconds she held out her hand. 'Is my finger swollen?'

Sonny shook loose confetti from her veil. 'You're only wearing the ring an hour. Wait until you have it on twenty years.'

ACKNOWLEDGEMENTS

I want to thank my wife Patricia, for being there.
My sister Eilish for her candid comments and enthusiasm.
My son Piaras, his wife Marissa, and my grandson Fionn for being on call. My graphic artist, and computer guru James Smith for his expertise.
My mentor, and muse, the author Andrew Hughes.
Finally, I want to thank Rohan, Margo, and Jillian, all of whom contributed to the final result.

Printed in Great Britain
by Amazon

30045758R00209